10/85.

Wavecrest

Wavecrest

BILL KNOX

PUBLISHED FOR THE CRIME CLUB BY

DOUBLEDAY AND COMPANY, INC.

GARDEN CITY, NEW YORK

1985

All of the characters in this book
are fictitious, and any resemblance
to actual persons, living or dead,
is purely coincidental.

Library of Congress Cataloging in Publication Data

Knox, Bill, 1928–
Wavecrest.

I. Title.
PR6061.N6W3   1985   823'.914
ISBN 0-385-19987-2
Library of Congress Catalog Card Number 85-4428

For "J" crew, *Spartiate III*,
Clyde River Patrol

DAFS notice 1046

Closure of West of Scotland sea lochs

The penalty for contravention of the closure is a fine of up to
£50,000 and seizure of catch and gear.

The closure is a conservation measure to protect stocks of
immature herring which overwinter in the west coast lochs. The
prohibition is on the use of mobile gear and will not affect the
operations of the static gear fisherman.

Wavecrest

Prelude

The night was calm and cloudless over the long, dark scatter of islands which run like an outpost barrier off the west coast of Scotland. Moonlight glinted silver-grey on the low Atlantic swell and picked out the snowcaps of the mainland peaks.

Swirling round reefs, lapping shoreline edges, the sea quietly obeyed tide and currents. Finishing a journey which had begun the breadth of the ocean away, the long fingers of the Gulf Stream probed a layer of warmer water into the main channels.

Here and there among the islands a lighthouse blinked, fishermen worked on their boats, ships ploughed a wash through the sea. Bobbing on the swell, whole colonies of seabirds slept. Along the shorelines, a multitude of tiny night creatures, some microscopically small, scurried and scavenged.

The black stain of the oil slick came from the northwest, missing the outer islands. Pushed by the currents, pulled by the tide, originally covering a square mile of water, it was now reduced to half that size.

But it remained a killer, dark and thick, sticky and silent. Seabirds, their feathers saturated, unable to fly, tried to clean themselves with their beaks and swallowed oil. Where the slick brushed rocks or a shoreline, all crawling life suffocated beneath a tarry coating.

The slick moved on, with no mind of its own. Beyond a small patch of broken water where two currents met, it overtook a wallowing, half-submerged piece of wreckage which had once been the stern half of a dinghy. In moments a thick, black scum clung to the drifting wreckage and oozed over what remained of the transom.

The kittiwake struggled aboard, covered in oil, barely recognizable as a bird. Exhausted by the effort, she slumped down on the dead thing that lay inside the broken hull. A sudden struggling and splashing, and a gull had joined her.

The kittiwake made a hissing noise, just once, deep in her throat, but the gull didn't move.

They stayed that way, while the first traces of dawn began to show across the sky.

The dead thing beneath them wore a coarse wool sweater. Wearily the kittiwake experimented by rubbing her wing feathers against a sodden, knitted sleeve.

The gull just watched.

1

A large, almost stationary anticyclone south of Iceland meant that a light northwest airstream affected the Scottish sea areas Bailie, Rockall, Hebrides and Malin. The October sky was clear of cloud, and the morning sun shone on a gentle blue-grey swell flecked with small patches of foaming white.

The Piper Aztec was flying at an altitude of 5000 feet, at her cruising speed of 230 knots. To the men in her cockpit, the islands of the Inner Hebrides were a panorama of dark rocks and sea crags, white sandy beaches and green, patchy vegetation.

The Aztec's radio muttered briefly. Her pilot acknowledged the message, then changed the set's frequency.

"Hey, Skipper." He looked at his passenger in the seat beside him and indicated his headphones. "Hear me?"

Webb Carrick nodded. But for a moment his thoughts had been somewhere else. He'd flown the Aztec's route often enough before, but this time was very different, everything that lay ahead held uncertainties.

"Good." The pilot's voice held a hint of amusement. "Your baby is on her way; we'll rendezvous as arranged. But Control wants me to divert first." He gestured ahead, slightly west. "It's thataway."

A moment later, the twin Lycoming engines altered their note and the slim white aircraft began a slow, banking turn. In the equipment-crammed rear, the other member of the Aztec's crew became busy.

Carrick looked down again and got his bearings. They were north of Mull, and the Aztec's new heading would take them towards the small, uninhabited Treshnish Isles.

"What have you got?" he asked through his microphone.

"No idea," the pilot said. "Somebody says there's something. We'll find out."

Carrick gave a nod and sat back. The government-operated Scottish Fishery Protection Service's air reconnaissance section was tiny and hard-worked. It gave an understandably low priority to nuisance tasks, and giving him a lift probably fitted into that category.

He forgot about the aircraft for a moment, ignoring the way it bumped and shuddered through a patch of turbulence. His first real command—two weeks old now, he had the all-important telex signal from Fleet Support carefully folded in an inside pocket of his uniform jacket.

"Chief Officer Carrick from *Marlin,* to command *Tern.* Effective on completion familiarization course, Clyde. On handover, *Tern* to continue allocated duty until further ordered."

It had meant an immediate growl of congratulation from Captain James Shannon, *Marlin's* small veteran commander. Then saying goodbye to a ship which had been his life for three full years and to the thirty men of her crew, men he'd come to know like a family. There had been handshakes, more congratulations.

"*Tern.* That's a bit of a surprise to me, Mister." Captain Shannon waited until they were in the privacy of his day cabin before he betrayed a fleeting doubt. He had poured two generous drinks from a bottle of his private stock of malt whisky. "I'd have said you were in line for something bigger." He paused. "But you're being handed a chance and a challenge. Enjoy them both—and good luck."

They'd clinked glasses to that.

He'd been dumped ashore at Stornoway and had been flown south, to the Fishery Protection Squadron's west-coast base at Greenock. Then he'd been plunged into two weeks' concentrated instruction, ashore and afloat, discovering just how different things were going to be.

Different? Hardly anything was the same.

Fishery Protection cruisers like *Marlin* were four-hundred-ton ships built like miniature destroyers and sturdy enough to take the worst of winter gales. They policed the fishing grounds from the islands far out into the Atlantic.

By comparison, *Tern* was one of the first of a new breed of small, fast patrol launches. Their role was to operate close in among the islands, in law-enforcement situations where the big cruisers were handicapped by sheer size and where speed was a vital weapon. For the same reasons, patrol-launch crews were small, hand-picked teams—young enough to absorb new technology, experienced enough to use it.

Shannon had been right. *Tern* would be a challenge . . .

The Aztec dipped and made a sudden, sharp turn to starboard.

They were coming in low, swooping over the first of the Treshnish Isles. Another lay dead ahead. It had a deep bay, like a knife wound surrounded by high cliffs, shelter for a fishing boat that lay at anchor.

"Gift-wrapped," said the Aztec's pilot. "Ready, Charlie? Let's make it a one-pass job."

"One pass," confirmed the crewman in the rear. "Steady of hand and sharp of eye—that's me."

Craning round, Carrick saw the telephoto lens on the video camera the man held like a gun against one shoulder, the lens aimed out through the aircraft's Plexiglas window.

"Skipper, what do you think?" asked the pilot.

Carrick frowned. The fishing boat was growing larger. He could see the Norwegian flag flapping listlessly at her stern; there were two large, black, half-submerged shapes tied against her rusting hull. The distinctive shape of a harpoon gun at her bow clinched it.

"She's a shark boat—Norwegian. Looks like they've caught a couple of bull basking sharks." He watched a moment longer. "She's probably getting ready to tow them back to her mother ship."

The Norwegians had shark-fishing rights in the Minch and used them. The Aztec's pilot gave a disappointed nod.

"Mark her anyway, Charlie," he ordered.

They zoomed over at five hundred feet, the video camera purring. Carrick could read the name *Asmar* on the shark-catcher's bow. Some of her crew were using a compressed-air lance to give their catches extra buoyancy. Two glanced up and waved.

The video camera stopped, and the aircraft climbed rapidly to escape the cliffs. Linked to the Aztec's sophisticated navigational computer system, the videotape would also carry a printout of the Norwegian boat's exact position. It was standard practice, useful evidence if needed later.

"Go back to sleep, Charlie," said the pilot, satisfied. He winked at Carrick. "I'll wake you when we've got rid of our sailor."

They gained more height, swinging in a lazy curve towards the mainland. Charlie had retired back among his video gear, and Carrick sat with his eyes half-closed, listening to the drone of the engines. Yawning to himself, nothing in particular to do for the moment, the pilot glanced at his passenger again with mild curiosity.

Webb Carrick was thirty-one years old, five feet ten in height and with a stocky build to match. Outwardly the pilot saw just another sailor in uniform, wearing a white wool rollneck sweater below his dark blue Fishery Protection uniform jacket. This one had a broad-boned face, a weather-bronzed complexion, dark brown eyes and an untidy mop of darker brown hair. The first signs of a few crow's-foot lines were beginning to show around the eyes.

The pilot liked to believe he could judge character—except, of course, in women. His passenger's slightly thin lips and the brief words they'd exchanged left the impression that Carrick, apparently easygoing on the surface, might be a shade short on temper underneath.

He hummed a tune to himself, amused. He'd heard Carrick had been first officer on *Marlin*. If anyone could survive under that legendary old devil Shannon, he had to be good—or mad. Or, maybe, a little of both.

The Aztec droned on. At last the pilot nudged Carrick and pointed. They were now about five miles out from the mainland, approaching another group of islands. Most looked uninviting, but the nearest was a narrow green hogback of land with a broad and sandy beach.

"That's our landing strip." He pointed at the long glint of sand on the east side. "Kenbride Island—the air-ambulance boys discovered it first and still use it, even though they have to have their patients ferried out by boat."

"Nothing on the mainland?" asked Carrick.

"Nothing—unless you've a helicopter or like free-fall parachut-ing. But even with Kenbride you've got to catch low tide—and bar-ometric pressure. Do it wrong and you're likely to get more than your feet wet." The pilot paused. "Yes, and I think I see your new child—nice timing."

Still a tiny speck, a boat was approaching from the north, travel-ling fast, weaving a broad white wake between the other islands. A new voice murmured from the Aztec's radio, and the pilot gave Carrick a wink as he acknowledged.

Going down, the Aztec made a low-level pass over the beach. Then it turned, the undercarriage lowered. An initial bounce, a brief splashing as the wheels ran through a shallow pool, then they were on dry sand again and had stopped. The engines died. Leaning over, the pilot opened the passenger door.

"Thank you for travelling with this airline," he said solemnly. "Unfortunately a cruel management forbids gratuities from grateful passengers." He glanced back. "Heave his gear out, Charlie."

Carrick climbed down, caught his duffel bag as it was tossed after him, then watched the patrol launch as she came racing in.

The Blue Ensign of the Fishery Protection flotilla snapping at her stern, *Tern* was putting on a show—he guessed for his benefit. Riding strangely flat in the water yet cutting through the swell, she had to be making well in excess of thirty knots. A broad white bow wave was backed by the muffled, throaty roar of her engines.

Suddenly the roar died to a murmur and the white wake faded. Swinging round in a tight circle, the patrol launch anchored about a hundred yards out. Figures moved on her deck beside the prominent cockpit bridge, then he heard the whine of an electric derrick as an inflatable boat was lowered smartly from the cutaway platform at her stern.

A moment later the inflatable's outboard engine barked to life. Two men aboard, it headed for the shore.

Carrick began walking across the beach to meet them. But his eyes were still on *Tern*, her grey, stubby, broad-beamed hull and cream upperworks, her pulpit lookout and searchlight mounts, the high clutter of radar and radio aerials.

A home-made pennant was flying on a halyard. The light wind straightened it for a moment, and he chuckled. Crossed cocktail glasses, white on black, didn't have a listing in any official signal book.

The inflatable came in, nosed the sand, and one of the two men aboard left her in a single hopping jump. Then he loped up the beach towards Carrick.

"Glad to see you." He shook Carrick's hand in a vigorous welcome. "Tim Maxwell. Welcome to Wonderland."

"Wonderland?" asked Carrick.

"Wonderland," repeated Maxwell. "On this stretch of coast, I wake up every morning and wonder what the hell is going to happen next." He drew a deep, satisfied breath. "But starting today I'm due a month's leave before I move on."

"You've earned it." Carrick knew a little about Maxwell, a tall, thin man, sharp-eyed, wearing faded blue overalls and a fisherman's jersey. Maxwell, who had transferred out of the Research branch to command *Tern*, was now leaving to organize a new fishery patrol service for a group of Commonwealth islands in the Caribbean. "Thanks for the demonstration as you came in."

"That?" Maxwell dismissed it with a gesture. "Just a last gentle

workout—I was feeling sentimental. Dump your kit in the boat. I'll
go tell the flying machine gentlemen they'll have to wait for a spell."

The tall, thin figure loped off again, towards the aircraft. Settling
the duffel bag more firmly on his shoulder, Carrick walked down
towards the inflatable. The crewman aboard it had his back turned
and was tinkering with the outboard engine. But there was something oddly familiar about him.

"What the hell are you doing here?" asked Carrick.

The man turned and scratched a thumbnail along his unshaven
chin. A face like a piece of worn rock shaped a grimace.

"You know how it happens," said Clapper Bell sadly. "I felt like a
bit o' a change."

Carrick stared at him, still bewildered. Six feet of burly, ginger-
haired, stubborn Glasgow-Irishman, *Marlin*'s bo'sun, Chief Petty
Officer William "Clapper" Bell, was just about the last person he'd
expected to see. Together, they'd made up the fishery cruiser's
scuba-diving team. Ashore and afloat, creating their own rules about
discipline without ever discussing it, they'd formed a total working
partnership.

"You mean you're with *Tern?*"

"Have been, for a week." Clapper Bell sucked his teeth reflec-
tively. "Just gettin' to know the ropes, like. I thought one o' us
should—sir."

Carrick swallowed. The last time he'd seen Bell, the bo'sun had
been leaning on *Marlin*'s stern rail as the fishery cruiser sailed out of
Stornoway harbour. They'd had a drink together the previous night,
from a bottle Bell kept hidden in the ship's scuba-gear compartment. As he remembered it, most of the bottle's contents had gone
down Bell's throat.

"Do I ask how?" Another thought struck Carrick. "Did someone
decide I needed a nursemaid?"

"No." Bell frowned. "It would have been more like a keeper,
anyway."

They grinned at each other.

"So what happened?" Carrick ignored a wavelet which creamed
in and lapped his feet.

"A couple o' days or so after you left, I heard that *Tern* needed a
replacement," said Bell. "One of their CPOs got sandwiched between her and a fishing boat—got his ribs bashed in. So I made
noises to the Old Man, then some other people, and everything was
fixed."

Carrick didn't doubt it. When Clapper Bell really wanted something, he had surprising connections. Most went back to the Royal Navy medal ribbons he wore on his shore-going uniform.

"I may need a friendly face, Clapper." He looked out towards *Tern.* "What's it been like?"

"Different," said Bell unemotionally. "But all right." He glanced along the beach. Maxwell was loping back towards them from the aircraft. "Better heave that bag in. This one doesn't hang about."

Maxwell arrived, gave Carrick an amused glance and thumbed towards Bell.

"Today's surprise?"

Carrick nodded.

"Your problem, not mine." Maxwell drew a breath. "Well, the plane driver says the tide will only let him wait half an hour. So let's move."

Carrick helped him shove the inflatable out with the next receding wave. They scrambled in, the outboard engine rasped, and the little boat curved away from the shore.

The aircraft's half-hour deadline meant time was tight in terms of a handover. They boarded *Tern* without ceremony at her cutaway stern, left Clapper Bell to secure the inflatable, then Maxwell led the way up a short companionway ladder to the patrol boat's main deck.

"Better meet the crew first—they'll expect it." He gave Carrick a sideways glance. "Just you and four men to run the show may seem strange for a spell."

Carrick nodded. The point had been rammed home often enough during conversion training on the Clyde, when much of the time had been spent handling another boat of the same class. A patrol boat's crew consisted of her skipper, a second officer, an engineer officer and two chief petty officers.

Even a few years earlier it wouldn't have been possible. But *Tern* was new generation, a forty-five-ton package of pushbutton automation in a sixty-five-foot-long glass-fibre hull. Most of her control and navigation systems were duplicated, she had a sophisticated computer-stabilized radar system and the latest in communications transceivers. Then came her "three by three" power package—three massive turbo-charged V8 diesel engines, each driving one of her three big, fully feathering propellors, and, handling it all, slim, deep, spade-bladed treble rudders.

Each *Tern*-class patrol boat didn't leave much change from a million pounds to build and equip. Each had totally to justify the investment.

The lapping of the waves against the hull competed with the background murmur of a generator as Carrick followed Maxwell along the swaying deck to meet the three men who were waiting in a line beside the cockpit bridge. As a first meeting, it came down to handshakes, names and fleeting impressions.

Andy Grey, the second officer, was in his twenties, with a lean, pock-marked face and spiky black hair. He wore a blue battle-dress jacket with a single, very new gold stripe on each shoulder and he treated Carrick with reserved caution before ducking back into the bridge area. *Tern*'s engineer officer was next, a squat hairy man named Sam Pilsudski. He was the oldest, in his late thirties, with a smile which showed a mouthful of gold-filled teeth. A pack of cheroots protruded from the top pocket of his faded white overalls.

That left the other chief petty officer, Gogi MacDonnell, who doubled as cook and showed all the potential of being the most difficult to get to know. A lean, sad-faced man who spoke with a quiet West Highland lilt, MacDonnell wore a wool tammy hat and his overalls were tucked into cut-down fisherman's boots. His handshake was firm, but he had a suspicious glint in his eyes.

Pilsudski and MacDonnell soon left, going aft. Once they had gone, Maxwell turned and rested his hands on the deck rail.

"I'll miss this." He looked towards the shore for a moment. "How about you, Carrick? With your record, you could have expected to make captain, be given one of the protection cruisers. Disappointed?"

It was a fair question, but the first time he'd been asked directly. Being posted to command *Tern* was no promotion as far as the Department's payroll was concerned. He still rated chief officer, as before—and the same applied to all the launch commanders. "Skipper" was strictly a courtesy rank.

"No disappointment." He meant it. "I'm happy enough."

"Good." Maxwell still gave him a curious glance. "Well, I heard you had a chance earlier—and turned it down."

It had happened that way, but there had been reasons. Carrick said nothing.

"That's your business. But maybe someone wants to see you do penance." Maxwell paused, then nodded at the home-made pennant fluttering overhead. "I'll take that with me. We had a farewell party last night." He hesitated. "How do you react to advice, Carrick?"

"Usually I listen," said Carrick mildly.

"Then do your own thing?" Maxwell chuckled. "I won't bore you —I'd feel the same way. Just remember that on a boat this size you're not so much handling a crew as heading a team, and there's one hell of a difference. Sometimes diplomacy rules—or that's the way I've played it. On the other hand, you're still the boss." He glanced at his wristwatch. "Right, let's start the guided-tour bit."

They began it.

Below deck, a compact layout utilized every inch of space, often in ingenious ways. Bell and MacDonnell had small, separate cabins for'ard and their own crew-mess area with a wall-mounted TV set. Sam Pilsudski's cabin was midships, separated from his engineroom by not much more than a bulkhead, then from there a narrow companionway led aft, below the bridge, to the stern cabins for *Tern's* skipper and second officer. Their small "officers' territory" wardroom was overhead, at main-deck level. So was the patrol boat's immaculate little galley, a spotless, glinting area equipped with everything from a chest fridge-freezer to a microwave oven.

Maxwell showed it all, yet set a fast pace. Detailing equipment, pointing out problems real or possible, he swept Carrick along in a way that showed that the aircraft waiting on the island wasn't far from his thoughts.

But when they reached the last stop, the cockpit bridge, he halted, said nothing and let Carrick look around. If he had his own emotions, he didn't show them.

Running most of the width of the patrol boat's broad-beamed hull, with more floor space than anywhere else aboard, the bridge area was panelled in mahogany and had thick glass down to chest level on three sides. An area aft held storage lockers, radio equipment and a small lectern desk which substituted for a chartroom.

Slowly Carrick walked forward. In front of him was a layout which told more about *Tern* than any words.

"Take your time," murmured Maxwell.

Carrick nodded, feeling that his mouth had gone dry.

Two black, thickly padded, fully adjustable chairs on pedestals faced the bridge's closely packed array of instruments, dials and glinting, aircraft-style controls. Andy Grey occupied the right-hand chair and had turned to face them. He had one hand resting casually on *Tern's* surprisingly large, surprisingly slim-rimmed steering wheel. It had a wooden rim, which seemed totally out of place in its electronic surroundings.

"Take a break, Andy." Maxwell pointed towards the door. "We're almost finished."

Tern's second officer rose with reluctance, forced a quick smile and went out on deck.

"Edgy right now, our Andy," said Maxwell dryly. "I had a dog like him once—didn't like change. Don't let him sulk too much. On a boat this size, that's a luxury you can't afford." He paused and glanced around. "Well, this is the office. You know the layout."

"Yes." Carrick touched the rim of the steering wheel. It quivered beneath his fingers as some underwater eddy played with the patrol boat's rudder blades. The wheel was big for the same reason it was power-assisted, to give maximum handling sensitivity. "Blindfolded."

He meant it, literally. It had been one of the final tests.

"So they still do that?" Maxwell grinned. "All right, how much of a briefing did you get on the operational side?"

"Basics." To one side, a low hiss of static came from a radio set. Overhead, digital readouts glowed from the additional instruments located above the bridge windows. "I was told to take the rest from you."

"Typical," Maxwell said. "Well, I left a folder in my cabin—your cabin now. There's the usual confidential stuff, and I stuck in a few notes that could be useful."

"Thanks." Carrick faced him. "I'd like to hear some of it from you."

"If that's what you want." Maxwell looked both surprised and pleased, but warned, "There isn't much of it good. For instance, there's a brand new oil slick drifting about twelve miles north of here—brand new as far as we're concerned, anyway. A fishing boat found it at first light today."

Carrick grimaced. "Big?"

"Not particularly. It's presenting about half a mile across, no more, and breaking up. But nasty—it looks like heavy crude sludge." Maxwell opened a drawer as he spoke and took out two small glass bottles. They were sealed, labelled, and held a black, tarry substance. "I had a look on the way down, collected the usual samples, and I'll take them out with me."

"One less job for me," said Carrick. The samples would be analysed, identified chemically in terms of possible source. If it was heavy crude sludge, it meant the captain of an oil tanker had carried out some illegal, time-saving tank cleaning while under way, then had flushed the results into the sea—and to hell with the consequences. But there was another, more immediate problem. "Where is it heading?"

"Keep your fingers crossed," advised Maxwell. "It could be turning, going out again. There's a dogleg current up there, maybe enough to keep the thing clear of land—though it may sideswipe a few of the smaller islands." He stuffed the bottles into a pocket of his overalls, turned again and brought down a chart from one of the shelves. "Now, let me show you real trouble. Welcome to Patrol Box Tango."

Carrick helped spread the linen-backed Admiralty chart on the desk, then looked at Maxwell again.

"Done your homework?" asked Maxwell.

He nodded. By the simple expedient of drawing inked lines on a chart, Fishery Protection divided all the sea around Scotland into patrol sectors. On the west coast, that meant box-shaped areas from the mainland out across the storm-funnel waters of the Minch to the islands of the Outer Hebrides and beyond. Anyone in Fishery Protection knew Box Tango by reputation. Anyone going into it made very sure he learned what he could in advance.

"At least life isn't dull," murmured Maxwell, as if reading his mind.

"I had that feeling." Carrick considered the chart for a moment. "Now it's getting worse."

Someone had carefully shaded the Box Tango sector in an appropriately angry yellow. Kenbride Island was on the southern limit, and Tango angled north from there in a line which took in some sixty miles of rocky mainland coast. Then it reached out into the Minch, gathering in a navigational nightmare of islands and reefs, a chart area studded with symbols which told of wrecks old and new, other markings in red which showed where an occasional lighthouse warned off any ship foolish enough to stray in without reason.

"The yellow was Andy's idea." Maxwell sounded apologetic. "But it helps—you can see how things are. On the one hand, there are some good deep-water channels. On the other, there's pure patrol-boat territory, sudden death to anything much bigger—and the same goes for most of the so-called harbours. Until we came along, half of the fishermen on this coast weren't sure we really existed."

Carrick grinned. "And when they found out?"

"They like their fun," grunted Maxwell. "I brought *Tern* on station three weeks ago. The second night, while we were at anchor, someone used us for target practice with a rifle. It knocked hell out of the glasswork."

"Better than being ignored," mused Carrick.

"Ignored?" Maxwell wasn't particularly amused. "We've got a nickname too. Anytime they chat about *Tern* on radio, they call her the Baby-sitter Boat. The trouble is, they're right—that's why we're here."

Carrick nodded. His briefing at Department level had been in more formal language, with talk of Commission of European Communities agreements. But the bottom line was the same. He would be baby-sitting.

The new economic offshore wealth around Scotland came from the giant gas and oil production platforms in the North Sea and the new Celtic Sea fields. But there was another wealth—the annual catches of herring needed by Europe, catches which had been reckoned in millions of tons.

Had been. For too many postwar years, the hungry modern trawler fleets, from both sides of the Iron Curtain, had decimated fish stocks. Until suddenly, unbelievably, boats began returning empty. The herring shoals no longer existed.

Europe's herring spawned in the deep-water sea loch inlets of the Scottish northwest coast, where the residual warmth of the Gulf Stream gave their young the chance to survive the winter. Forced into it, Europe had changed the rules—tight fishing-limit quotas were being backed by a new order that from October until March the Scottish spawning grounds were totally closed to trawls and nets. Any pirate flouting the ban could be fined a crushing £50,000 sterling. His catch, his gear, even his boat could be confiscated.

The Department briefing added a footnote. Patrol Box Tango was rated by fishery research scientists as the "richest and largest of the herring nursery areas."

"Ever meet *Puffin*'s skipper, Johnny Walker?" asked Maxwell suddenly.

"I know him," Carrick said cautiously. *Puffin* was another of the *Tern*-class boats; Walker wasn't one of his favourite people.

"*Puffin* is working in our box. Department moved her in ten days ago to lend a hand. I've been operating both boats as a team." Maxwell eyed him deliberately. "I checked, and you're Walker's senior by a couple of the proverbial short hairs—so *Tern* stays command boat."

Carrick didn't comment and decided not to ask how Walker felt about it. He'd find out soon enough.

A hoarse screech sounded above the background noises of the patrol boat, and a large black-backed gull banked out of a diving turn just outside. Still screaming, it vanished, and Maxwell was leaning over the chart again.

"You know we've had a few raids on the nursery areas?"

"Alleged raids," said Carrick. "That was the phrase used."

"Damn Department jargon." Maxwell rested one finger like a pointer on the yellow-shaded sector. "They're happening. If I was a trawler skipper, I'd maybe try it myself—one night of fishing in any of these sea lochs, get away with it, and they might as well have their own private gold mine."

"How do you hear about them?"

"The usual way—some static-gear fisherman, working legally, lobster fishing or long-lining, starts howling that his gear has been wrecked or trawled away." Maxwell shrugged. "We've had two reports of boats almost rammed in the night, other stories about warning shots, general minor mayhem."

"Organized?"

"Organized enough to make sure we're always left like idiots." Maxwell turned away and prowled the bridge. "I've used Dunbrach harbour in Priest Bay as a base, because it's a useful midpoint in the sector and, more important, the few other harbours are even smaller or dry out. From there, I've run varied patrols, operated random sweeps—the lot." His mouth tightened. "But every time, we've been in the wrong place or too late. It's like someone was reading my mind."

"Someone ashore working for them?"

"It has to be that way," admitted Maxwell. "And he has the right connections."

Carrick nodded a slow agreement. West-coast fishermen operated like an offshore Mafia, particularly when at sea. They used their own private radio codes to speak to other boats from the same port —or wives ashore. Any unexpected sighting of a "fishery snoop" grey hull brought an immediate warning for friends and neighbours.

But the sea loch raids sounded like the work of large trawlers, not local boats. Trawlers, whatever their nationality, were foreigners, loathed and usually excluded from the coded chatter.

Unless someone had the right connections.

The black-backed gull had returned, had landed on the foredeck.

It stared in at them, screamed a derisive challenge, and a lump of cotton waste hurtled in answer from somewhere aft. Startled, the gull flapped away while a voice shouted a curse.

"Gogi," explained Maxwell absently. "He doesn't like bird shit on his deck." He frowned at his wristwatch. "I'll have to move. Look, if you want an alternative harbour to Dunbrach then try St. Ringan, to the north. But watch the approach—it's tricky."

"I will," promised Carrick. "What about contacts?"

"Your best is Jimsy Fletcher in Dunbrach. He's the local postman and their special constable, plus a few other things. He'll help if he can. But steer clear of a family named Rose—they're trouble, including the women." Maxwell grimaced. "And whatever you do, don't tangle with a character called the Bagman—anything in uniform is his natural enemy. He lives like a beachcomber, but he can eat little people like us for breakfast."

"Maybe I should come back with you," suggested Carrick.

"No chance, friend." Maxwell opened a locker, brought out his skipper's cap with the gold Fishery Protection badge above the peak and looked at it. "I'll miss a few things but, hell, I'm not going to get emotional now."

"Good luck," said Carrick.

"To both of us." Maxwell grinned, rammed the cap firmly on his head, then straightened. His right hand came up in a crisp salute. "She's yours, Skipper. Permission to go ashore?"

"Permission granted." Carrick returned the salute, matching the formality, knowing the moment mattered to the lean, overalled figure. "And thanks."

They shook hands, then he went with Maxwell to the stern, where Clapper Bell was waiting in the inflatable. Maxwell's gear was already aboard and he scrambled down. The outboard engine fired and the little boat rasped away towards the shore and the waiting aircraft.

Carrick glanced round.

The cocktails pennant had gone from the rigging.

Port and starboard diesels ticking over, a shimmer of blue smoke pulsing from their stern exhausts, *Tern* was ready to get under way by the time Clapper Bell had returned from the island. As the inflatable was brought aboard, they saw the Piper Aztec take off from the beach landing strip. It climbed rapidly, then turned south and rocked its wings in goodbye.

It was their turn to move. Bell was back in the coxswain's position, Carrick in the command chair, Andy Grey standing behind them.

"Andy." Carrick glanced round. "We'll head back to Priest Bay, normal patrol speed. Course?"

"Steer—uh"—Grey's eyes flickered quickly to the compass binnacle—"bring her round to zero-three-two."

"Zero-three-two," said Bell amiably, the wheel already spinning.

"Medium pitch, and taking her to two thousand r.p.m." Gently, conscious of at least one critical spectator, Carrick opened the two outer throttle levers. "Stay around, Andy."

They started to move, the hull vibrating as the diesels began growling. Carrick caught another glimpse of the Aztec, a dwindling speck in the sky, then turned his attention back to the patrol boat. Gathering speed, throwing up spray, she left a curve of white wash behind her as she came round on her triple rudders.

A few seconds more, and the vibration altered as her bow came up. Hands still on the throttle levers, Carrick waited for the next moment as the patrol boat bucked along.

It came. *Tern* suddenly settled into that strange and level hull position and the vibration eased. He grinned to himself, checked the instrument dials and sat back.

"Heading?"

"Zero-three-two." Clapper Bell gave a fractional wink. "On course, Skipper."

"Right." He slipped out of the command chair and motioned for Grey to take his place. "Take over, Andy. I'll be in my cabin."

His second officer nodded and combed a hand quickly through his spiky black hair. Leaving the bridge, Carrick headed aft along the narrow companionway. He reached the steps which led down to his cabin, then caught a glimpse of Gogi MacDonnell through the open door of the galley. Sad-faced as ever, still wearing his wool cap, MacDonnell was nursing a coffee mug. Changing direction, Carrick joined him.

"Any more of that?" he asked.

"Always is, sir," said MacDonnell. Shuffling around, he produced another mug and filled it from a large brown pot.

"Thanks." Carrick took the mug and sipped the slopping, scalding coffee. "Where do you come from, Gogi—originally?"

"Not around here," said MacDonnell. "I'm Outer Isles, Skipper—Barra way."

"Fishing folk?"

"Aye." MacDonnell allowed himself a slight flicker of a smile. "Always have been. I was myself."

"Till you switched sides?"

"Some saw it that way." MacDonnell shrugged. "I wanted a change."

Carrick nodded. A fisherman who stepped across the line as MacDonnell had done usually lost a few friends.

"You know this part of the coast?"

"One way and another, yes." MacDonnell's lean features didn't alter. "And before you ask, Skipper, yes, I know a few folk ashore, around Dunbrach and Priest Bay." He took a swallow of coffee, then dumped the empty mug in the galley sink. "But I'm still an outsider, almost as much as you are. It's not just the uniform that goes against us—on this coast, you need five generations of family in the local churchyard before you're accepted."

"You tried for Maxwell?"

MacDonnell nodded.

"Keep trying. I'd appreciate it," said Carrick quietly.

He finished his coffee, then went down to his cabin. Inside, the door closed behind him, he drew a deep breath and looked around. His bag was lying on the bunk, propped against the inner skin of the glass-fibre hull, quivering a little in sympathy with its surroundings.

The cabin was smaller than he'd had on *Marlin,* but with a better finish, plenty of locker space and a separate compartment which held a washbasin and toilet. The shower cubicle, which he shared with Grey, was located outside.

It didn't take him long to unpack, and his own things scattered around took away much of the strangeness of his surroundings. He learned a little in the process, like watching his shaving kit, placed on the smooth surface of the tiny dressing table, promptly slide to one side and stop against a bulkhead. His heavy duffel coat swayed gently on a hook behind the door, and the cabin porthole, above the bunk, gave him a spray-blanketed view out just above *Tern's* water-line.

He'd get used to it all. Finished, Carrick took the folder Tim Maxwell had left, glanced at the contents, tucked it into a locker to study later, then sat on the edge of the bunk and rubbed a thumb along his chin.

Just at that moment Carrick could have used a cigarette. But he'd more or less stopped using them and his last pack, still almost full, was one of the things he'd left behind when he'd said goodbye to the fishery cruiser.

The steady roar of the diesels throbbed through him as he stayed on the edge of the bunk, putting together the way he'd found things.

Box Tango would have been enough on its own. But having *Puffin* and Johnny Walker for company, under his orders, wasn't a totally welcome surprise. He could certainly use help—but *Puffin* hadn't been mentioned before he flew up. He knew just enough about the way minds worked at Fleet Support to realize it could have been deliberate.

Why? Carrick considered his reflection in the dressing table's little mirror, remembering other occasions.

There was always a reason. It had been almost the first lesson he'd learned when he had switched from a deep-sea Merchant Navy life and had been given the black warrant card which declared Webster Carrick held an appointment as a British Fisheries Officer.

A sea-going policeman—part of the offshore law-enforcement agency for the Scottish fishing grounds, an agency with responsibility for several thousand square miles of dangerous seas and treacherous coasts, the hunting ground for an international line-up of fishing boats.

A thin scatter of protection cruisers and the new patrol boats flew the Blue Ensign with gold anchor badge of the service. Without as much as a deck gun, they used that flag as their authority—backed by a combination of speed, diplomacy and sometimes hard-fisted logic.

It wasn't easy. The multimillion-pound fishing industry, an industry of fiercely independent individuals, always wanted bigger catches and bigger profits. Home fishermen or foreign, small drifters or ship-sized factory trawlers, each had its own rights or restrictions —with plenty of skippers contemptuous of controls, ready to run the risks involved, gamble with lives as well as livelihoods.

Fishery Protection held the line. Sometimes that meant boarding or arresting; sometimes it meant rescue and a grudging, wry respect.

But when there was a puzzle, there was always a reason.

The thought sparked another. Swearing under his breath, Carrick reached for the wall-mounted ship's phone beside the bunk and pressed the bridge button. There was a short buzz, then Clapper Bell answered.

"That oil slick," said Carrick. "Are we near it yet?"

"Near enough, Skipper," said Bell. "Just about within spitting distance."

Carrick heard a brief mutter at the other end, then Andy Grey came on the line.

"Sorry, sir," said his second officer quickly, almost tensely. "Bell's right. Maybe I should have called you. I—"

"You're not a mind-reader," said Carrick. "Reduce speed and stay on the edge of the thing. I'll come up."

He replaced the phone. The diesels were slowing as he left the cabin. By the time he climbed the companionway steps and went through to the cockpit bridge, *Tern*'s broad-beamed hull had curtsied down and her white wake had become a narrow, milky ribbon of disturbed sea. Clapper Bell was still behind the wheel, but the door on the port side was open and Andy Grey was out on deck.

"Out there." Bell pointed in the same direction. "That's Handa Island."

The island was a grey mass of high, bare rock about a mile off the port beam. Between it and the patrol boat, a long stretch of sea was covered in a blanket of black oil. Carrick could smell the oil in the air, could see how it smothered the light swell except at the edges, where isolated patches had been broken away by tide and current.

"How close do we go?" queried Bell, his main attention on *Tern*'s controls.

"Keep easing in," ordered Carrick. A miniature snowstorm of white specks, seabirds taking to the air, had risen from the island. He watched them circle for a moment. "Cut your speed all the way back."

He went out on deck, caught a glimpse of Gogi MacDonnell spectating near the stern, then joined Grey.

"Tim Maxwell hoped we might be lucky." Carrick indicated the oil-covered water. "Any real change in this muck's position?"

"I think so, sir." Grey's young, pock-marked face frowned. "The slick was about a mile south of Handa when we came down. Yes, it's on the turn."

"That's the way we want things." If the slick had turned, was moving back out into the open Minch, it could break up faster—and it would be in someone else's patrol box. "Take a positive position fix, then signal Department."

Grey nodded and went back into the bridge.

Murmuring on, rolling a little in the swell, *Tern* began to encounter some of the drifting patches of oil on the edge of the slick. Where they touched, they left black streaks along her waterline.

"Gogi MacDonnell won't thank you for that," said a dry voice at Carrick's elbow. "He gets paranoid about keeping a clean ship."

Carrick turned. Sam Pilsudski had come up on deck, an unlit stub of cheroot jammed into one corner of his mouth. The engineer officer slouched nearer, the light breeze ruffling his long hair and giving him the appearance of a tousled sheepdog.

"I've seen worse." Pilsudski nodded at the slick. "Bigger, anyway."

"You can keep them," said Carrick grimly.

"Right." Pilsudski gave enough of a grin to show a flash of gold teeth. "Ever think of how most of them look, like a man could walk on them?"

"Try it on your own time," advised Carrick.

"Maybe." Pilsudski's voice lost its humour. "Then—well, maybe not."

They were passing another drifting patch. A large, dead seabird was half-buried in the tarry sludge, a blackened shape with one big wing spread like a tarnished, broken fan.

"And there'll be plenty more like it," said Pilsudski. "Notice those birds over on Handa? There must be damned thousands of them."

No one ever really knew how many birds died in an oil slick, how slowly or how painfully. Carrick decided he had seen enough. Glancing round, he signalled through the bridge window to Clapper Bell. Bell nodded, and the diesels began to change their note.

"Skipper." Pilsudski's voice was harsh and quick. "Hold it."

Another patch of oil was drifting towards them. Something floating with it was too big to be any kind of bird.

"Hell," said Carrick sickly.

He gave a swift, chopping signal and *Tern*'s engines faded again.

They used a boathook to guide the body round to the sternwell deck, brought it aboard and laid it on a piece of old canvas Gogi MacDonnell had hastily produced. It was caked in sludge but, using a rag, Carrick cleaned down to a white face and staring, dead eyes. Then to half-opened lips edged with a thin, oil-scummed froth which always meant death by drowning.

"Well?" He sat back on his heels and looked round. "Know him?"

Clapper Bell and MacDonnell were standing behind him. Pilsudski had made a strategic withdrawal to his engineroom and Andy

Grey had the helm. The two chief petty officers exchanged a glance and shook their heads.

"He's not dressed like any kind of fisherman," said Bell slowly. "But I haven't heard of anyone missing."

He was right. A padded nylon jacket, once red, was buttoned up to the neck and topped denim trousers. One foot was bare, the other still wore a rubber-soled canvas shoe.

Tight-lipped, Carrick stooped again and unbuttoned the padded jacket. Thick oil clung to his fingers in the process. Then the jacket fell open—and he stared.

"Jesus," said Clapper Bell softly in a way that was no blasphemy. "He's a woman."

A woman who had been wearing a thin flannel shirt, now sodden and clinging to her dead body like a second skin. Gogi MacDonnell hesitated, then removed his woollen cap as a vague mark of respect. For the first time, Carrick saw that MacDonnell was totally bald.

"Where the hell did she come from?" asked Bell of no one in particular, and no one answered him.

She had probably been in her forties. Under the oil, her medium-length hair was light brown. But there was nothing in the jacket's pockets to identify her, no jewellery apart from a small gold wedding ring on one finger, no hint of what might have happened.

"Cover her up." Carrick got to his feet, looked at the oil oozing over the canvas, and saw MacDonnell's expression. He knew what the man was thinking. "But leave her on deck—it won't make any difference now."

Turning away, he went quickly to the bridge. When he arrived there, Andy Grey eyed him nervously.

"I've sent the signal with the oil slick's position, sir," reported Grey. He hesitated. "Should we send another now, about the body?"

"It can wait." Carrick flopped into the command chair and sighed. "Andy, stop calling me 'sir' every other minute. It makes me feel old. Understood?"

"Yes, si—Skipper." Grey looked at him strangely.

"Then let's get out of this." Carrick found a clean rag and tried to clean the worst of the oil from his hands. "Resume course, full ahead."

"Resume course, full ahead, Skipper," repeated Andy Grey.

He opened the throttle levers and *Tern*'s diesels began to gather speed. A first thin wind-borne curtain of spray began to spatter over the canvas-wrapped body at her stern.

Handa Island and the oil slick were soon far behind them.

2

For another half-hour, the patrol boat travelled north along the bleak, barren, almost empty mainland coast. The wind veered a few points, some cotton wool cloud drifted in overhead, but the sea stayed calm.

Webb Carrick used it as a time for settling in, for quietly observing the ways of *Tern*'s crew. Few orders were really needed as they carried out their tasks. They knew what to do and when, did it without fuss or question, totally at home in their small, noisy world.

They passed an elderly coaster plugging south with a pen of sheep as deck cargo. The only real excitement, enough to bring Sam Pilsudski up from his engineroom and coax Gogi MacDonnell out on deck, was a hunting pack of killer whales. *Tern* overtook them on her port quarter, a dozen sleek, black-backed, white-bellied shapes, travelling fast, almost on the surface, ravaging death on the move for anything big enough and unfortunate enough to cross their path.

Priest Bay, when it showed ahead, had green hills as a backcloth. A ten-mile sweep of sand and shingle beach and shaped like a broken saucer, the bay ended to the north with a narrow spit of high land which served as a natural breakwater. Beyond the spit lay Loch Ringan, one of the main designated herring nursery areas.

That left the Hound Islands to the west. Several miles out from the mainland, scattered like a half-strung necklace, they showed as a series of saw-toothed outlines on the radar scan. The Hounds had a reputation to match—ships of any size stayed away from them.

For the moment, the Hound Islands were just part of the scenery. Priest Bay was still unfolding and, using the bridge glasses, Carrick followed a tiny ribbon of road to where sunlight glinted on windows. At first sight, Dunbrach harbour looked pleasant but unimpressive, a typical enough fishing village. Clustered together on the rising ground, cottages and other buildings backed the solid grey stone of the harbour wall. Some boats were in. He could just make out the tips of their masts.

But another part of the bay was becoming visible from behind a fold of land. Carrick blinked in surprise as two huge black hulls suddenly seemed to fill the lenses. Instinctively he tightened the focus and stared again.

Two big ocean-going oil tankers, riding high and empty, lay at anchor close into the shore in what had to be deep water. He made a puzzled guess that their anchorage was two miles east of the village, then lowered the glasses.

"What about them?" he asked sharply.

"The tankers?" Andy Grey half-turned in his seat. "They've been there for months, Skipper. It's the usual story—no work for them."

"So they're parked up here," said Clapper Bell, raising his voice to make sure he was heard. "Fifty-thousand tonners, both o' them— the *Ranata* and the *Ranassen,* Danish-owned, Panamanian-registered."

Carrick grimaced.

Unemployed tankers had become a sad part of the shipping scene. The worldwide glut of tanker tonnage became worse every time oil prices took another rise; even some of the massive supertankers now spent months quietly rusting at their moorings. Down on the Clyde, he had seen five tankers anchored in a sad, unwanted line.

But, even using the best deep-water channel in from the Minch, bringing a pair of fifty-thousand-ton ships into Priest Bay must have been a hair-raising experience for their captains.

"Who was the genius who chose Priest Bay?" he asked with heavy sarcasm. "Does he have a name?"

"Yes. You could even meet him, Skipper," said Grey. "Magnus Andersen—he owns the Rana Line, and the rest of his money is in oil." He sucked his teeth with a degree of envy. "Andersen bought one of the Hound Islands a couple of years ago as a hideaway, and spends a lot of time there. I saw him in Dunbrach a couple of days ago."

"An' I saw what was with him," interrupted Clapper Bell with a lecherous grin. "She's tall an' blond, and she wasn't his mother." He sighed. "You know, if I had that kind of money—"

"You haven't." Carrick cut him short and turned to Grey again. "Andersen. Is he friendly in our direction?"

"He knows we exist," said Grey warily. "We haven't troubled him and he hasn't troubled us, Skipper."

"We'll try to keep it that way," murmured Carrick. He thumbed Grey out of the command chair, took his place and settled back

against the padding. "Clapper, bring her round ten points to starboard. I want a look at these tankers."

It was sheer curiosity. There was no way the oil slick to the south
could have originated from the two tanker ships in Priest Bay, but
they were still unexpected neighbours.

A few minutes later *Tern* made a leisurely half-speed pass about two
hundred yards out from the anchored ships. The great black, rust-
streaked hulls towered above the little patrol boat, totally shutting
out any view of the land as she cruised along. But they had a sad,
almost brooding air, tethered by those massive anchor chains, con-
demned to wait until someone, somewhere, might want them.

A line of washing was drying on the *Ranata*'s foredeck and a thin
stream of water was cascading from her side. A man appeared near
the stern, looked down at them and gave a lazy wave. There was no
sign of life on the *Ranassen,* but some recently dumped garbage was
floating near her.

"Two caretakers aboard each of them, and a maintenance team
come visitin' now and again," explained Clapper Bell as *Tern* cleared
the *Ranassen*'s bow. They could see the shore again and a small,
obviously new wooden jetty. "Fresh groceries once a week, everything laid on—can't be bad, having a berth like that."

"Would you do it?" asked Carrick.

"Me?" The big Glasgow-Irishman winced at the thought. "No.
But ask me in another twenty years. I could have changed my mind
by then."

Carrick grinned, then answered the engineroom phone as it
buzzed.

"Skipper?" Sam Pilsudski seemed to believe in shouting. "Sorry,
but I'm going to have to shut everything down for an hour as soon
as we're in Dunbrach."

"What's the problem?" Carrick checked the instrument dials as he
asked. "Everything looks all right here."

"It's technical. You don't have to understand," said Pilsudski.
"I've got a hot bearing down here."

"You've got your hour," said Carrick resignedly.

An overfall patch of lumping swell lurked outside Dunbrach harbour, but the actual approach, lining up two signal beacons and
keeping them parallel, was simple enough. The patrol boat loitered
in towards the clustered houses and the harbour entrance, the clear
water beneath her showing weed-covered rock. Other rocks, some

Hound Islands—the one out on Little Drummer Island. Who wants to go visiting there? Man, I suppose it could have been weeks before anyone really worried about them."

The group on the quayside had been listening and were beginning their own muttered discussion. Not all the glances coming Carrick's way were friendly and, although there were other questions he wanted to ask, the time wasn't right.

"We'll get her ashore," he said quietly.

They helped, soberly, silently, and Carrick joined them on the quay. The woman's body had been placed a few paces away, resting on some empty fish boxes, and the other men went farther along the quay, to where another group had gathered. Only MacTaggart was left beside Carrick. The fishing skipper lit a cigarette and held it cupped in one hand.

"You're Maxwell's replacement?" he asked after a moment.

Carrick nodded.

"Hard luck." The man made it a grunt. "You could have had a better start."

He seemed ready to say more but stopped it there as an old red van came speeding into the harbour from the village. It slowed, weaved among the quayside obstacles towards them, then stopped and two men got out. The driver, slightly built and wearing overalls, had thinning sandy hair and metal-rimmed spectacles. His passenger was in postman's uniform, older, stockily built.

The postman led the way across, gave MacTaggart a casual nod and faced Carrick with considerably more interest.

"*Tern*'s new skipper, eh?" He spoke with a dry West Highland lilt, gave a slight smile and added, "Not the best of welcomes, Mr. Carrick. Still, as it says in the Book, 'We speak that we do know, and testify that we have seen.' "

"Right, Jimsy." The slight figure beside him had a faint lisp. "John, chapter three, eh—verse ten."

"Verse eleven." The postman fumbled in one pocket, drew out a crumpled handkerchief, tried again and briefly offered a battered warrant card. "Credentials—I'm Jimsy Fletcher, the special constable here." He indicated his companion. "This is Hammy, my brother. He's our village undertaker."

Hammy bared his teeth in what was meant to be a smile. "Part-time only, Skipper. Mainly I run a wee plumbing business—there's not enough people around Dunbrach to make a living out of burying them."

Carrick shook hands with them both. A plumber who was an undertaker, a postman who was a part-time constable—it happened that way and sometimes more along the sparsely populated coast. A part-time special constable like Jimsy Fletcher was given the equivalent of a few days' police training a year and had "real" police on call from the nearest divisional office if things got rough. Jimsy looked the older of the two brothers, probably in his late forties, heavier in build, with watery blue eyes. But there was still a strong family resemblance in looks, and they shared the same shade of sandy hair.

"Both of them now, husband and wife. We expected that." Jimsy Fletcher paused, watching Hammy amble off towards the dead woman. MacTaggart went with him. "Well, Hammy will take care of the arrangements. There's no one makes a better coffin." He gave a sigh. "But it'll mean the usual paperwork—no avoiding that."

"When was the last time anyone saw Keenan or his wife?"

"Alive? I don't know yet," said Fletcher. "There's still some of this morning's mail to deliver, then I'll start asking." He scratched his chin and looked hopeful. "Will your people take care of what we could call the offshore side of things—for now, anyway?"

"We could go out to their lighthouse and take a look around," agreed Carrick slowly. "But I'd rather wait until *Puffin* gets back. Anything else?"

"Yes, Skipper, there is—in a way." Fletcher sucked his teeth and made it an innocent smile. "You'll know about *Puffin?*"

"Tell me," invited Carrick.

"It seems some foreign trawlers were busy pirating again last night, north of here. Skipper Walker heard about it and thought he'd go and take a look. There's—ah—well, a connection."

"Then connect," said Carrick.

"The man who found Bob Keenan brought back some wreckage." Fletcher stuffed his hands in the pockets of his postman's jacket and looked carefully out to sea. "Bits of Keenan's boat. There's a story these damned trawlers were poaching in Loch Ringan three nights ago, then left in a hurry. Now suppose one rammed Keenan's boat and just kept on going—" He paused again. "That would be offshore, wouldn't it?"

"It would." The story, easily built on rumour, could fan a lot of trouble. "I'll have to see the wreckage, talk to the crew who found Keenan."

"There's only one man involved—he always sails on his own."

Fletcher's interest shifted from the sea to the fish boxes behind Carrick.

The other Fletcher had produced a home-made wooden stretcher from his plumber's van and had recruited MacTaggart and two other fishermen to help him. Using it, they carried the woman's body to the van and loaded it aboard. The rear doors slammed shut and Hammy nodded to his brother.

"One man, then," said Carrick. "What's his name?"

"Well, he's not always cooperative," said Jimsy Fletcher cautiously. "You'll need to remember that."

"I'll try."

Fletcher shuffled his feet. "Around here, folk just call him the Bagman. You won't have heard of him."

"You're wrong." Carrick took a deep breath and resisted a sudden urge to kick Dunbrach's special constable on the seam of his postman's trousers. But Fletcher had him trapped. Tim Maxwell's warning about the Bagman looked like coming to life. "So where will I find him? Or are you going to come along?"

"No, I must get that mail delivered," said Jimsy Fletcher hastily. He gestured quickly at the slipway side of the harbour. "Try Reiver's repair yard. If he isn't there, he has a house of sorts along the shore."

"Thanks," said Carrick.

"You're welcome." Fletcher began rapidly edging away. "And—ah—as it says in the Book, 'He that doeth wrong—' "

"Usually makes a profit." Carrick was cruel.

Jimsy Fletcher swallowed, finished his retreat to the van and clambered in. It drove off at a dignified pace.

Gogi MacDonnell was aft, using a mop and bucket to wipe away the oil stains still on his deck. The engineroom for'ard hatch was open and a tuneless whistling from below showed that Sam Pilsudski was happy enough working on his engine problem. But neither Clapper Bell nor Andy Grey was visible. Carrick went back aboard and found them in the little for'ard mess area. Bell was talking quietly and the young second officer was listening with a worried expression on his thin, earnest face.

Whatever they'd been discussing, it stopped when Carrick entered. Grey got to his feet. Clapper Bell stayed seated and gave a quick warning frown that Carrick shouldn't ask.

"I'm going ashore," he told them. "I've got to find the Bagman—he brought in the other body."

Bell and Grey exchanged a wincing glance.

"I know," agreed Carrick. "But I'm boxed in. Andy, still no word from *Puffin?*"

"None, Skipper." Grey shook his head.

"Keep a listening watch till I get back. Don't call them." Carrick had his own notion why *Puffin*'s commander was staying silent. He turned to the Glasgow-Irishman. "Clapper, you and Gogi take a turn ashore for an hour. Keep your ears open for gossip about the Keenans or what might have happened to them—you know what to do."

"No problem." Bell gave an understanding grin.

"But don't stray." Carrick knew he didn't have to say more. "Now, how much trouble should I expect from this Rose family? Are they all as thorny as Grandpa?"

"They're unpredictable," said Andy Grey feelingly. "If we'd rammed Grandpa, they'd either have declared war or just fallen about laughing." He glanced at Clapper Bell and got a nod of encouragement. "The Roses are like a—a tribe of sea gypsies, Skipper. They live out of the village—nobody seems to know how many of them there actually are. They run a string of old boats, they're into everything from fishing to dealing in scrap metal, and Jimsy Fletcher reckons they're always feuding with someone."

"He should know." Carrick gave a slight smile at the mention of Dunbrach's special constable. "Are we on their hate list?"

Grey shook his head. "No more than you'd expect. Some occasional hassle ashore, but nothing worse. Tim Maxwell tried to keep it that way."

"Grandpa maybe rules, but Danny Rose seems the one to watch," said Clapper Bell. "Danny is the old devil's favourite son—and the kind who should be kept in a cage. He goes around in his own version of cowboy boots, and he'll use them to kick anyone's ribs in when he feels annoyed." He looked down at his large fists and grinned. "But there's a cure for that."

"Leave him to someone else," Carrick told him bluntly. "We've enough on our plate."

He left them, went below and entered the engineroom. Sam Pilsudski's domain, a box-shaped area with a metal floor, was dominated by the three grey-painted diesel units. They were flanked by two large generators and the rest was pipes and valves, scattered dials and a snaking web of armoured cabling. One of the diesels was partly dismantled and Pilsudski stood at a bench, muttering to himself as he worked.

Pilsudski heard Carrick's footsteps on the metal, turned and raised a quizzical eyebrow.

"Skipper?"

"How's the problem coming along?" asked Carrick, glancing at the scattered parts on the bench.

"The bearings thing, Skipper?" Pilsudski's overalls were open to the waist, showing an expanse of hairy chest and stomach; his hands and face were black with oil. He rubbed a hand down his chest, transferring some of the oil in the process, and reached for one of the cheroots in his top pocket. "Fine; not as bad as I thought."

"Good," said Carrick gently, then gestured toward the bench. "Yet that looks more like a pump unit. Strange—and a lot less vital, isn't it, Sam?"

"Uh—" Pilsudski forgot his cheroots, then grinned. "Yes, I got things wrong."

"Sam, I learned the old 'hot bearings' dodge on my first ship," Carrick told him. He looked slowly around the glinting engineroom and shook his head. "If you want maintenance time, you'll get it— anytime I can genuinely manage it. But no more scare stories."

Pilsudski gave an embarrassed nod.

"So we forget it." The last thing Carrick wanted was any kind of quarrel with his engineer officer. "But we've got to go out again. How soon till we're operational?"

"Give me another half-hour." Pilsudski was positive, then curious. "Does that mean you've heard from *Puffin?*"

"No," said Carrick.

"That figures." Pilsudski scratched under one arm and scowled. "There could be better times to say this, but you could have trouble with that bird on *Puffin*. What he needs is—is—"

"A kick up the tail feathers?" suggested Carrick.

Pilsudski laughed and turned back to his bench.

Two of the Dunbrach boats were going out. Carrick stopped on his way along the quayside, watching them. They were open-decked long-liners, each with a whale-back bow shelter, a small for'ard wheelhouse and a blunt transom stern.

Long-liners were a dying breed. They fished with hook and bait—

a thousand hooks on a line that could be over half a mile long, often several lines to a boat. Lines paid out at the chosen fishing ground, then left floating, buoyed at each end. Long-liners hoped for prime demersal fish, cod and whiting, and their catches brought top market prices for quality.

Both boats leaving had a crew of three aboard. A man stood at the stern of one, waving to a woman and a small child standing near the end of the harbour breakwater. The woman waved back, then the boats had gone, bobbing and pitching as they met the swell. The woman turned, took the child by the hand, and they started back towards the village.

Carrick pursed his lips. By now, every woman in Dunbrach probably knew two bodies had been brought ashore. That kind of news struck home in a fishing community, stirred secret fears, left wives thinking of their men at sea. If rumours spread about how the Keenans might have died, then Dunbrach could quickly become an emotional powderkeg.

He began walking again, past piled fish boxes and lobster pots, the drying nets and the moored boats. The air smelled of diesel oil and fish, rotting seaweed and the occasional whiff of stale bilges. The few men around, some gossiping and others working, generally ignored him.

That was usual enough. But he sensed something more, a sullen, low-grade bitterness, and heard the occasional muttered insult directed at his back. Fishery Protection might be the traditional enemy, but when pirate trawlers came raiding and local fishermen lost gear and suffered, then Fishery Protection was supposed to do something about it.

So far, they'd failed—and Fishery Protection couldn't afford to be seen to fail.

He was glad to reach the slipway and Reiver's repair yard. Surrounded by rusted, scrapped machinery and stacked timber, the yard was simply two big brick sheds with corrugated-iron roofing. One had an open front and sheltered a thirty-foot clinker-built lobster boat. The hull propped up by steel cradles, the little wheelhouse stripped down and some of the decking ripped away, it was at the halfway stage in a refit.

But no one was working there, and Carrick turned to the second shed. He opened a door, went in and discovered a brightly lit workshop area. But, again, despite the neon tube lights blazing overhead, there was no one in sight. He went past a purring oil-fired furnace and benches littered with tools, skirted round a portable welding unit, and stopped at the far end where an open-topped Land-Rover stood with the rear axle jacked up and one wheel removed.

"And what the hell do you want?" asked a voice behind him.

A small, thick-set man, grey-haired and wearing mechanics' overalls, limped out from a little cubbyhole of an office which Carrick hadn't noticed. He had a wrinkled, gnomelike face.

"I'm looking for the Bagman," said Carrick.

"He's been—and gone." The small man limped a couple of steps nearer and gave Carrick's uniform a critical glare. *"Tern's* new skipper, aren't you?"

Carrick nodded.

"You found Keenan's wife." The gnomish face became friendlier. "I'm Joe Petrie, the yard foreman—the lads are on their lunch break. If you want the Bagman, try where he lives—east of here, along the beach. Do you know him?"

"No."

Petrie chuckled. "If you go, don't expect a welcome."

"I want to see what he salvaged when he found Keenan," said Carrick. "It could matter."

"It could." The little man beckoned. "There's not a lot, but he asked us to keep it till people like you came along."

Limping ahead, Petrie led the way to the stores area, partitioned into separate bays. In one, otherwise empty, the broken stern section of a small boat was propped against the wall. Streaked with black, tarry oil, a pool of water still forming under it on the concrete floor, the splintered wood was flanked by pieces of smashed planking.

"I knew that boat," said Petrie. "It was maybe a shade heavy, but sturdy enough for any weather—and Bob Keenan could handle it." He shrugged. "So could his wife—living out on that damned lighthouse, they'd plenty of practice."

About four feet of the stern section remained intact, with scars on the transom to show where an outboard motor had been mounted. But the hull had been shattered, the timbers splintered like matchwood.

"You don't get damage like that on rocks," mused Petrie. "Anyway, we've had good weather lately. It had to be—well, like this." He chopped the edge of one hand against an open palm. "I'll bet a year's overtime that boat was run down, hit by something big and in a hurry."

"I'd wait," murmured Carrick. "Why risk your money? We've a Department laboratory staff who get paid to run tests and decide— and they'll want all this."

Petrie glanced round as he heard the shed door creak open again. Then he grinned as a woman came in, closing the door behind her. Dark-haired, in her late thirties, tall and heavily built, she had a plump, round face and wore a sheepskin jacket over a wool sweater and tweed skirt.

"You're back early," accused Petrie.

"When you're talking to a bank manager about an overdraft, he doesn't waste time." She smiled and turned her attention to Carrick. "So—you're Chief Officer Carrick. I know about you. Sam Pilsudski's a friend of mine. Need any help?"

"All I can get," said Carrick dryly.

"Maybe you do." She gave Petrie a slight nod which sent him on his way. "I'm Norah Reiver. For what it's worth, which isn't too much right now, I own this yard."

They shook hands. She had a grip as strong as most men.

"How do you like *Tern?*" she asked.

"I'm still the new boy. But I've no complaints," Carrick told her.

"Good." Norah Reiver said it absently and pointed at the salvaged wreckage. "Well, this is advice, not help. Maybe people didn't know much about Bob Keenan and his wife, but they were liked. The way they died, some of the stories that are going around, there could be a lot of anger building up. Some people are saying the word to use about this is 'murder.'"

" 'Some people'—including you?"

"I'll wait." Her broad face was serious.

He nodded. "How well did you know the Keenans?"

"We talked a few times. They brought in an occasional thing to be repaired." Norah Reiver put her hands in the pockets of her sheepskin jacket. "The last was that old generator behind you—it's ready for collection."

Carrick turned. The generator, small and portable, wasn't just old. It was a museum piece.

"We had a problem getting parts," explained Norah Reiver. "But they weren't worried. They kept it as a reserve machine, and got their electricity from another one we sold them last year. I don't turn down work, not with six men's wages to pay."

Carrick nodded, his attention straying from the old generator to its nearest neighbours, two wooden crates the size and shape of ammunition boxes. But the name Seibe Gorman stencilled on their sides told him a different story. Seibe Gorman was known world-wide for its diving equipment.

"What about these?" he asked.

She shook her head. "No, they're for our Danish oil baron—Magnus Andersen, over on the Hound Islands. He's a scuba enthusiast. I radioed him that the crates had arrived and he's sending a boat over. There's a couple of thousand pounds' worth in that lot."

"Nice." Carrick felt a moment's envy, but a possibility stirred in his mind. "What about the Keenans' generator? Did they know it was ready?"

"You mean could they have been sailing over to collect it?" The big woman beside him shook her head again. "They weren't in any hurry—I told you, it was their spare. And they didn't have a radio link. I knew they'd just look in the next time they were over in Dunbrach."

"Tell me about them," he asked again.

"You'd do better asking Jimsy Fletcher," she said. "Before he delivers a letter, he does everything short of steam it open."

"I'll buy him a kettle."

Norah Reiver chuckled. The shed door opened again and two young men in mechanics' overalls came in. She waited until they passed, heading for the Land-Rover.

"I don't know much. The Keenans were a quiet couple—didn't talk much about themselves." She shrugged. "I'd say they were in their mid-forties. They were certainly from England and they bought the old lighthouse about five years ago."

"What about children, relatives?"

She shook her head. "None I know about."

"Why did they move north?"

"They just decided they didn't want to live in a city anymore and did something about it. It—well, it seemed to work for them."

Carrick nodded. A regular trickle of people tried the same escape route, for the same reason. Most soon decided they'd made a mistake.

"What about money?"

"They counted their pennies, but they paid their bills." She paused, puzzled, vaguely irritated. "Does it matter?"

"Probably not." Except he'd wiped that tarry sludge from a dead woman's face. "Can you keep the boat wreckage until we collect it?"

"Of course." An electric drill began rasping at the Land-Rover. She ignored the noise. "Have you talked to the Bagman yet?"

"He's next on my list."

"I see." A faint twinkle showed in her eyes. "He's difficult—we've had some rows. But I like him."

"Does he have any other name?"

"David Smith—now and again Jimsy has to deliver a letter." Norah Reiver grimaced. "But even Jimsy can't get more out of him than that."

Joe Petrie had come limping back and was waiting impatiently. Carrick thanked her and left, and Petrie gave him a grunt as he went past. Outside, sounds of hammering and sawing came from the boat shed—the yard lunch break was over.

A lamppost and a District Council notice board marked the boundary between harbour and village. The lamppost was being used by a mongrel dog, the notice board had a poster about a church hall concert, a notice that the mobile dental would now call on Tuesdays instead of Thursdays, and a timetable for the local bus service.

On the other side, Dunbrach's main street amounted to about a score of shops and houses facing the sea and a small, almost empty car park with a war memorial in its centre. Behind it and along the shore was a scattering of small stone-built cottages, almost all with white walls and dark slate roofs, television aerials and tiny gardens. A farm truck rattled past, taking the main road which wound up into the hills. Two old men were gossiping on a seat beside the war memorial; the few other people in sight included young girls in denims and a scattering of ambling fishermen admiring the passing scenery.

Carrick turned right, following the shore. A track skirted the front of a small schoolhouse, ran past a few more cottages, then ended at the edge of the beach. He went on, crunching over shingle and dried, crackling seaweed, then rounded a low hummock of ground covered in rough grass.

Ahead of him, farther along the curve of Priest Bay, he could see the black hulls of the two anchored oil tankers. But he was only a stone's throw or so away from the tumble-down remains of an old cottage built close to the foreshore. It faced out towards a fragile wooden jetty where a small fishing boat was tied up, bobbing gently with the light incoming swell.

Half of the cottage roof had fallen in, but the rest had been patched with planks of wood and a strip of roped-down tarpaulin. One window was a gaping hole, another had been blocked with a sheet of tin, and smoke curled from the surviving chimney. Someone had even attempted a patch of garden.

Carrick went nearer. The muffled wail of bagpipe music reached him, competing with the murmur of the waves and the way the light wind rustled through the coarse tufted grass inland. The tune was a pibroch lament with some tricky fingerwork. The piper had to be inside the cottage.

He reached the jetty and stopped where it touched the shingle. The boat, a sturdy, broad-beamed open dinghy, was about fifteen feet long and clinker-built, with an inboard kerosene engine and a whaler's pointed stern. Work-stained, badly in need of a coat of paint, she had the name *Kelpie* branded on her bow. Among the jumble of fishing gear stowed aboard lay a scrap of lugsail and a lowered stub of a mast.

But the wail of pipe music had stopped. The cottage door creaked open and a tall, thin, bearded man stepped out into the daylight and stood in silence for a moment. Then, an ancient, thigh-length leather jacket flapping loose around him, a bulging canvas pouch slung over one shoulder, the figure came stalking across the shingle. When he stopped, he was about three paces away.

"I'm looking for David Smith," said Carrick.

"You've found him." The dark, hooded eyes held no hint of welcome—or anything else.

Over six feet tall, probably about sixty years of age, of skeleton build with a skull-like face to match, the Bagman had skin the texture of worn granite. His roughly trimmed beard, like his hair, was black but liberally sprinkled with grey. Under the jacket, which fitted where it touched, he wore a coarse wool sweater and stained moleskin trousers. His ankle-length boots were laced with fishing twine.

"You brought in Keenan's body," said Carrick.

"I did." The hooded eyes didn't blink. "Then I heard you brought in his wife."

Carrick nodded.

"They were decent enough people." The curt voice softened for a moment, then the bearded mouth tightened again. "What do you want from me?"

"A few details now. Then some kind of statement later."

"A statement?" The Bagman used the word like an unpleasant

taste. "I don't have much time for statements, forms—or uniforms, Skipper."

"I was warned," said Carrick.

"Well, you came." The Bagman showed a trace of amusement. "Not much I can do about that."

He beckoned with a bony hand and Carrick followed him over to the cottage and inside.

They went through a tiny, shabby lobby into a room which might have been a forgotten corner of a maritime junkyard store. Dusty lamps and an old lifebelt lay in one corner beside a broken ship's wheel. Cork fishing floats overflowed from a wooden box; a partially mended net was slung between an upturned barrel and a metal stand.

"Let's get it done with—I've plenty else to do." The Bagman cleared two frayed armchairs, unceremoniously dumping anything lying on them onto the bare floor. "What are you after?"

"Not a lot." Carrick settled in the nearest chair. "Begin with where and when you found Keenan."

"He was about a mile northeast of Handa Island—I saw some birds perched on what looked like a spar of wood. But it wasn't." The pouch still dangling from his shoulder, the whipcord-thin figure bent to feed some fresh billets of driftwood onto the fire which burned in a blackened stone hearth. "If the time matters, I suppose it was round nine A.M." He glanced round. "I sailed around for a bit, but didn't see anything else. Where was the woman?"

"East of Handa, a couple of hours later."

The Bagman nodded and continued to tend his fire. Behind him, a scarred table was littered with the remains of a meal. Behind the table, a stuffed, moth-eaten sea eagle glowered down from a Victorian glass case. A modern pump-action shotgun rested on nails above the fireplace stonework.

"Handa isn't exactly on your doorstep," said Carrick. "What took you down there?"

"A man can sail where he wants." The hooded eyes gave a baleful glare. "I was there—that's what matters."

"All right." Carrick nodded. "Tell me about the wreckage."

"That's easy enough to remember." Rising to his feet, the Bagman scowled at his visitor. "You want to know why? Because the man was jammed into that stern section, like he'd died clinging to it, with most of it under the water." He gave an impatient, dismissive gesture with one bony hand. "I brought it into my boat, then I collected a few bits and pieces."

"I've seen them," said Carrick.

"Then you know," said the Bagman stonily. He sighed. "Talking makes me thirsty. You'll join me in a dram?"

Carrick nodded. The offer wasn't gracious, but old customs still lived on the west coast. A visitor under anyone's roof had to be offered hospitality.

A whisky bottle without a label and a chipped tumbler came from a cupboard. Opening the canvas pouch, the Bagman brought out a battered metal cup and wiped the rim on the sleeve of his leather jacket. He splashed a generous measure of whisky into both and handed the tumbler to Carrick.

"Slainte." The Bagman took a quick swallow from the cup. "This comes from—well, one of the Outer Isles. A man I know has his own wee still, one a few Excisemen would like to find."

"That's not my worry." Carrick sipped the illicit whisky and had seldom tasted better. He tried to probe on. "You know boats. What did you think when you saw that wreckage?"

"That it had nothing to do with me." The Bagman took another swallow from his cup, then sat on the edge of the other chair, lips sucking at a stray tendril of beard. "But—all right, I'll say this much. I saw a boat smashed that way once, years ago. It happened in fog—she was run down by a cargo ship."

"In fog." Carrick looked at him steadily. "When was the last time Priest Bay had fog?"

The Bagman shrugged. "A month ago, maybe more."

"No fog, good weather. And you know the sea around the coast and the islands. You know the tides, the currents."

The thin, bearded figure gave a suspicious frown but said nothing.

"I'm trying to work out why you made the trip down to Handa," said Carrick softly. "Maybe you knew something had happened between here and the Hound Islands. Maybe you worked out when and where the results might turn up."

"Did I?" The Bagman stiffened where he sat and gave a low growl of anger. He drained the rest of his whisky at a gulp, then replaced the tin cup in his pouch. "Man, maybe there are things happening around here. But I've sense enough to want no part in them—I did what I had to do, and I'll do no more." He nodded curtly towards the door. "So finish your drink, then take your silly wee uniform back to your silly wee boat. Get out."

"All right." Carrick took his time over the last of his whisky, set the tumbler on the floor and got to his feet. "If you change your mind, let me know."

The Bagman snorted and stayed seated.

Leaving the cottage, Carrick closed the door. The wind had strengthened again. A chopping swell was beginning to fill the bay and looked worse down where the oil tankers were anchored. He grinned to himself, thinking of a different storm that might have erupted inside the cottage if he'd stayed much longer. Maybe he could have handled things better.

He started to walk along the front of the cottage, heading in the direction of the village. Passing the ruined, roofless section of the old building, he caught a glimpse of a mud-spattered motorcycle propped under a crude shelter inside. Something else caught his eye. Three small white feathers were clinging to the crumbling stonework beside him. There were others, some larger, lying on the ground. Stooping quickly, Carrick gathered the nearest, fingered them briefly, then tucked them in an inside pocket.

He glanced back. There was no sign of a face at the cottage window.

Carrick was glad. Because now he had an idea why the strange, aggressive individual inside hadn't wanted to talk about Handa.

He had been wrong. But it could wait—and it didn't alter his instinctive feeling that the Bagman knew much more than he wanted to tell.

The short walk back across the shingle towards the path to Dunbrach didn't give much time to think.

The way it ended as he stepped onto the path didn't help.

A shot rang out, a bullet slammed into the dirt near his feet, erupting gravel like a small volcano.

Carrick threw himself down. Another shot, a sharp whipcrack that meant a high-powered rifle, following seconds later, and the second bullet glanced off a rock close to his head, then whined away in a wild ricochet.

There was no cover.

But there was no third shot, no sound except his own harsh breathing and the background murmur of wind and sea.

Carrick rose slowly, brushed the grit of the path from his uniform and drew a deep, steadying breath.

The shots had come from inland, from the rising ground beyond the narrow strip of grazing field which formed a boundary with the beach. Over on the far side, a few long-haired Highland cattle turned their soft brown eyes in his direction for a moment, then went back to nuzzling the grass again.

Nothing moved on the rise. The rifleman, whomever he had been, had probably gone.

Carrick sighed, decided to leave things that way.

But someone round Dunbrach had a killing sense of humour. Had two people already died to prove it?

3

Two long-distance fish trucks, big refrigerated units with an English wholesaler's name on their travel-stained sides, had been added to the Dunbrach scenery. Deserted, their drivers off for a meal and a rest before loading and the long haul to the cities, they occupied a considerable portion of the parking space in front of the village war memorial.

Webb Carrick was almost level with them, on his way back to the harbour, when Clapper Bell loitered into sight. Hands in his pockets, a cigarette dangling from his lips, the big Glasgow-Irishman gave what was intended as a surprised grin—the kind that usually meant he wanted something.

"Where's Gogi MacDonnell?" asked Carrick suspiciously. "You were supposed to stay together."

"We did the rounds, then he reckoned you'd be hungry when you got back. He's aboard, in the galley—I said steak, he said no way." Bell removed what was left of the cigarette, flicked it away and looked hopeful. "I could use a beer, Skipper. This business of trotting around an' picking up gossip builds up a man's thirst."

"I know. You've told me before," said Carrick. He knew the rest. Anytime Clapper Bell had money left in his pockets there was something wrong. Back on *Marlin,* it had been reckoned Bell would have had to buy a brewery to square his drinking debts. "All right, it's my shout—again. Where?"

Happily, Clapper Bell led the way.

It was a short walk. Located in a lane a stone's throw from the war memorial, the Long Galley Inn was a place that had seen more than one century pass by. A low building with thick stone walls and narrow, bottle-glass windows, it had a moss-covered slate roof and an entrance door which was two steps down from the level of the lane.

They went in. There were dark oak beams overhead, the stone floor was patched with concrete and the bar counter showed the scars of generations of use and misuse. The air smelled of stale smoke and cheap disinfectant, a fruit machine glowed silently against one wall, and a group of four fishermen standing at the counter were the only other customers.

"Back again, Malky." Bell nodded at the barman, who was fat, with a droopy ginger moustache. He glanced at Carrick. "Uh—"

"Two beers." Carrick paid for the drinks when they came, ignoring the silent stares from along the bar. "Over here."

He led Bell over to a table, where they sat with their backs to one of the bottle-glass window slits. Nursing his beer in one massive paw, Bell took a long, noisy gulp, then wiped the foam from his lips.

"Feel better?" asked Carrick.

"A lot." Bell gave a contented sigh, set down the glass and looked at it for a moment. "Do we forget the 'Skipper' bit for five minutes?"

"I bought the beer, didn't I?" reminded Carrick.

"Yes." Bell gave him a friendly, lopsided grin. "So how did you make out around the village?"

Carrick told him, briefly. The Glasgow-Irishman listened impassively through most of it, but gave a soft, sympathetic chuckle when Carrick finished by telling how he'd been fired at along the beach.

"If they missed, they meant it that way," was his verdict. He paused and took another swallow of beer. "Ach, things look stormy —and I don't mean the flamin' weather. My turn?"

Carrick nodded. "Anything you've got."

"Start with the Keenans, then." Bell set down his glass and rubbed a finger round the rim. "The main story goin' around is that they must have been run down by the trawler that raided Loch Ringan three nights ago."

"Nobody saw a trawler," said Carrick wearily. "All we've got for evidence is some damaged gear. Until we get the postmortem reports we don't even know when they died."

"There's another notion bein' spread." Bell scowled in the general direction of the fishermen at the bar counter. "It's that maybe it wasn't a trawler—that maybe it was *Tern* or *Puffin*, that the way we've been charging around the Minch at night—" He stopped and shrugged.

Two of the fishermen sauntered over to the fruit machine, fed it some money and began playing. Carrick watched them, his face impassive but feeling a cold surge of anger. It was a cleverly malicious rumour—and a patrol launch could have smashed the Keenans' boat like an axe hitting an egg box.

"Who's spreading the story?" he asked.

"A woman Gogi knows heard it from one of the Rose bunch. She's not the only one." Bell reached into his pocket, then struck a match with a flick of his thumbnail and lit a cigarette. He drew briefly on the smoke. "Hell, it had to happen, Webb. We're natural targets."

Carrick nodded. Fishery Protection got plenty of nastiness thrown their way, had to accept it, try to ignore it. He took a sip of his drink without really tasting it, seeing the men at the fruit machine finish without winning and drift back to their friends. One of them glanced in his direction and made a low-voiced comment. His companion gave a quick, sly grin.

"Pick up anything about the Keenans as people?" he asked Bell.

"A scrap or two, that's all. They hadn't much of an income, but he drew some kind of disability pension. His wife used to be a school-teacher." He flicked ash from his cigarette and blinked as it landed in his beer. "They didn't spend much time away from the island, and the last they were over on the mainland was about a week ago. Bob Keenan told a couple o' people down at the harbour that he'd have to hire a lawyer—he'd had a fallout with his next-door neighbour."

"Next door—you mean Andersen, the Dane?"

"Mr. Oil Money." Bell nodded.

"What kind of fallout?"

"No idea." Bell raised an eyebrow. "How about Norah Reiver— didn't she mention it?"

"No."

"She probably didn't know." Bell ignored the ash in his beer and took another gulp, following it with a satisfied belch. "She's—uh— pretty friendly with our Sam Pilsudski." He grinned. "Sam's inclined to be sensitive about it."

The fruit machine began gobbling money again as another pair of fishermen tried their luck. The ginger-moustached barman, with nothing better to do, drifted over towards the window table. Carrick shook his head and the man shrugged, then turned away.

"Time to go?" Bell looked disappointed.

"Almost." Carrick laid both hands flat on the table. "Once you've told me about Andy Grey. What's going on, Clapper?"

Bell hesitated and sucked his teeth. "Ach, I've sorted it out."

"But I still want to know."

"You won't thank me," said Bell reluctantly. "Andy's problem is *Puffin's* skipper—your absent friend Johnny Walker."

Carrick winced. He'd already enough to settle when the other patrol launch returned, but now, if there was more . . .

"What about Walker?" he demanded.

"He's young Andy's brother-in-law—married to an older sister. Andy only joined our mob a few months ago; he's still a temporary appointment on *Tern,* and it won't be confirmed till the end of the year." Bell gave a long, hard snort. "All right, it seems he's made a few mistakes. Tim Maxwell didn't mind, but Walker put the boot in hard, every time."

"Why?"

"Ask Walker," said Bell. "Anyway, when they got word you were coming, what happened was Walker told Andy you were the original hard-nosed bastard—that if he put one foot wrong you'd have him on a Department report bad enough to scuttle him."

"Damn." Carrick rubbed a hand across his forehead. "You sorted Andy out?"

Bell nodded. "He's worth it. Give him time."

"And keep Walker off his back?" Carrick promised himself he would. "Clapper—"

He saw Bell wasn't listening. The big man's eyes had narrowed; his attention was on four newcomers who had just walked in through the Long Galley's low doorway.

"Trouble," said Bell.

Three were in their late twenties, casually dressed, and the barman's quick, anxious smile when he saw them showed they weren't strangers. The fourth, small, wizened and elderly, still wearing the same oilskin jacket, was Grandpa Rose. When he saw Carrick, he gave a quick snap of his fingers and muttered to the others.

They nodded. Two walked over to the fruit machine and the previous players immediately faded back to the counter. The third, tall and well built, with black curly hair, stayed with the old man and followed him to a table near where Carrick and Bell were sitting. Watching, Carrick realized the younger man's height owed at least a couple of inches to his footwear—scuffed but expensive Western-style boots with slim, elevator-type heels.

"That's Danny Rose," murmured Bell. "The one I warned you about." He had already considered the two at the fruit machine. "They won't try anything big—the odds aren't right."

The barman came scuttling over with glasses and a whisky bottle as Grandpa Rose settled, Danny beside him.

"Good lad, Malky," said the old man in a soft purr of a voice. He watched the barman fill both glasses, then thumbed towards the two men at the fruit machine. "See to them while you're at it." He gave a hard sniff as the barman departed. "Danny, there's something different about this place today. You notice?"

"I notice." Danny Rose gave a coolly amused glance in Carrick's direction. Clean-shaven and muscular, good-looking despite an old, deep scar under one cheekbone, he had a heavy gold identity bracelet on his left wrist, and the way his denim jacket hung loose gave a clear view of the sheathed diving knife attached to his broad leather belt. "Do we ask him over?"

"I've got to apologize to him, haven't I?" Grandpa Rose gave a wheezing laugh, turned and beckoned. "Spare a moment, Skipper?"

"Watch the old devil," muttered Bell out of the corner of his mouth as Carrick got to his feet.

"I'll try," said Carrick softly. "Go play the fruit machine, Clapper." He crossed to the other table but ignored the chair Danny Rose pushed towards him.

"Well, Mr. Carrick." Grandpa Rose grinned up at him, showing a mouthful of blackened teeth. "We sort of met at the harbour, eh? Did I worry you?"

"You knew what you were doing," Carrick answered dryly, conscious that Clapper Bell was strolling over to the fruit machine.

"Uh-huh." For a moment the older man's face froze, as if he was making a quick reassessment. "Did that maybe make two of us?"

"Try it again and find out," invited Carrick.

"It might be dangerous." Danny Rose rocked back in his chair, a mocking expression on his face. "What happens if you people sink a boat? Do you stop to say sorry?" He raised his voice for the benefit of the fishermen at the bar counter. "What about that poor slob Bob Keenan and his wife? What happened to—"

He ended there, sprawling backwards as Carrick deliberately kicked the chair from under him. Hitting the stone floor with a thud, Rose lay open-mouthed for a second, then came scrambling up, one hand dropping to the knife at his belt, balancing ready on the toes of those Western boots.

"I wouldn't," said Carrick softly. He had the distance measured to the whisky bottle, the only weapon handy, ready to grab it. But he was trying for something more important than the outcome of a brawl. Every man in the bar was watching, waiting. He raised his voice. "Do you want reality?"

Puzzled, Danny Rose hesitated.

"I know the story." Carrick made every word count, as it had to. "Probably you've all heard it—that one of our patrol boats ran down the Keenans and left them to drown." He had to keep his eyes on Rose, could only sense the men's reaction. "Convenient, isn't it? But ask yourself how it started, and why. Two people you know drown—and someone is twisted enough to see it as a chance to stir trouble."

There was total silence, then a brief, sudden scuffle over at the fruit machine. It ended. Clapper Bell stood with an innocent expression on his broad face, but one of Rose's men was leaning against the wall nursing his mouth and the other, moaning softly, was clinging to the machine for support.

"Danny." Grandpa Rose used his son's name like a sharp whip-crack, taking another quick glance at the watching faces. "You got what you asked for—now leave it. Pick up that chair."

Danny Rose swallowed but took his hand away from the knife. Then, still scowling, he stopped and put the chair upright again.

"That's better." His father relaxed. "I came here for a quiet drink, nothing more." Pausing, he scratched at the white stubble of beard on his chin and frowned at Carrick. "Skipper, you're not a patient man."

"I can be," said Carrick. "When it pays."

"Maybe." Grandpa Rose gave a doubting snort. "But the whole thing started as a damfool joke, didn't it, Danny?"

"I wasn't the comic who dreamed it up," countered his son sullenly. He gave Carrick a scowl of grudging respect. "That trick with the chair—I didn't like it."

"I did," countered Carrick.

Someone chuckled. Grandpa Rose joined in with a cackle. In the background, the man clutching the fruit machine had stopped moaning.

"Join us for a drink, Skipper," suggested Grandpa Rose unexpectedly. "We'll forget the uniform. Right, Danny?"

Danny Rose forced a grin of agreement.

"Another time." Carrick shook his head. "I'm due back aboard *Tern.*"

"Then pay us a visit, see how we operate, eh?" urged Grandpa Rose. "A wee bit of salvage work, a wee bit of fishing and most things in between—it'll interest you." He eyed his son slyly. "Danny can show you around."

A grunt which might have meant anything came from Danny Rose.

"I'll let you know," said Carrick.

He signalled to Clapper Bell, who hadn't moved.

The fruit machine's lights were still glowing. Easing the man clinging to it to one side, Bell gave the machine's start button an absent slap, then walked away as it began purring.

He joined Carrick, and they had reached the door when the fruit machine stopped and money began clattering out.

"Hell," said Bell sadly.

But they left without looking back. Carrick waited until they were out of the Long Galley lane before he spoke.

"What happened with your two?" he asked.

"Nothing much." Bell grinned. "I just persuaded them that you an' Rose were having a private quarrel." He ambled on a few steps. "Pruned him back a bit, didn't you?"

Carrick shrugged. Sea gypsies like the Rose family came tough and resilient; Grandpa Rose and Danny weren't the type who forgave and forgot.

But for the moment, at least, he might have won.

Five minutes later *Tern* had manoeuvred out of Dunbrach's tiny harbour and swung on a west-northwest course, towards the Hound Islands.

Carrick was in the command chair, and he had Andy Grey behind the steering wheel. As soon as the patrol launch was under way, running on her outer engines, Carrick acted. He'd already warned Sam Pilsudski what he planned and the midship diesel was ticking over, ready.

"Let's wind her up, Andy." He reached forward for the remaining throttle lever and gradually brought in the midship engine. *Tern* responded with an increased surge of power and he winked at his second officer. "It's time I found out what she can do."

Andy Grey nodded and gripped the steering wheel a shade tighter.

Still gathering speed, white curtains of spray drenching from her bow and pattering like a rainstorm on the bridge windows, *Tern* carved through the swell in her flat, pugnacious attack angle. The instrument dials for all three engines swung up to 2300 revolutions, full ahead, and the digital speed readout flickered past 30 knots.

Carrick spared a thought for Sam Pilsudski, down beside the roaring, air-gobbling diesels with those protective earmuffs jammed on his head. But he had a feeling that Pilsudski was probably enjoying himself, and *Tern* at speed became a steadier platform, vibrant, living, taking her designed role and loving it.

"Andy." Another heavy curtain of spray battered the bridge glass, where they now had the wipers sweeping. He saw the increased tension on Grey's features, his white knuckles against the dark wood of the wheel. "Nature calls. She's yours—sit back and enjoy it."

Grey turned a startled face. But Carrick was already out of the command chair. He went aft and down the narrow companionway stairs, then stopped outside his cabin and waited. Like any small, fast craft, *Tern* was sensitive to how she was handled. Already the hull had taken on a stiffer, uncomfortable vibration as if in protest. Carrick winced in sympathy but didn't move—and gradually, at first almost imperceptibly, the vibration began to ease again as Andy Grey began really to accept his role.

"Now, think with her, not against her," he muttered under his breath. It wasn't the only lesson Andy Grey had to learn, but it was the most important—and one that only *Tern* herself could teach. "Blend into her, boy."

Then he grinned, suddenly realizing why he'd done it, remembering how Captain Shannon on *Marlin* had stomped off the fishery cruiser's bridge at the height of a force eight gale—leaving only Carrick and a helmsman.

Probably Shannon had hidden himself away somewhere too, and at least the helmsman had known his job. Andy Grey was on his own.

He let another couple of minutes pass, then felt confident enough to climb the aft stairway to the tiny wardroom. As he reached it, Gogi MacDonnell stuck a surprised face out of the galley across the passage.

"Skipper?" MacDonnell gave an instinctive glance for'ard, as if he was trying to see through to the bridge. "Uh—?"

"Who hasn't eaten yet?" demanded Carrick.

"Well"—MacDonnell scratched the tiny area of skin visible between his ear and his knitted cap—"just you. But—"

"I want a mug of soup and a sandwich, fast, carry-out style—or

I'll cut the plug off your microwave," Carrick told him cheerfully. "Where's Clapper?"

"Below deck." MacDonnell still looked worried. "Sorting out the scuba gear. He said we'd maybe need it."

"We might." Every now and again Clapper Bell seemed able to read his mind. "All right, Gogi. Shift."

Gogi MacDonnell shifted. He emerged again in record time with the soup and some cold sausage jammed between two doorsteps of bread. Carrick took them with him, made his way back to the bridge and paused for a moment at the lectern-shaped chart table.

Outside, there was still the same moderate, lumping swell and the same drenching spray as *Tern* powered her way on. Viewed from the rear, Andy Grey was still hunched forward in his chair, his total attention on his task. But he was nursing the wheel rim, not choking it; his whole attitude showed more confidence.

"All okay?" asked Carrick easily, sliding back into the command chair. He took a first bite of the sandwich without even looking at Grey. "I made a detour."

"All okay, Skipper." Grey almost grinned at him, then gestured ahead. "Here comes someone else in a hurry—that's Magnus Andersen's favourite toy."

Small, black and slamming through the swell, another fast boat was heading towards them from the Hound Islands, apparently on course for Dunbrach. Carrick used the bridge glasses, studying her lines, noting her bullet-shaped bow and the way she sat low on her rounded stern.

"She's travelling." He gave a soft, appreciative whistle. The other boat, practically a racing shell, had two figures in yellow waterproof tops just visible in the shelter of an open cockpit. Behind them was the bulge of a low cabin fairing. From her looks, the black boat might be capable of matching *Tern* for speed in fair weather. But he imagined she could be hell to handle in a rough sea. "If that's Andersen, is he always in a hurry?"

"Always—in anything." Grey said it enviously. "At least, anytime I've seen him."

Carrick lowered the glasses as the black boat passed them at a distance of about five hundred yards. One of the figures in the cockpit waved an arm in greeting, then the other craft was astern, still heading arrow-straight towards Dunbrach, pitching and heaving as she crossed *Tern*'s wake.

The Hound Islands, a string of black basalt cliffs topped with green, stretched four miles from northeast tip to southwest tail with Little Drummer Island as their northern tip. They were open to the worst fury of the Minch's winter gales and it showed. The black rock began at sea level, where foam marked the mouths of caves and gullies. Above that, strange shapes had been carved and worn by the elements. Some resembled groups of pipe organs, others could have been tall cathedral pillars; there were places whorled and patterned like giant wood knots.

Tern made her approach towards Little Drummer at reduced speed and with suitable care. The island was small and whalebacked, with an odd, deep notch almost down to sea level near the southern end. The lighthouse, a squat, white pillar, sat at its highest point like a small crown, and a steep, winding path, visible to the eye, led from there down to a narrow concrete landing stage.

"Come down to slow ahead both, fine pitch." Carrick watched and waited while the two outer diesels changed their murmur. The midship engine was already stopped. "Steer fifteen degrees port."

"Fifteen degrees port." Andy Grey repeated the order and fed the wheel through his hands. As the patrol boat answered and began her approach towards the landing stage, he took another glance at the island and whistled softly through his teeth. "It wouldn't be my idea of home."

"You'd be no good as an estate agent. Call it a desirable detached residence with privacy and sea views," said Carrick dryly. He gauged their progress. "Midships. All right, she'll do at that."

He glanced at the sonar readout, which had been twitching and quivering in nightmare style. The reasons were all around—stray outcrops of rock which either broke the surface or showed as swirling foam. They'd collected an audience of gulls, crying and swooping overhead, and there were other spectators, sleek grey seals, basking here and there along the shore.

Clapper Bell and MacDonnell were on deck, readying the patrol launch's lines and fenders. MacDonnell stopped and pointed as a seal's head popped into view in the water close alongside. A pair of big, innocently fearless eyes considered the intruding strangers, then the seal unhurriedly submerged again.

They murmured on, close to a final fang of rock, then *Tern*'s fenders creaked as she nudged the barnacled concrete of the landing stage. Another minute and they had tied up, the patrol boat's engines were silent, and even Sam Pilsudski emerged on deck.

He made towards Carrick, then blinked as a low booming noise, like a distant explosion, echoed round the rocks. It faded, then had gone.

"What the hell was that?" asked Clapper Bell.

Gogi MacDonnell grinned at them. "Just the Drummer." He gestured with his calloused hands. "When the tide's right, the sea scours in under a rock overhang." He slapped his hands together. "Like that—right now, you'll only hear it now and again. But in the winter, when there's a storm, I've heard the Drummer banging when we've been fishing a mile offshore."

"Yet they lived with it." Carrick looked up at the lighthouse as another, softer boom reached his ears. Keenan and his wife could have been no ordinary people. He drew a deep breath. "Time we started. Sam, you stay aboard and mind the store. Clapper, you and Gogi have a general look around—Andy and I will take the lighthouse." He turned to Pilsudski again. "If you need it, recall signal will be one klaxon blast, repeated. Emergency recall, two blasts."

"Two." Pilsudski scratched his chest. "What's an emergency?"

"If it happens, you'll know," said Carrick dryly.

Beckoning Andy Grey, leaving Bell and MacDonnell to make their own decisions, he went ashore, crossed the landing stage and started up the track.

They heard the Drummer again when they were halfway up the slogging climb. By the time they reached the top, comparatively level ground covered by a mixture of coarse grass and stunted heather, Andy Grey was panting. The lighthouse tower was not much more than a stone's throw away—but there was something wrong. The heavy door at its base lay open, creaking in the wind.

When they got nearer, they saw why. The wood around the lock was splintered, as if it had been attacked by an axe or a heavy hammer. The lock itself was shattered metal.

"Skipper—" Andy Grey combed a hand through his black mop of hair, bewildered. "What the hell happened?"

"Someone beat us to it," said Carrick in a flat, angry voice. "Come on."

They went in. The lighthouse's living quarters were at ground level, small rooms leading off the central area where steep iron steps curved upwards towards the tower. The Keenans had converted them into a bedroom and living room, a small kitchen and a smaller bathroom.

Every one had been ransacked, books swept from shelves, drawers hauled out and emptied, cupboards left bare. Even the bedding had been ripped from the mattress and the mattress itself thrown to one side. It was the same in the kitchen and bathroom. Anything and everything had been left ripped, torn or discarded.

"When?" asked Grey.

Carrick shook his head.

He went on alone up the spiral stairway. One floor up, there was a storeroom and a small workshop. The storeroom door had been locked and now hung almost off its hinges. Inside was turmoil.

Another turn of the iron steps and he was at the start of the glinting cogwheels and rods of the clock mechanism which had once controlled the Little Drummer light. A brass plaque on the wall, still polished, commemorated the light's official going into service in the year 1860. He went on again, one more turn of the upward spiral, and reached the lantern gallery with its great, dominating, now unused lens—a lens which, despite its weight, balanced on a mercury float in a way that meant a touch would have been enough to move it.

The light sources, a tall electric bulb and a standby acetylene burner, were still there too. A spider had woven a new, fragile web between them and the lens. Frayed and faded, the cotton blinds which had shielded the lens from direct sunlight still hung at the thick glass windows all round.

A small door led on to the railed, open outer-gallery platform. Carrick opened it, stepped out, and the wind tugged at his clothing and rustled the cotton blinds behind him. Far below, he could see *Tern* sitting like a toy boat at the island's landing stage.

But it was the rest which almost made him gasp. He could have been on the Aztec aircraft on its surveillance patrol. He was looking down the whole length of the Hound Islands chain.

First and nearest, largest in the chain, there was Bochail, where Magnus Andersen lived. He could see the roof of a large house and some outbuildings, then another gap of sea which looked like a deep-water channel but was marked as foul water on the charts, and two more islands beyond that.

He glanced west, while the Drummer boomed again below. The view was out across a wide sweep of the open Minch with a faint blur on the horizon which had to be one of the Duter Islands. Suddenly, urgently, he hurried round to the other side of the railed gallery, then stopped again.

From north to east, a panorama of sea and mainland, he was looking across at the heart of Patrol Box Tango. There was the wide mouth of Loch Ringan, the nearest of the herring nursery areas, and the tiny white cottages of St. Ringan village. Lower down, from Dunbrach harbour onwards, most of the whole wide sweep of Priest Bay lay exposed. He could see small specks of fishing boats at work, the two laid-up tanker ships, even what might be a truck moving on a road.

All that, with the naked eye. Carrick drew a deep breath, thinking of what Bob Keenan and his wife could have seen with a telescope or a pair of high-powered glasses. Seen by day—or by night.

The wind felt strangely colder. He went back into the lantern room, closed the door, then clattered his way back down the iron stairs to the living quarters.

"Anything, Skipper?" Andy Grey, squatted down beside a litter of books and papers, gave him an inquiring glance.

"The same as here, all the way up." Carrick shook his head.

"Vultures, whoever they were." His second officer's pock-marked face tightened with anger. "They can't be long gone, Skipper. I mean, even if they headed out for the island the moment they heard about the Keenans—" He paused and frowned. "Unless they were already out. There's always gossip on the fishing waveband, and if they heard that way—"

"Maybe." They were the obvious possibilities, but there was another—that someone had known the Keenans' fate before their bodies were recovered. Carrick looked around the room again. "What about here?"

"What you'd expect." Grey grimaced up at him. "There's a little jewel case lying empty in the bedroom, a cash box over there forced open. No way of knowing what's gone, Skipper." He lifted a framed photograph from the floor. "Seen this?"

Carrick took the photograph. The glass in the frame was broken, but the print was still intact. It showed a group of smiling men in uniform—a familiar enough uniform. He shaped a silent whistle of surprise.

"Customs officers in full rig. Could be a dockside rummage squad," suggested Grey. He grinned a little. "The last Merchant Navy trip I did, the ship was done over by a rummage squad at Liverpool. Hard men—they practically took her apart."

"They hang on," said Carrick, frowning at the print. "Keenan—?"

"Customs waterguard officer, retired." Grey motioned towards the scattered papers. "There's old identification and more photographs in that lot."

"He had some kind of health breakdown." Carrick set the photograph down on a table. What had started as a thin tendril of doubt, of nagging suspicion, was growing fast. Keenan might have said nothing about his former Customs background—that made sense near a freebooting fishing community. But training died hard. If he had come across something, seen something from that lighthouse eyrie, would he have ignored it? Trawler crews on a big-money poaching raid weren't the only kind of pirates still afloat. "All right, there's not much more we—"

He stopped. An edge of brass tubing just protruded from under an overturned chair in the far corner. Going over, he righted the chair, then picked up a big, old-fashioned brass telescope and a folding triple mounting. The telescope was a Barr and Stroud, with War Department markings.

"Nice." Grey rose to his feet and came over. "Not many as good as that around anymore." He paused and rubbed a thumb along his chin, puzzled. "Some people would give a lot of money for a glass like that. Wonder why they didn't take it?"

"If I get the chance, I'll ask," said Carrick more curtly than he meant.

But he knew Grey was right. Even the most modern-minded of seamen would have grabbed the brass telescope he was holding. It was more than a precision instrument with powerful lenses; it was something that captured the very essence of what the sea could mean.

A good telescope—a saying he'd once heard, handed down from the days of square-rigged ships, drifted into Webb Carrick's mind. A good telescope would allow a sailor to count the hairs on a dockside whore's chin from ten miles out. At least, that was the polite version.

Yet it had been left behind.

And when the one-time Customs man had used it, what had he seen?

He placed the telescope and the tripod stand beside the photograph on the table, gestured silently towards the door, and Andy Grey followed him out.

Another soft boom sounded from the Drummer as they reached the open air again. Outside, there wasn't much more to see. They found the generator shed, a stone-built bunker. The door was unlocked, the old, original lighthouse generators inside rusty and use-less, the Keenans' small, modern unit occupying a corner beside them. A smaller shed was a pumproom, providing the lighthouse's water supply, apparently tapping some underground spring.

But nothing else.

"Before we go"—Andy Grey gave a concerned glance towards the lighthouse—"well, shouldn't we secure that door, Skipper? Suppose more scavengers come visiting?"

"We can nail it up." It would only be a gesture. Short of leaving a guard, there was no way the dead couple's home could be protected overnight on the empty island. By tomorrow Carrick hoped it would be someone else's worry.

He swore under his breath as a thin klaxon blast sounded from the direction of the landing stage. A few seconds passed, then it was repeated; Sam Pilsudski wanted them back.

"Fix that door, but don't make a meal of it," he told Grey. "I'll go down."

He loped across the rough ground to the start of the steep path to the landing stage. Down below, *Tern* still lay moored as before. He could see Sam Pilsudski out on deck. But he could also see the reason for the recall signal, the slim black boat completing a slow, tight turn in towards the shore. Magnus Andersen was paying a visit.

Carrick made his way down to the landing stage and boarded *Tern* moments before the other boat murmured alongside the patrol launch. A tall man wearing a yellow waterproof suit passed a bow line across to Pilsudski, then scrambled aft and tossed another to Carrick. The lines secured, the two hulls touched.

"*Tak* . . . thank you." The tall man, in his mid-fifties, clean-shaven, with strong features, close-cut greying hair and clear blue eyes, stepped across to *Tern*'s deck. He gave Pilsudski a nod but came towards Carrick. "Chief Officer Carrick? Magnus Andersen, from Bochail."

Carrick shook hands with the well-built Dane. Behind them, the black boat's engines stopped.

"I came to see if I could help." Andersen's voice was deep and soft, with only a trace of accent. "We went over to Dunbrach, on a small errand—then I heard about the Keenans." He shook his head. "A terrible thing. Hard to believe."

"We still know very little." Out of the corner of his eye, Carrick saw the black boat's other occupant beginning to emerge from the cockpit. "When did you see them last?"

"About a week ago." Andersen shrugged. *"Ja,* about that. It is hard to say it now, but things weren't good between us. The less I saw of them, the better I liked it. You knew that?"

Carrick nodded. But he was looking at the young woman who had just stepped aboard *Tern.* Almost as tall as Andersen, wearing a similar waterproof suit, slim in build, she had short, straw-coloured hair, high cheekbones and the same keen, clear blue eyes.

"I nearly forgot." Andersen gave a mock sigh, but an undisguised pride entered his voice. "My daughter Marget, Chief Officer—she isn't too pleased with me. She feels we should have waited, till later."

"Till we were needed." Marget Andersen gave Carrick a calm, almost apologetic smile. She had white, even teeth. "Maybe you are busy enough. But if we can help—"

"Anyway," agreed Andersen. He gestured up at the lighthouse. "Perhaps there are things to do—"

"No. Somebody got ahead of us." Carrick paused while the Drummer gave one of its periodic booms in the background. "They broke in—the whole place has been looted."

Father and daughter stared at him.

"I don't understand." Marget Andersen looked bewildered. "We were told no one knew about the Keenans—"

"Until this morning," said Carrick.

"Ja, but that would be time enough for some," said Magnus Andersen. "I know these fishing people—they like to pretend to be slow. But when it matters, they can move quickly." He pursed his lips. "Is it true that it was the Bagman who found Bob Keenan?"

Carrick nodded.

"Then isn't it even possible he made a detour here, to Little Drummer, before he took Keenan's body to Dunbrach?" The man's blue eyes were hard as he spoke. "Chief Officer, I can claim Viking ancestors. They were supposed to be experts at pillage. But if they returned today, they could learn a few lessons along this coast."

"Right now, anything is possible. It could have been anyone," said Carrick deliberately. "Even—"

"Even us, their nearest neighbours?" suggested Marget Andersen quietly and without rancour. She glanced at her father. "He's right, *Fader."*

Andersen shrugged, but said nothing. Carrick was glad.

"When did you last see the Keenans, Miss Andersen?" he asked.

"About a week—the same as my father." She used her hand to brush back a stray lock of damp hair from her forehead, and a small emerald ring glinted in the sunlight. "That was three—no, four days after I arrived." She saw more of an explanation was needed. "I live and work in Copenhagen. This is a holiday visit."

"Marget prefers to live her own life—and why not?" Andersen gave a wry smile and stuffed his hands in the yellow jacket's pockets. "Sometimes, of course, I have—well, other company, Chief Officer. But I value privacy. I bought this island to get it."

"And you tried to buy Little Drummer to make sure of it?" Carrick saw Clapper Bell and MacDonnell coming over the shore rocks towards the landing stage. They weren't hurrying. "That's the story I heard in Dunbrach."

"It's true. The Keenans were on this island when I came to Bochail—and at that time we were friendly enough." Andersen pursed his lips as the Drummer gave another soft boom. "You hear that? To me, even in winter, it sounds like a heartbeat. I don't like boardrooms and desks. I escape to here every time I can."

"What went wrong between you and the Keenans?"

"A simple thing. But it mattered. I am a widower; I have been for a long time. I told you I sometimes have company." Andersen gave a wary glance at his daughter, but she nodded. "Look, I discovered I was being spied on—not by Keenan, but by his wife. She even used a damn telescope sometimes, from that lighthouse tower."

"While you had company." Carrick managed to stay straight-faced. "You're sure?"

"*Ja*. I have a good pair of binoculars." Andersen ignored the irony of the situation. "Maybe the woman had nothing else to do, but would you like it to happen?"

"Probably not. So you offered to buy them out?"

"At a fair price, but they turned me down." Andersen was wearing thin rubber yachting shoes. He rubbed the toe of one along the rough concrete of the landing stage and sighed. "Sad. If they had agreed, if they had gone away—well, this couldn't have happened." He paused and shrugged. "So—we can't help here?"

"Not right now," said Carrick. "Maybe later."

"If we can, we will," promised Marget Andersen. She touched her father's arm. "We should get back home anyway. Remember that phone call you're expecting—the one from New York."

"You mean the one I hope comes from New York," corrected Andersen. He gave a wry twist of a grin. "Tanker talk, Chief Officer—a possible time-charter deal, and a good one. I might even need one of the Priest Bay ships, get it earning again." Unexpectedly he changed the subject. "Norah Reiver told me you were interested in my Seibe Gorman shipment. Is diving one of your sidelines?"

Carrick nodded. "Sometimes it has to be."

"Good." Andersen was pleased. "Then I want a chance to talk with you sometime—I can always learn from a professional. In fact, once things—well, quieten, we could maybe dive together over at Bochail. Marget would like it too. She's better under water than most men." He winked. "Or so she keeps telling me."

"It's a family trait," said his daughter, but smiled. "Yes, you'd be welcome."

Father and daughter said goodbye, then went back aboard their powerboat. The engines rumbled to life, the straw-haired girl at the controls, and as Carrick cast off the mooring lines and tossed them across to Magnus Andersen, he noticed the boat had the name *Helga* in small gold lettering at the stern.

"*Farvel*, Skipper." Andersen gave a wave across the widening gap as the slim hull began moving. He raised his voice to a shout above the engine noise. "I almost forgot. Your other boat, *Puffin*, is back. That part-time policeman character said you'd want to know."

The Dane waved again, then clambered down into the *Helga's* cockpit. She eased out carefully at first, then, clear of the shoal rock, she began to gather speed.

"That daughter of his knows how to handle a boat. Probably most other things too," mused Sam Pilsudski, ambling over from *Tern's* bow and leaning on a deck rail. He watched the white wake building as the powerboat streaked away. "Not bad. The boat, I mean—that's a Thorneycroft hull and my bet would be a pair of turbo-charged BMW diesels. She's a beauty."

"The boat, you mean," said Carrick solemnly. But he'd have said the same about Marget Andersen and he had the feeling that she would be equally capable in anything she tackled. With an effort, he got back to what mattered. "Any signal traffic for us while I was ashore?"

"Yes and no." Pilsudski took a fresh cheroot from his top pocket and gave the tip a tentative bite. "*Puffin* was trying to raise us—that was after she sent a high-speed signal to Department."

"Did you answer?"

"No." Pilsudski shook his head in mock innocence. "Hell, what do I know about radios? I'm the engineer officer."

Carrick nodded and let him go. Clapper Bell and Gogi MacDonnell had come back aboard, and Andy Grey was scrambling his way down towards the landing stage. His crew was almost complete again.

"Find anything along the shore?" he asked the two chief petty officers.

"Not a lot, Skipper," said Bell. "But there's a patch of beach where a small boat could come in. That's where we got these."

He dropped a cigarette lighter and a small tin box into Carrick's hand. The lighter was a cheap plastic type, probably made by the million. The tin contained half a dozen hand-rolled cigarettes.

"They were on a rock, like someone forgot them," explained Bell. He glanced at MacDonnell for agreement. "There were marks on the shingle, though. Like a dinghy had been dragged in."

"It could have been," said MacDonnell cautiously.

"Any way up to the lighthouse from there?" asked Carrick.

"Yes, but it wouldn't be too easy." MacDonnell grimaced. "Still, if someone didn't want to be seen at the landing stage—"

"Someone didn't." Carrick gave the lighter and cigarette tin back to Bell, then reached into his pocket. "Gogi, what do you make of these?"

He showed MacDonnell the bird feathers he'd collected outside the Bagman's tumble-down cottage. Frowning, the ex-fisherman took one and rubbed it between his fingers.

"Gannet, Skipper." He was positive. "They've got that special touch of colour among the white. Then—well, one of those others you've got, the black one, is from a wingtip. Gannet. But—"

"Did you notice any gannets along the shore here?"

MacDonnell looked at Bell, met a blank stare and shook his head.

"Gannets." Carrick pursed his lips. The gannet—islanders often called them *gughas,* the great sea ducks—was an easy bird to recognize. Big, heavy, greedy, aggressive, it often had a six-foot wingspan. But it was a bird which usually lived in remote island colonies, thousands of birds to one colony. "Where's the nearest you'd find them?"

"In numbers?" MacDonnell didn't hesitate. "Back down at Handa Island, Skipper. I saw plenty there this morning, when we found the Keenan woman's body."

"That's what I thought." Carrick put the feathers away as Andy

Grey loped along the landing stage and jumped aboard. "Thanks, Gogi." He turned to Grey. "All secure up there?"

"Nailed shut, Skipper, like you wanted." Grey seemed pleased with himself.

Behind them, the Drummer boomed again—heavily, almost angrily. Beyond the shoal rock the sea was taking on a darker colour and becoming lumpier. The wind direction had changed again and there was more cloud in the sky.

"Start up and cast off," ordered Carrick.

Puffin was in Dunbrach. He had something different to sort out there.

4

The late afternoon sun was veiled by more cloud as *Tern* made the return crossing to the mainland. By the time she entered Dunbrach harbour, a first few specks of rain had begun to show on her bridge windows.

More of the fishing boats were out. But *Puffin* was at the west quay and there was space by her stern. Carrick brought *Tern* in, made an unhurried swing in the harbour's cramped space and berthed a few feet from her sister's stern. One of *Puffin's* crew caught the mooring lines as they were tossed across, attached them to two of the quay's iron bollards, then vanished back aboard the other patrol boat. There was no sign of her skipper or anyone else.

"You know where I'll be," said Carrick. He had left *Tern's* bridge and Andy Grey had followed him out on deck. "I want a private talk with your brother-in-law—it could get violent at the edges."

Grey nodded gloomily. "He's still family, Skipper."

"Your family, not mine. Just make sure nobody sets a hoof off this boat till I get back." Carrick paused, seeing a complication in postman's uniform heading their way with long strides. "There's Jimsy Fletcher—you'll have to cope with him for now. Take him below, pour a drink into him, two if necessary—keep him occupied."

Going up on the quay, he boarded *Puffin* at her stern. As he started along her deck, the crewman who'd helped with the mooring lines appeared again.

"Lookin' for the skipper, sir?" He gave Carrick a wary but friendly grin. "He's in his cabin, cleaning up. If you want to wait in the wardroom—"

"I don't," said Carrick. "What's your name?"

"Tam Kennedy, sir." The man, lanky and dark-haired, stiffened under Carrick's gaze. "CPO Bo'sun, sir."

"Bo'sun, go tell your skipper I want to see him now, on the bridge. Who else is aboard?"

"No one, sir." Kennedy moistened his lips. "They went up to the village. But—"

"Tell him," said Carrick quietly.

"Sir." The man headed below.

Carrick walked to *Puffin*'s bridge, went in and pushed the door shut behind him. He could have been back aboard *Tern*—the layout was identical. But there were cigarette burns along the ledge of the instrument panel, something dark and sticky had stained the matting under the command chair and a twisted tangle of signal flags lay stuffed in a corner like so much dirty washing. He drew a finger along the top of one of the radio cabinets, looked at the greasy grime he'd collected and decided he was acting like a nosing maiden aunt. Yet ship-keeping standards on *Puffin* obviously weren't as good as they could be.

He waited, then heard footsteps coming from aft and a moment later Johnny Walker almost erupted into the bridge.

"Well?" Walker, a bulky, pudgy-faced individual with short, thinning fair hair, glared at him. Carrick's age, a few inches smaller, he was in his shirtsleeves and had been shaving. There were traces of shaving soap on his cheeks and his hands gripped the ends of the towel still round his neck. "What's the imperial summons about, Carrick? Who the hell said you could board my command and start ordering my crew around?"

"You're bellowing like a bull, Johnny," said Carrick softly. "We've something to sort out. You know it—give me enough encouragement and I'll do it the hard way."

Walker flushed and took a deep, snorting breath. "Now look—"

"This stays private, Johnny—if you've sense." Carrick's words cut him short. "Where's your bo'sun?"

"Gone ashore." *Puffin*'s skipper flicked the towel from his neck and tossed it aside, still glaring. "Well?"

"This morning."

"Independent action." Walker scowled. "You've heard of it?"

"*Tern* and *Puffin* work together. You went batting off north without as much as a grunt on the radio."

"That?" Walker shrugged. "Maybe we had a radio fault."

"You got it fixed in time to signal Department," said Carrick. "You know why you did it; so do I. I'm the new boy; you want to score points." He didn't wait for an answer. "Was there a trawler raid?"

"False alarm," said Walker reluctantly. "It happens. I filed a negative report." He shifted slightly to the defensive. "Hell, you don't know how things are in this damned Tango patrol box—"

"But I'm learning fast," said Carrick. "So far I've got two dead bodies and a story being spread we're to blame. I go out to Little Drummer and I find the Keenans' place raided."

"The lighthouse?" Walker stared at him and swallowed. "I'd heard about the rest, but—"

"But it happened while you were chasing your tail up north." It was unfair, but Carrick had to be brutal. "So before anything else happens, let's settle this. Department made this a two-boat operation. Whether you like it or not, whether I like it or not, we're a team—with *Tern* as senior boat. Accept it. Otherwise—"

"Otherwise what?" Walker was suddenly wary. "If you're thinking of going moaning to Department—"

"No. Because if I did, the odds are you'd lose *Puffin* and you know it." Carrick shook his head. "But if you want a war, you can have it, make your own troubles—and some for me. Your choice."

For almost a minute Walker said nothing, his pudgy face hard to read. Then, at last, he sighed. "You're the boss. I pushed my luck. Settled?"

Carrick nodded. It was better to say nothing.

"Hell, the way things are I should almost thank you." Walker gripped the back of the command chair with both hands and scowled. "All the time we've been here the situation has been sliding from bad to worse—and now we've got the Keenans. I'd back the idea they were rammed by a trawler."

"The last Loch Ringan raid?"

"Three nights ago—it was real enough." Walker nodded. "The lobster syndicates over at St. Ringan are still howling about how much gear they lost."

"What about sightings?"

"None that stand up. But the trawlers will be back." Walker tapped his fingertips on the chair. "Look, these damned sea loch nurseries are stuffed full of fish, and the pirate trawlers must be clearing a fortune each time."

Carrick knew it was true. One brief night-time hit-and-run raid, perhaps a couple of hours' actual fishing, and a trawler probably cleared more in hard cash than a patrol boat's crew earned in six months. Balancing that against the risk of prison and the other penalties, many a trawlerman might be tempted.

Around Dunbrach, the risk factor seemed to have become artificially slim.

"You've tried. Tim Maxwell tried. How do you feel about it? Do they have help ashore?"

"They must," said Walker sourly. "Nobody gets that lucky."

"That's why I want to try something, starting tonight." Carrick rescued one of *Puffin*'s signal pads and a pencil from among the clutter on a shelf. "I'll show you. Tell me what you think."

A few rough lines drawn on the signal pad were enough. The plan was basically simple, one that had begun shaping on the way back from Little Drummer.

"Take this as the mainland, these as the Hound Islands. Any trawler has to come in from the Minch after dark and get out again well before dawn. There's no time to play thread-the-needle through the reefs, so she has to use one of the safe routes." He used the pencil again, marking them in. "Notice anything?"

Walker rubbed at the flecks of shaving soap still on his chin. "I'd forget the top channel," he said. "It's close to the shore all the way, too much risk of being spotted. But the others"—he became more interested—"you're right. They funnel together northwest of the Hounds, then fan out again." He frowned. "But that's still a lot of water."

"And that's why we'll use one boat as an early-warning radar picket." Carrick marked a cross northwest of the doodled islands. "She can cover the funnel sector, track anything creeping in from the Minch and where it looks like heading."

"It might work." Walker chewed his lower lip, most of his rancour faded, the possibility exciting him. "But the picket boat has to get out there without being spotted. That's been our trouble—we've been tagged every move we make."

"Then we get ourselves untagged."

"All right." Walker gave a grudging nod. "You or me?"

"Turn about. *Tern* tonight, *Puffin* tomorrow, and on from there." For the moment, Carrick accepted that Johnny Walker was willing to work the way he wanted even if he couldn't forecast how long it might last. "The second boat stays inshore, on listening watch. If we get lucky, then it's a joint intercept pattern."

"And if something goes wrong?" Walker answered his own question. "Hell, we haven't much to lose. I like it."

"Good." Carrick leaned back against a bulkhead. "How do you feel about your crew, Johnny?"

"My crew?" Walker looked surprised. "No problems—I've got Kennedy and the other CPO is Rab Shaw, who knows his stuff. Bill Martin, my second, was on *Skua*—he says you know him. Amos Lynch is engineer officer. They're all right. Why?"

"I've got a good bunch on *Tern,*" said Carrick. "That includes young Andy Grey. Stop needling him, Johnny. He may be your brother-in-law but he's not on *Puffin.*"

"Has he come moaning to you?" Genuine surprise showed on Walker's pudgy face.

"He hasn't said a word. Just stay off his back."

Walker scowled. "Andy needs to be pushed, for his own good. I promised my wife I'd kick him into shape. He's—"

"He's my worry."

"Tell that to my wife." Walker swore under his breath and took a sideways kick at the litter of signal flags. "But if that's the way you want it, fair enough." He gave a long sigh. "About tonight. When do we sort out details?"

"Now," said Carrick.

It took only a few minutes. Walker listened, found no particular faults and was in a reasonable humour again by the time Carrick finished.

"We could give someone a nasty surprise—scare the hell out of him at the very least," he said happily. "Carrick, you know the only thing really wrong with you? You're not married, so you don't know what happens when your wife wants something done."

"She can't be any worse than Department," said Carrick.

"I wouldn't gamble on it," said Walker, slumping down in the split padding of his command chair. "You'd lose."

Carrick grinned. It was a new insight on the flamboyant, head-strong Walker everyone knew about. Maybe the fastest way to get *Puffin* cleaned up would be to suggest her skipper's wife might be on her way to visit.

He said goodbye, left Walker still slumped in the command chair and went back aboard *Tern.*

Jimsy Fletcher was settled happily in the wardroom, a glass of whisky in front of him, his postman's jacket unbuttoned, a smile on his face, Andy Grey in close, dutiful attendance. From the state of the bottle on the table, Grey had taken Carrick's advice in literal style.

"You're back then, Skipper." Fletcher made it a beaming state-ment of fact as he saw Carrick enter. "I've just been telling this lad some of the problems, the responsibilities of representing the law on your own, the way I do. It's no easy task being a special constable. But as the Good Book says—" He paused and sipped at his glass. "Well, another time."

"Mr. Fletcher preaches on Sundays in the mission hall," said Andy Grey woodenly. "He says we'd be welcome to look in."

Carrick nodded without comment, then let Grey escape before he turned to Fletcher again.

"You heard how things were at Little Drummer?"

"Aye." Fletcher scowled. "Villains. They must have come from farther up the coast, or off a foreign boat. Nobody in this village would stoop so low."

"You know your sinners better than I do," said Carrick dryly. "Any other reason you're here?"

Fletcher finished his drink first and gave a hopeful glance at the bottle. When there was no response, he gave a slight sigh.

"Just to tell you what's been happening. The medical people decided they didn't want to come here to do the autopsies. My brother Hammy is having to drive the bodies all the way to Inverness." He brightened. "Mind you, he'll charge mileage. Another thing is that I'm to get a wee bit of help. There's a detective inspector and a sergeant arriving sometime tonight—I'll have to give them a bed at my place. Eh—will you be here to meet them?"

"Sorry." Carrick shook his head. "We'll be out."

"Oh." Fletcher showed his disappointment, then interest. "Why?"

"I'm taking *Tern* north, along the coast," lied Carrick. "*Puffin* will probably do the same, to the south."

"I see. Aye, those damned trawlers." Fletcher eyed Carrick with a touch of caution. "How did you find people when you looked around the village?"

"Some of them found me," Carrick told him.

"Aye." Fletcher frowned. "I mean how did you get on with the Bagman?"

"We talked. I believed most of it." Carrick chuckled at the memory. "We'll get that wreckage shipped out tomorrow for tests." One thing still puzzled him. "Exactly what does he keep in that damned bag?"

"A wee bit of everything." Fletcher sighed. "He says he likes to be ready for emergencies. Tools and spare shoes, food and—and drink." He eyed the whisky bottle wistfully. "There's no harm in that, I suppose."

"None," agreed Carrick.

Sadly Fletcher gave up and rose to leave.

"Back to work—I've tonight's mail to send off south, then I suppose I'd better get ready for those detectives arriving." He sniffed in disapproval. "What good they'll do I don't know. Still, I suppose it's as it says in the Book—aye, Corinthians three, verse nine. You'll know it?"

"Tell me," said Carrick.

" 'For we are labourers together,' " said the postman solemnly. His face darkened a little. "Mind you, these days some get paid a damn sight more than others."

Tern sailed on schedule, two hours before dusk. But the time that remained while she was in harbour passed quickly. Carrick had reports to write and two long signals to send off to Fleet Support at Department headquarters in Edinburgh, then Johnny Walker came aboard from *Puffin.* He'd combed his thinning red hair; he wore an almost clean white shirt and tie and he offered a couple of minor alterations to their plan. They were sensible, and Carrick agreed— then noticed how Walker gave Andy Grey only the slightest of nods as he left.

Norah Reiver was another visitor, but her quarry was Sam Pilsudski. They stayed on deck, talking quietly for several minutes, then she left and Pilsudski went below. The next thing Carrick heard was some loud, cheerful whistling coming from the engineroom.

Later, the patrol boat worked across to the other quay and Dunbrach's refuelling berth. She queued behind two fishing boats until it was her turn for the heavy black oiling hoses to come aboard.

Tern's diesels gobbled sixty gallons an hour in normal operations, more when she was pushed, and the supply meter clicked steadily, almost alarmingly, until her fifteen-hundred gallon tanks were topped up. At last, Sam Pilsudski was satisfied and the oiling hoses were uncoupled. The patrol boat stayed a little longer, taking on fresh water, then that ended.

"Everything buttoned up, Skipper," reported Clapper Bell, sticking his head into the bridge. He winked. "We've been gettin' the treatment out there—where are we going, what are we doing? So we told them the fairy story, like you wanted."

"Let's hope they believe it," said Carrick. He took a final glance around and was satisfied. "Showtime, Clapper. Stand by to cast off."

Stern first, *Tern* eased out from the refuelling berth. Watched by a considerable audience of fishermen, she idled round until her bow came in line with the harbour entrance. Johnny Walker was leaning over a rail at *Puffin*'s stern and gave a casual wave. Then *Tern*'s outer diesels began throbbing a thin blue haze of exhaust fumes and she was under way, the wind and a moderate swell meeting her as she cleared the shelter of the stone breakwater.

The Fishery Protection ensign flapping and cracking at her stern, a first new drenching of spray across her deck, the patrol boat pitched and rolled for a few moments while her bow came round again. Then, with a deeper, throaty growl, she began to build up speed and became a grey arrowhead leaving a white shaft of wash which pointed north.

Half an hour later, the weather still uncertain and blustering, *Tern* had entered Loch Ringan for the first time since Carrick had taken command. Cruising peacefully at fifteen hundred revolutions along the loch's southern edge, making a deliberate circular tour of the big sea loch nursery area, she gave all the appearance of carrying out a routine patrol inspection.

Gogi MacDonnell was taking a turn at the wheel. Carrick had told him to stay about a hundred yards out from the shore and then had left him to it.

Loch Ringan, flanked by mountains and several miles long, varying between two and three miles wide, had the village of St. Ringan on the north shore near its entrance, and not much more. A few small farmhouses clung to the lower slopes of the mountains, and sheep grazed on sparse grassland or nosed their way along the foreshore. Some hardy tourist campers had pitched two bright orange tents where a stream—not much more than a trickling burn—came down from one bald rise of rock.

But there was life in plenty beneath *Tern*'s glass-fibre hull, life that teemed and swam, that registered on the patrol boat's sonar scan as a constant electronic chirping and clicking that translated on the bottom-contour view screen into densely packed shoals of fish. The Loch Ringan nursery held herring by the million, pampered them with trapped Gulf Stream warmth which raised the temperature those few vital degrees higher than the open sea.

Webb Carrick watched the rest of it from the railed-in lookout pulpit above the bridge. Wearing a duffel coat against the wind, using the bridge glasses at the personal focus mark he'd scratched on their adjusting screws, he saw other, larger fish break the surface here and there. Plenty of predators fed on herring—and only some were under water. A profusion of seabirds were flying above the loch, from the inevitable gulls to fulmars and dark shags, even a few large-beaked, gracefully ugly cormorants. Every now and again one would make a stabbing, splashing dive to claim its share.

Even a nursery could be one of nature's killing grounds.

He gave up after a spell and let the bridge glasses dangle by their strap round his neck until *Tern* reached the head of the sea loch and started her swing along the north shore.

Every report of the trawler raid three nights back, no matter how vague, had said it had been along the north shore. Soon he was using the glasses again, seeing the evidence for himself. Here a cluster of smashed lobster creels had been washed ashore, there a collection of floats which had supported a pattern of long-lines bobbed in a useless cluster. Farther on, there was even the half-submerged remains of a smashed boxwood store pen, where some fisherman had kept his catch of crabs in floating captivity until he wanted to market them.

It was all typical, all as he'd seen often enough before. He could picture the trawler, working in darkness, ground chains and heavy boards scouring the sea bottom, her great, purselike nets scooping up any fish that couldn't escape their gaping, moving maws.

Suddenly Webb Carrick felt lonely and undecided. He let the glasses hang by their strap again, stuck his hands in the duffel coat pockets and allowed himself the luxury of a sigh.

Maybe the Keenans had died that way, their boat smashed down by a fast-travelling trawler, callously left to drown. But maybe something very different had happened for very different reasons.

He could talk about it with Johnny Walker, as *Puffin*'s skipper. He could discuss it with Clapper Bell. A couple of real police would be in Dunbrach when he got back there in the morning.

But when it came to a Fishery Protection involvement, he was the man on the spot. Right or wrong, any decisions would be his and he'd be stuck with them.

Command experience. Webb Carrick grimaced to himself, idly watching a pair of workboats fishing some distance ahead. Whatever was going on between the mainland and the Hound Islands, he felt as helpless as a man handed a tin whistle and a pyjama cord and told to perform the Indian rope trick.

A vague shimmer, narrow and lacking any real form, lightly discoloured a ribbon of water close ahead and across *Tern*'s path. For a moment it only half-registered with him. Then, as the patrol boat growled on, the shimmer became a barely submerged tangle of rope and clinging, drifting nets.

Carrick grabbed the telephone handset linked to the bridge.

"Nets." He shouted the warning. "Dead ahead. Stop engines!"

The shimmer disappeared under *Tern*'s bow wave. Seconds later the starboard outer diesel stopped, but a shudder ran through the hull in the brief moment before the port engine fell silent.

Suddenly *Tern* lay dead in the water, rolling oddly and sluggishly in the swell.

Carrick scrambled down, ignored the startled faces behind the bridge windows and ran aft along the deck. Somehow Clapper Bell was already at the cutaway diving recess below the stern transom, peering down into the lapping water, swearing at the world at large.

"Bad?" asked Carrick.

"Not good." Bell moved aside to let him get closer and pointed.

Carrick groaned. Down on his knees, all he could see of the port outer propellor shaft and screw was a hideous tangle of rope and a twisted curtain of net which seemed to go down into the depths forever.

"Looks like it fouled some o' the rudder gear too," said Clapper Bell helpfully. "Hard luck, Skipper."

It had happened, it would have to be unhappened—unless he crawled *Tern* back to Dunbrach like a wounded duck, risking the other screws being jammed. He got to his feet and saw the rest of his crew waiting in the background.

"Sam?" He raised a hopeful eyebrow at Pilsudski.

"Shouldn't be any real damage," was Pilsudski's judgement. He scratched his chin. "On the other hand—well, we'll have to find out."

"Who hit the stop buttons?"

"Second officer, Skipper." Gogi MacDonnell gave Grey a slight sideways grin. "Like greased lightning."

"Andy." Carrick nodded his thanks and drew an embarrassed grin. Every moment had counted. He glanced at the shore and saw they were barely drifting, the mass of rope and net holding *Tern*'s modest tonnage like a large sea anchor. "All right, now we clear it."

"Who's 'we'?" asked Clapper Bell. "You're skipper. I can—"

"We," snapped Carrick with a touch of asperity. "So move. Both sets of gear."

"Power mad," said Bell amiably, and got busy.

Five minutes later, suited up, aqualung harnesses on their backs, Carrick and Bell duck-dived down under the patrol boat's hull. Despite the Gulf Stream, the sea chilled through Carrick's neoprene wet suit for the first few moments. Then he forgot it as he finned along, studying the problem, his air regulator valve clicking its steady, reassuring rhythm.

It could have been worse. From a diving viewpoint, it could hardly have been easier. They were close enough to the surface to have plenty of light, the tangle of rope was totally confined to the port shaft and screw and only a ragged swath of torn net clung round the outer rudder. The rest would be a long, slow business of cutting through the tightly wound rope.

Kicking round, he signalled to Clapper Bell and the Glasgow-Irishman finned nearer, a thin plume of exhaled bubbles rising from his scuba gear. Bell shaped a question mark with one hand and tapped the big, saw-edged diving knife strapped to his leg. Carrick nodded.

They set to work, almost side by side. Despite the chill, Carrick soon felt sweat running down his face as he hacked and cut at the tough, thick rope. It was part of a main trawl hawser, and what had happened, why it should be there, was a mystery on its own—but a mystery that could wait.

Small fish flicked past. Clapper Bell lost his balance as one coil came free from the glinting stainless steel of the propellor shaft and performed what amounted to a tumbling somersault to get back. But he winked at Carrick through his face-mask glass.

They worked on, some of the small, darting fish losing their initial fear and becoming brave enough to nibble at their arms and legs, one even nudging against Carrick's face mask. After thirty minutes, *Tern*'s rudder gear was clear and more chunks of rope had been sawed from the propellor shaft.

Then, without warning, it all went wrong.

One minute Carrick was sawing at yet another turn of the thick, unyielding rope. The next, it seemed to snap. Snaking and twisting, all the remaining rope uncoiled from the shaft, flicked through the water and caught him round his waist. Suddenly he was dragged down, enveloped in more rope and swathes of net, trapped and helpless, being slowly pulled head first towards whatever lay below.

The fall ended gently enough, on thick bottom ooze which rose like a muddy soup, then settled again. Overhead, Carrick could see more of the trawl net billowing and quivering, one layer above another, teased by the currents, equally liable to float or sink.

Pressure pain was building behind his eyes. Carrick equalized it by forcing some air into the face mask, then tried to think. His aqualung was still functioning; for the moment there was plenty of air left in the twin cylinders. His right arm was caught in one tangle of net but he twisted round and managed to see the reading on the depth gauge strapped to his wrist.

The needle quivered on 160 feet.

Twenty-six fathoms. At that depth, the time his air would last was cut by more than half. He tried to assess the rest. He'd lost the diving knife on the way down, he could only move his left arm a few inches, but his left leg was free.

When you're in trouble, think first and fast . . . a demon of a naval diving instructor had hammered the rule home until everyone on Carrick's course had used it as a comedy line. But it meant don't be a damned fool and make things worse.

Carrick forced himself to stop struggling, then steadied his breathing until the demand valve was working again at a slow, steady rhythm matched by the streaming bubbles of exhaled air rising to the surface.

They'd see them on *Tern*. The patrol boat carried a spare aqualung set, and Andy Grey's record showed he'd some basic scuba training.

But what about Clapper Bell? All Carrick could recall was a fleeting impression of a burly, suited figure fighting to escape from a clutching curtain of torn net.

That damned net. He studied what he could see of it in the dim bottom light, tracing it against the patches of waving weed and isolated pinnacles of rock. Badly torn, it looked like the type used by a medium-sized trawler. Why it had been floating like a curtain, how they'd disturbed what partial buoyancy it had possessed, didn't matter. But it was a puzzle on its own. This one had been abandoned, yet a trawl net could cost several thousand pounds to replace.

That wasn't what he had to think about.

How much time had passed since he'd been dragged down. How was his air lasting out?

He wasn't the only life trapped by the trawl net. A large cod, trapped by the gills, was still twisting, tail thrashing, only a few feet away.

Suddenly Carrick realized he was struggling again. He gained some movement in his right arm and as a bitter reward a fold of net settled over his face mask. Cramp twisted painfully at his legs. He felt cold seeping through his body. He wanted to shout, to swear, to plead for help.

Something flicked at his head. He twisted his neck round, saw only net, then the net quivered and a hand came through, gripping his shoulder.

The hand was withdrawn, but he couldn't have imagined it. His air supply still had to be okay, it hadn't been just his mind.

The net quivered again, kept quivering, began to part. A knife glinted, slicing busily, and two scuba-suited figures were working out there. His shoulders, then his right arm came free. The nearest figure pressed close, face mask to face mask, then Clapper Bell shoved another knife into Carrick's hand.

Three knives at work freed him in minutes. Clapper Bell eased him clear, then tapped his air cylinders and pointed at the surface. The other diver hovered nearby, waiting.

Carrick nodded.

The big cod was still fighting, still trying to escape. Carrick kicked towards it, carefully used the knife to cut it loose from the mesh and watched it swim away. Then he thumbed to Bell and the other figure and they began rising, staying well clear of the trawl.

His two hovering nursemaids stayed with him while he made two decompression stops on the way up. Then they broke surface close together. *Tern* was waiting for them, her engines murmuring, someone waving from her deck.

Webb Carrick spat out his breathing tube, then looked round at the two men bobbing beside him in the swell. Clapper Bell was nearest. The other shoved back his face mask, and Andy Grey peered at him.

"How do you feel, Skipper?" asked Grey anxiously.

"Fine." Carrick made an attempt at an indignant scowl. "But what the hell kept you?"

"Beautiful the way you said that—like poetry." Clapper Bell took a slopping wavecrest across the face but couldn't stop grinning. "Ach, we just decided there'd be hell to pay if we went back without you."

Carrick matched his grin, then took a long, deep breath of the clean, salt-fresh air and tried to stop himself from shaking. He'd surfaced with exactly three minutes' reserve in his air tanks.

"Everything's freed. Sam says there's no damage," reported Grey, drifting nearer. "We're back in business."

Carrick nodded. A few short, snakelike pieces of cut rope were floating nearby. He spoke to Bell and waited until the Glasgow-Irishman had collected a couple.

Then they began swimming for *Tern.*

The agreed charade still had to be played out. Under way again, *Tern* made an apparently leisurely business of completing her circuit of the sea loch, then nosed her way into the harbour at St. Ringan. The tide was well out and a few boats lay stranded in mud. The others were clustered tightly near the harbour mouth and the patrol launch squeezed in beside them.

St. Ringan was smaller than Dunbrach but otherwise there was little to choose between them—and once again the Fishery Protection flag didn't receive a particular welcome. Inviting them aboard, Carrick warned two of the local skippers about the drifting trawl net but said nothing about what *Tern* was doing. He left that to Gogi MacDonnell, who went ashore, returned with a paper bag filled with groceries from the village store, and was suitably indiscreet when he gossiped at the shop counter.

Dusk was greying in as *Tern* left again, steering north, making a leisurely progress about half a mile out from the shore, her navigation lights switched on. Carrick kept things that way for half an hour, until darkness had totally arrived. Then the patrol boat gradually widened her distance from the coastline.

There was enough cloud overhead to ensure little moonlight. *Tern*'s size and low silhouette made her hard to spot at any distance on the average fishing boat's radar. When he passed the word to darken ship and only the soft red bridge lights remained, the patrol launch blended totally into the night.

They steered west, engines murmuring, picking a careful passage through the waiting maze of shoals and reefs, committed, but with time to spare. It amounted to a blend of seamanship and *Tern*'s electronics, and both had been used to the full before she reached the chosen picket position six miles north of the Hound Islands. Creeping into shelter on the leeward side of a line of rocks, the patrol boat anchored. To the northeast, on the far mainland, a lighthouse flashed on the horizon. Another showed to the west.

At 2300 hours, *Puffin* radioed from Dunbrach that she had sailed on her south patrol sweep. Johnny Walker made the call himself and sounded suitably bored. But it was the other half of the plan—*Puffin* would go through the same "darken ship" routine, then ease back into Priest Bay.

Aboard *Tern,* Sam Pilsudski emphasizing his engineer status by snoring loudly in his cabin, the rest of her crew settled into a routine of radar and anchor watch duty. Carrick had the 2 A.M. turn, and until then he lay fully dressed on his bunk, unable to sleep, feeling the jerking motion of his little command, hearing the slap of the waves against her hull, willing the phone above his head to buzz.

It didn't. A few minutes before he was due to be called, he gave up. Pulling on his shoes, shrugging into his duffel coat, he climbed up to the bridge.

"Skipper." Andy Grey, a shadowy figure in the faint red bridge lights, greeted him with a shake of his head. "Nothing yet. Fairly quiet."

Carrick crossed to the glowing radar screen. All he saw was the inevitable sea clutter and an electronic mush to the far west which meant rain, yet he'd detected a small doubt in Grey's voice.

"Tell me."

"It was odd, Skipper—that's all." Grey half-stifled a yawn. "It happened near the start of my watch. All I'd had till then was one or two inshore contacts—small craft, nothing trawler size."

Carrick nodded. Line boats, drift netters, clam fishers—any and all of them were liable to work at night and were easy enough to sort out on a radar screen.

"So what was odd?"

"Weird is maybe a better word." Grey was sure of that much. "I was checking the north sector, your bottleneck area. Then I noticed two contacts to the south, off the Hound Islands." He grimaced. "One had come out of Priest Bay, the other must have been around somewhere, masked by the Hounds."

"And?" Carrick tried to keep his patience.

"They met about midway, stayed together three, maybe four minutes, then split again and went back the way they'd come." Grey saw Carrick's lack of reaction. "The thing is, Skipper, it happened again—about half an hour ago."

Carrick blinked. That was different.

"Same pattern?"

Grey nodded. "Everything." He yawned, openly this time. "Weird."

"What's the last you saw of them?"

"One getting back into Priest Bay, the other I'm not so sure about —I lost it in a rain squall clutter." The second officer shook his head. "They must have been up to something, I suppose."

If Grey had called him—Carrick stopped it there. *Tern* was hunting a trawler, not spying on the Priest Bay area; Andy Grey had at least been alert enough to notice the movements outside the target sector.

"Anything else about them? Size, speed?"

"Bigger than us, but not much—both of them. Speed—no, nothing unusual, Skipper. Maybe ten to fifteen knots. But—"

"Leave it for now. Log it in the morning."

Grey nodded, said good night and went below. Carrick leaned his hands on the edges of the radar screen and stared at its display for a long moment, feeling as puzzled as Grey had been.

But whatever had happened, there was nothing they could do about it. Not now.

Rain began pattering on the bridge windows as another small squall passed over. He sighed, gave up and settled down in front of the radar set.

Nothing happened during his watch. Clapper Bell took over at 4 A.M., growling and unsociable, and this time Carrick was asleep almost as soon as he reached his bunk. At 6 A.M. Gogi MacDonnell shook him awake and thumped a mug of tea on the locker beside him.

"Wrong night, Skipper," he sympathized. "Ach, well, you can't win them all."

It was still dark, but the sea's mood hadn't changed. Half an hour later, *Tern* was under way again, creeping back towards the coast. By dawn, the start of a grey, misty morning with rain still in the air, she was within sight of the mainland and heading south towards Priest Bay. Before long she passed some long-liners bucking their way north from St. Ringan, and there was an immediate chatter of partially obscene comment on the fishing wave band.

St. Ringan was a low blur not far ahead when a call rasped in on the Protection frequency.

"Black Label calling. You awake, Whisky Straight? Switching on the fan."

Carrick was in the command chair, with MacDonnell at the wheel. He shrugged at MacDonnell, switched to the secondary Protection frequency and keyed in the scrambler unit before he lifted the microphone handset. Johnny Walker's sense of humour wouldn't win prizes when it came to a choice of call signs. But, even allowing for distortion, he didn't sound happy.

"We're awake, Johnny." He scowled at the microphone. "I'm on my way in. No score."

"Then how about getting a move on?" suggested Walker. "I'm in Dunbrach—got back about ten minutes ago, as scheduled. There's trouble." He paused and gave a noise like a chuckle. "And you've got the command boat, so that makes it yours."

Carrick swore to himself, then pressed the "Send" switch.

"Go on."

"Somebody did a torch job on Reiver's repair yard overnight—burned it down. The visiting constabulary have grabbed your friend the Bagman for it." Walker paused again and seemed to be talking to someone at his side. "I've to tell you the Keenan wreckage was lost."

"Thanks," said Carrick.

"Look on the bright side," said Walker. "They can't blame this one on us. See you."

Carrick slapped the handset back on its hook, took a deep breath, then nodded to MacDonnell.

"All full ahead, Gogi," he said.

"All full ahead," repeated MacDonnell, and reached for the throttles.

Eyes closed, Carrick nursed his head in his hands and tried to hide exactly how he felt. Yet again, it seemed that Patrol Box Tango had won. *Tern* and *Puffin* had both been in the wrong place at the wrong time.

And *Tern* was command boat.

The smell of burning hung over Dunbrach harbour, and a few dark wisps of smoke were still rising from the repair yard. *Tern* came in quietly past the breakwater, then tied up beside *Puffin* at the west quay. There was a hail from the other boat's deck. Carrick stepped out from the bridge and saw Bill Martin, her second officer, standing at her rail.

"Skipper, I've a message for you from my boss," Martin told him across the gap. "He's gone back up to the yard—things have got worse. They've found a body." He shook his head and beat Carrick to it. "That's all I know; sorry."

Carrick glanced round. Sam Pilsudski was almost at his elbow, a sudden, pleading look in his eyes.

"All right, Sam," he said quietly. "I could use company."

They went ashore and strode quickly along the quay. At the slipway end they had to push their way through a small crowd of onlookers, then had their first close-up view of what had happened. The yard's main building was a gutted, roofless ruin. But Pilsudski gave a grunt of relief and pointed. Dishevelled, obviously distressed but unhurt, Norah Reiver was just coming out of what had been the main door. She was with Walker and two strangers, one of them a woman.

"Wait, Sam," ordered Carrick.

He went forward on his own. Walker saw him first and for once looked glad to see him.

"You heard?" he asked.

Carrick nodded.

"It was Joe—Joe Petrie, my foreman," said Norah Reiver in a tired voice. "Joe—he was one of our originals. He worked for my father."

"They found him under a wall," said Walker. "Not very pretty. They'll move him soon as Jimsy Fletcher's brother-in-law gets here." He indicated the two strangers. "I forgot. Chief Officer Carrick, this is Inspector Hume and Sergeant Dee—the visiting law."

"Ernie Hume. She's Kate." Detective Inspector Hume completed the introduction with a handshake. He was middle-aged and heavy-faced, dressed in a brown tweed suit topped by a military-style raincoat. He had the kind of voice that could make even a pleasantry seem a threat. "Saw you coming in."

"Better late than never," said Carrick. He glanced at Hume's sergeant and drew a slight, sympathetic smile. Kate Dee was angular, not unattractive, and about his own age, with dark hair and darker eyes. She wore a grey corduroy jacket over a faded blue shirt and denim trousers, the trousers tucked into short, high-heeled leather boots, and had a leather handbag slung over one shoulder. He thought of the Bagman, but something else mattered first. "Norah, I brought Sam with me."

She looked at Hume. He nodded, and she gave Carrick a grateful glance, then went over to join Pilsudski.

"Good friends?" asked Hume heavily, watching them meet. He grunted to himself. "Doesn't matter. One hell of a little package we've got here, Carrick. Your two bodies, the lighthouse break-in, and now this. You want the story?"

Carrick nodded.

"Show him, Kate." Hume dug his hands in his raincoat pockets and scowled. "I want some thinking time."

The dark-haired woman beckoned, and Carrick followed her into the acrid air of the gutted building. Charred wood crunched beneath their feet, an ember still glowing here and there. The partition walls had gone or been reduced to skeletons; the Land-Rover he'd seen the previous day was a burned-out shell. He paused, trying to remember where the boat wreckage had been stored, and Kate Dee understood.

"It burned." She gave a slight shrug. "Norah Reiver helped us look. But that's probably where the fire started—was started."

"You're sure it was that way?" asked Carrick.

"We're sure that's how it looks," she corrected. Her mouth tightened a little. "Over here—"

It was a spot where fallen roofing beams and other debris had been dragged to one side, leaving a thick covering of powdered ash on the concrete floor. Carrick took a step forward, then felt his stomach heave.

The upper half of Joe Petrie's body had escaped the worst of the flames, even though the hair had been singed from his head. But most of his clothing had been burned away and one leg had been charred to the bone. He lay on his back, almost as if he'd been asleep and hadn't wakened.

Carrick moistened his lips, remembering other bodies, other fires, even if most of them had been at sea.

"How did he die?" he asked.

"No obvious wounds—"

"But not the fire, Sergeant?"

"It doesn't look that way." Kate Dee's dark eyes considered him soberly. "But Ernie—Inspector Hume—is keeping quiet about that. We haven't even hinted at it to Special Constable Fletcher. Particularly not to Special Constable Fletcher. Not till we're sure." She indicated the charred body on the floor with a mixture of pity and disgust. "Seen enough?"

"Yes." He turned away. "Was he married?"

"A widower."

Carrick was glad.

They went back out into the open. Detective Inspector Hume

greeted him with a grunt, then glanced impatiently at his wrist-watch.

"Where's Fletcher got to?" Hume shoved his hands back in his pockets. "He said five minutes—but it's always the same with these damned specials. He probably went home for breakfast, and that's more than I've had." He turned to Kate Dee. "Where'd you leave the camera?"

"In the car."

"Get it and add a couple of general views of this place to what you got inside—we may need them." He heaved a sigh as she went off. "That's how it goes in this part of the world, Carrick. Half the time we have to do our own scene-of-crime work—though with this one we'll have to bring in some experts, day-trip style."

"But you think you've got your man?"

"Yes. And a good idea of what happened."

"Tell me," said Carrick.

"It's simple." Hume scuffed a shoe along the ground and considered the mark he'd made. "Petrie lived in a cottage just behind this place. Somebody broke in here—we found a side door jemmied open. Petrie must have noticed something wrong, dressed and come over. Then"—he shrugged—"the fire was spotted soon after one A.M. At least, that's when Fletcher was told and hauled us out of our beds. It was well alight by the time we arrived, and Dunbrach doesn't run to a fire brigade—just a hose and some buckets. So it burned down."

"Then you arrested the Bagman. Why?"

"Witnesses. And there's no formal arrest. He's officially helping with inquiries," said Hume. "Fletcher has a couple of fishermen sitting on him somewhere."

"I asked why," said Carrick flatly.

"You mean motive?" Hume shrugged. "Well, you've lost that wreckage from the Keenans' boat, haven't you?"

"He brought it in," Carrick reminded him. "You said witnesses. What kind?"

"My kind." Hume didn't hide his irritation. "Stick to the sea, Carrick. This is dry-land stuff. Your Bagman, or whatever his name is, has a motorcycle, and the family who spotted the fire heard a motorcycle leaving. Your Bagman was seen skulking around the harbour at about midnight. Then something you don't know, because you were out on patrol by then—he turned up just before the yard closed last night and had one hell of a row with Petrie. Petrie wouldn't say why afterwards, but they almost had a punch-up on the spot. Norah Reiver saw it, and she wasn't alone. And—"

"Aye, and I've just let him go," said a dry, mild voice, and Jimsy Fletcher ambled in front of them.

"You did what?" Hume's beefy face flushed an awesome purple.

"Let him go." Dunbrach's special constable gave a pixylike grin. "Ach, you wouldn't want to look a fool, would you, man? We found him in bed, didn't we, fully dressed, even his boots on, snoring like a horse and smelling like a distillery?"

"Fletcher—" Words failed Hume. He stuffed his hands even deeper in his pockets as an alternative to violence, and glared. "You'd better make sense. My prisoner—"

"Detained for questioning," murmured Carrick.

Both ignored him.

"You see, I didn't notice his motorcycle anywhere at the cottage," said Fletcher. "That's what kept me away—that and Hammy having to get a new bath out of his van before he could use it for moving the body. Use the van, I mean—"

Hume began a low, throaty growl.

"Jimsy," Carrick warned softly.

"Sorry, Skipper." Fletcher scratched his chin. "Well, you see, I asked around. The Bagman had a drink or two too many last night in the Long Galley. Then he fell off that machine of his near the harbour, at about midnight. That's when folk saw him."

Detective Inspector Hume swallowed hard. "Go on." The growl had become a croak.

"What they didn't see was Hector Brown arriving—Hector runs the garage in the village and he's the helpful kind. Anyway, Hector loads the Bagman and his bike into the garage pick-up truck. He takes the Bagman out to his cottage and dumps him in bed, the way we found him. The bike is in Hector's workshop and it can't be used until it's repaired."

"He still had his boots on." Hume surrendered with ill grace. "Why the devil didn't that damned beachcomber open his mouth, tell us?"

"He says you didn't ask him," said Jimsy Fletcher. He shook his head. "And then—well, it's like John ten, verse five, Inspector. 'For they know not the voice of strangers.' He says he didn't like the look of you anyway."

"The perverse, twisted son of a—" Hume kept the rest of it between his teeth, then drew a deep breath. "All right. Can you move Petrie's body now?"

The special constable nodded. His brother was already backing his plumber's van up towards the shed.

"Then get on with it." Hume turned towards Carrick, still trying hard to keep control. "I'll have to see that lighthouse. I talked to Walker and he said he'll take me out on *Puffin*. But he needs your agreement."

"You've got it." Carrick was surprised at Johnny Walker's sudden regard for protocol. "What about here?"

"I'll leave Kate—Sergeant Dee. She can hold what's left of the fort till I get back." Hume paused and eyed Carrick with a minimal degree of hope. "Have you any ideas?"

"We had some radar sightings," said Carrick tentatively.

"Radar?" Hume snorted at the word. "Electronic whimwham stuff is your province, not mine. What about people?"

Carrick shook his head. But the radar sightings after midnight had to matter—and a few other things were nagging hard at his mind.

"Then let's leave the radar thing till I get back from the Keenans' lighthouse." Hume dug his hands into his pockets again. "I'd better get down to that boat."

"Have a good trip," said Carrick.

"Out there?" Hume looked out beyond the harbour at the lumping grey sea and almost shuddered. "Tell them to drive that thing carefully. I get seasick looking at a goldfish bowl."

"I'll talk to Walker," promised Carrick.

Johnny Walker would love it.

5

Hunched at the stern rail like a martyred gorilla, Detective Inspector Ernie Hume was aboard *Puffin* when she sailed for Little Drummer a few minutes before nine A.M. But he disappeared below the moment the patrol boat met the first of the waves outside the harbour breakwater.

Webb Carrick watched the departure from the quayside. He'd talked briefly to Johnny Walker, just long enough to establish that *Puffin*'s crew hadn't seen anything during the night which might explain the strange radar contacts noted aboard *Tern*. He'd expected that. At least Walker was still in a cooperative mood, cooperative enough to agree that the radar-picket idea was worth trying again.

He could smell breakfast cooking aboard *Tern*. He called down, and Clapper Bell appeared at the for'ard hatchway.

"Has Sam come back?" asked Carrick.

Bell shook his head.

"We won't be going out for a spell. Pass the word—but nobody strays too far. Anyone going ashore keeps his mouth shut and his ears open."

Bell grinned and vanished again.

Some fishing boats had sailed. Others were getting ready to leave, blue exhaust rising in clouds as cold engines coughed to life. Excitement over, Dunbrach was trying to start another day, and no one had time to spare Carrick a glance as he went back towards the slipway. Joe Petrie's body removed, curiosity satisfied, the last spectators had drifted away from what remained of the Reiver repair shed.

But it wasn't deserted. When he went into the gutted, almost roofless shell, Carrick found Sam Pilsudski and Norah raking through the fire-blackened remains of what had been the office area.

"There's damned little left of anything, Skipper." Pilsudski gave a sideways kick at the charred remains of what had been a desk and it collapsed among the ashes. He gave a sympathetic scowl at the tall, heavily built woman beside him. "It's a total mess."

"The bank made sure I'm well insured." Her broad face grey and drained, Norah Reiver gave a slow, bitter glance around. "I'll survive, but I can't replace Joe Petrie." She paused, then touched Pilsudski's arm. "At least Sam has been here to help. I needed him."

Pilsudski gave an embarrassed grunt. "I haven't done much. Uh—Skipper, any problem if I stay on for a spell longer?"

"No. Do that." Carrick heard movement farther down the shed and glanced round. Kate Dee and Jimsy Fletcher had just come in through another door. "We'll be in harbour until *Puffin* gets back."

"Thanks." Pilsudski gave him a wry, lopsided grin.

Carrick left them struggling to open the heat-warped drawer of a filing cabinet and walked over to meet Fletcher and the woman sergeant.

"Hello again, Skipper." Fletcher nodded cheerfully. "Well, that's my brother Hammy on his way to Inverness with Petrie's body. Two round trips in two days—much more business like this and Hammy will be able to buy a new van. Not that I'd want to see it happen, but—"

"Business is business," agreed Carrick. He glanced at Kate Dee. "Your boss is on his way on *Puffin*. He didn't look too happy."

"He wouldn't." She left it at that.

"And that leaves you in charge, Sergeant?" suggested Fletcher craftily. "On the police side, I mean. But as I'm the special constable here—"

"We'll both have to suffer," asked Kate Dee with an ice-cool edge. "You understand that, Jimsy—don't you?"

Fletcher hesitated, swallowed and flushed to the roots of his sandy hair. Then he nodded.

"Good." She gave him a slight smile. "We'll keep it that way."

"Jimsy." Carrick decided it was safe to intervene. "Why were you so keen to prove the Bagman didn't burn this place?"

Jimsy Fletcher blinked, even more confused.

"I wondered about that too," mused Kate Dee. Brushing a strand of dark hair back from her forehead, she frowned. "Jimsy, you told us he was trouble."

"He is," protested Fletcher, embarrassed. "But—och—folk stick together in this village." He sought refuge. "Like it says in Romans, we 'Rejoice with them that do rejoice, weep with them that weep.' "

Carrick nodded. Around Dunbrach, it might be more a case of hanging together in case they hanged separately.

"You'd miss him?"

"Maybe he's odd. But we need him," Fletcher said. "Man, he's a magician when it comes to shell fishing. Any time he wants, he brings that boat of his sailing in loaded down with mussels." He shook his head with a degree of envy. "Some go south to market and probably end up in your top London restaurants. The rest—well, any long-line skipper grabs them for bait. They'll swear the Bagman's mussels catch the best fish for miles!"

"What about his other sidelines?" asked Carrick dryly.

"I can't say I really know, Skipper." Jimsy Fletcher wasn't a very good liar. He cleared his throat awkwardly and forced a smile at Kate Dee. "Sergeant, I'll have to leave you for a spell. There's the morning's mail ready to be delivered."

"Then you'd better get to it," she agreed wearily. "I'll just try to manage without you."

Jimsy Fletcher winced and looked hurt. But he still seemed glad to leave.

"You've bruised him," said Carrick as the man went out.

"Just enough." For a moment, despite their surroundings, a twinkle showed in her dark eyes. "Some of these villages still haven't heard that women have the vote." Then she paused. "Skipper—"

"Webb."

"Webb. If I bruised him, you worried him. What was that business about sidelines?"

"David Smith, our Bagman, probably knows more than he'll admit about a few things," said Carrick. "Did you meet him?"

"Meet him?" Kate Dee wrinkled her nose. "I helped drag him out of the rat-nest he calls a bed. Then Ernie Hume had me go through that damned bag he totes around." She saw Carrick eye her own leather shoulder bag and reacted indignantly. "I can guess what you're thinking but don't say it—and I tell you that bag of his holds the biggest collection of male junk I've ever seen!"

Carrick grinned and glanced along the shed. Sam Pilsudski and Norah Reiver still seemed to be struggling with the same filing cabinet.

"I'm due another talk with the Bagman. Want to come?"

She frowned. "How about breakfast first?"

"That's what I'm hoping he decided."

"All right," agreed Kate Dee. "I've Ernie's car keys. But I think better when I've eaten—and I've been up more than half the damned night."

He gave her a sympathetic grin, but pointed towards the door.

They went towards it, picking their way through fallen debris. Then, at the door, Kate Dee suddenly stumbled, almost fell, and swore as she grabbed at Carrick for support. She tried another step, swore again, and looked down at her Western-style boots. The heel of one had been broken off.

"I'll find it." Carrick hunkered down, raked a hand through the ash and debris and exposed the edge of a metal foot grid set into the floor. "There's your culprit."

"Just find the damned heel, then maybe I can stick it back on." She hobbled nearer.

He chuckled, raked with his fingers again, tugged, then sat back, triumphant. "Here."

"That's not mine. It's too big." She scowled at the broken portion of boot heel in his hand. "What are they doing—breeding?"

Puzzled, Carrick tried again. In another moment, he found a second, smaller boot heel.

"That's it. Thanks." She grabbed the new discovery, then considered it ruefully. "What do you think?"

Carrick didn't answer her. He was frowning at the first boot heel he'd found jammed in the grid. It wasn't a woman's size. But it was still narrow, elevator-style, enough to add a good couple of inches to any man's height.

He'd only seen one man around Dunbrach who wore that kind of footwear—Danny Rose.

"What's wrong?" asked Kate Dee, her change of voice matching his mood.

"Which door was forced last night?"

"This one." She stopped. "And he'd leave the same way."

"In a hurry. If someone lost his boot heel, he wouldn't stop to look around."

"Someone?" Kate Dee raised an eyebrow.

"A particular someone." Carrick nodded grimly. "All right, let's see if we can get you back on an even keel."

"Why bother?" she asked. "These people probably prefer to see women barefoot."

Carrick helped her to hobble out of the shed and across a patch of waste ground to where a black Ford Granada was parked. She flopped into the driver's seat of the unmarked police car, hauled off the offending boot and tossed it to Carrick.

Only part of the heel had snapped away, and some nails still protruded. He picked up a handy stone from the ground, used it as a hammer and tapped the broken portion back in place.

"It won't hold for long." He slipped the boot on for her. She had small feet, with neat, well-formed toes. "Don't blame me if it goes again."

"I won't." She produced a pack of cigarettes from the pocket of her grey jacket as Carrick came round and settled into the front passenger seat. "Use them?"

"I'm trying to say 'I did.' " He shook his head.

"I tried a doctor and hypnosis." Kate Dee lit a cigarette with the dashboard lighter. "Then I discovered what he really had in mind." Amused at the memory, she drew on the cigarette and glanced at Carrick. "That other boot heel—"

"Later. And I'd have to prove it."

She sighed, started the car and set it moving.

By road to the Bagman's cottage was a considerably less direct route than the path along the beach, and it ended in a short, jolting ride down a pot-holed apology for a track. When Kate Dee stopped the car and they got out, Carrick could just make out the line of the road behind them. A bus was travelling along it, heading in towards Dunbrach.

"Don't expect an exactly friendly welcome from him," he warned as they walked down towards the Bagman's cottage.

"After this morning, there's no chance." Kate Dee chuckled to herself, then nodded towards the sullen, whitecapped waves breaking along the shore. "But from the look of that, I think Ernie Hume would swop places with us."

Carrick spared a moment's sympathy for the absent detective inspector. Heavy grey clouds, the kind that meant rain, were beginning to pile up again on the horizon. By the time *Puffin* returned to harbour, her reluctant passenger was going to be in need of care and attention. But he was unlikely to get either in much measure from his dark-haired sergeant.

Inevitably they'd been seen from the cottage. When they reached the door it was open and the Bagman stood there, no sign of welcome on his thin, bearded face. He was in his shirtsleeves, his arms folded, but for once he wasn't carrying his canvas pouch.

"What's this you've brought with you?" he asked Carrick acidly, gesturing toward Kate Dee. "You Fishery snoops are bad enough on your own. But—" He stopped and peered at her. "You're that damn woman policeman. Dragging me off somewhere again, are you?"

"Don't tempt her," said Carrick mildly. "Be nice and she might even apologize." He ignored the gasp of protest at his side. "You didn't make things easy for anyone, and you know it."

"I didn't hear them ask for help." A devil of amusement lurked behind the words, then the Bagman stood back. "All right, come in. I'm in a forgiving mood."

Muttering under her breath, Kate Dee allowed him to shepherd her ahead of them. They went through to the same room Carrick had seen before. He'd guessed correctly: the Bagman was in the middle of breakfast. A plate, a brown mug and a knife faced a loaf of bread, some butter still in its wrapping paper and a blackened coffee pot.

"Some coffee?" asked the Bagman.

"No, thank you." Kate Dee shook her head politely.

"Well?" The Bagman sat down, carved himself another slab of bread, coated it heavily with butter and took a first bite. "What is it? More questions about last night?"

"Later." Carrick reached inside his pocket and brought out the little collection of bird feathers from his first visit. "Let's start with these."

The Bagman stopped chewing. His thin, skull-like face stayed impassive.

"Gannet feathers, every one of them." Carrick placed the collection in front of the man. "You're from Lewis. That's one of the few islands where the gannet rates as good eating, a local delicacy."

"True." The Bagman gave the slightest of nods. "Most other folk would find them too oily to stomach. But if you've known the taste from childhood—" He shrugged.

"A gannet hunter needs a license and permits, and they're hard to get." Carrick spoke almost gently. "But a man who hunts gannet without them could land in jail."

"So I've heard." The Bagman was unemotional. "There are gannets by the million, Skipper. More than any of your conservationists could count in a lifetime. And, aye, maybe a few gannet are killed. But it's not wanton killing. Like you said, for us they're a delicacy."

Carrick glanced at Kate Dee. She was puzzled, trying to understand, watching them both.

"I'll tell you what it's about, Sergeant," he said. "I want our friend to tell us how many people around here buy gannet from him."

The Bagman's bearded mouth twitched, but he said nothing.

"You wouldn't say why you went down to Handa Island, and that's the reason." Carrick didn't pause. "You didn't want to admit you'd been gannet hunting, didn't want to risk a hefty fine or a prison term." He turned to Kate Dee. "You know how gannets are killed? A hunter lands at night, climbs the rock and clubs the birds down while they're sleeping."

"There are other ways," said the Bagman, his eyes straying to the shotgun on the wall above the fireplace. "If—supposing a man did hunt a *gugha* or two around here, it might be as an obligement, Skipper. An obligement to a few old friends—old in years." He straightened a little, defiant. "He wouldn't look for any profit—not from folk like that."

"And I wouldn't want to send a man to jail for it," said Carrick softly. "Particularly if that man started being sensible, started realizing that we're really talking about murders."

"Murders?" The Bagman repeated the word gravely.

"The Keenans—I don't believe it was any kind of accident." Carrick let it sink in for a moment. "And maybe Joe Petrie's death makes the total three."

"Petrie?" The dark, hooded eyes showed total surprise. "But—"

"Tell him, Kate," said Carrick.

She hesitated. "We're not certain—"

"But you think it." The Bagman drew a deep breath. "If that's the real way of things I'll help—if I can."

Carrick was ready. "You quarrelled with Petrie yesterday. Why?"

"A watch. Bob Keenan's wristwatch." The Bagman was still holding the chunk of bread in his hand. He scowled and tossed it aside. "It was a gold watch, a good one—Keenan always wore it. But it wasn't on his body."

"And Petrie thought you'd taken it?"

"He thought—and he offered to buy it from me." He turned to Kate Dee again, as if he found it easier to talk to her. Or that it mattered more she believed him. "There was no watch on Keenan's wrist—not when I found him. That's what I told Petrie. He called me a liar."

"I believe you, David." She used his first name quietly. It could have been a trick of the flickering firelight from the hearth, but her angular face seemed to have softened, to hold a degree of sympathy. "There was nothing more?"

"No." He hesitated. "At least, nothing more I want to talk about."

"Then we'll leave it—for now," Carrick agreed. "What about last night, when you were trying to drink the Long Galley's gentry dry. Were any of the Rose family around?"

"I didn't see any of them. Not then."

"Later?"

"At the harbour." The Bagman gave a crooked grin through his beard. "You could say I wasn't too steady by then. But I saw Danny and some o' his relatives sailing a boat out."

"Danny Rose—you're sure?"

"Danny. I know that devil well enough."

Carrick nodded, masking his interest. "When did they sail?"

"About midnight." The Bagman paused, then added stonily, "I didn't have a watch."

"Where were they heading?"

"I wasn't too interested—in anything." The wry, crooked grin showed again. "Skipper, it's been a while since the last time I had more drink than I could handle. But that quarrel with Joe Petrie set me off—God rest his soul."

It was all he could tell them about the boat which had sailed. The next thing he remembered with any real clarity was being wakened in the cottage and taken back into the village.

The Bagman walked with them when they returned to the Ford. He opened the driver's door for Kate Dee as a delivery van rattled past on the road, heading farther up Priest Bay.

"More groceries for those layabouts on the tankers. They get through enough food to feed a regiment. That's soft living, Skipper —not that anyone ever gets aboard to sample it."

Carrick raised an eyebrow. "Any reason?"

"Orders, they say. But who's going to steal a damn great hulk of a tanker?"

"No one around here," said Carrick. "Not unless they had a buyer." He went round to the passenger side, then paused with the door half open. "I'll be back again."

"I know that." The Bagman gave a fractional nod. "Skipper, I'll give you one piece of advice, for free. You know your job, that *Tern* of yours is a fine boat." The hooded eyes met Carrick's squarely. "I can't tell you more, because I'm not sure myself. But you're steering a dangerous course—that goes double anywhere near the Hound Islands. Fair warning?"

"Fair warning," agreed Carrick softly.

Turning on his heel, the Bagman strode quickly back towards his cottage.

It left Carrick plenty to think about on the drive back to the village, to think about with a growing frustration. If one of the boats seen on *Tern's* radar screen had been sailed out of Dunbrach by Danny Rose, what about the other, the one which had appeared from the Hound Islands. The timings between the two sets of sightings left a gap which coincided with the Reiver repair shed being set on fire. On its own, that wasn't enough. But if he'd known the questions to ask, what more might he have managed to squeeze from the strange, lonely man at that cottage?

The car reached the village, murmured on down a short street, then halted outside a grey two-storey house. Part of the ground floor was a shop, with a Post Office sign hanging outside.

"Breakfast." Kate Dee said it firmly. "No arguments—I'm starving." She winked. "Jimsy Fletcher rented us two rooms, bed and breakfast—I don't think Inspector Hume will grudge you having his."

They went in. Jimsy Fletcher was still on his mail deliveries, but his wife, a plump, plain, soft-spoken woman with a welcoming smile, ushered them into a small dining room which smelled of wax polish and clean linen.

Breakfast in the special constable's home was no two-minute grab-and-run affair. Thick, steaming porridge with cream was followed by massive portions of scrambled egg, finely sliced fried venison and beef sausages. Coffee and a small mountain of fresh toast amounted to mere incidentals.

Carrick gave up with his plate only two thirds cleared, fought off Mrs. Fletcher's concerned attempt to offer him more and settled for a final cup of coffee. Kate Dee did the same and sat back with a contented sigh.

He watched her light a cigarette. Over the meal, he'd learned a few things about her—not all of it what he'd expected.

She came from Edinburgh, where her father was a lawyer. But not many lawyer's daughters, studying ballet, stomp out of class, head north to the Highlands and join the police.

She'd applied to the Northern Constabulary because she preferred the hills to city life. She'd given up ballet because she'd looked once too often in a practice-room mirror and had realized she didn't have the wisplike build required of a ballerina. Six years service had taken her from uniform duty to CID work and finally to promotion to sergeant.

"How long have you been working with Detective Inspector Hume?" he asked.

"About a year." She settled farther back in her chair. "Any day now he'll maybe get used to it and stop complaining."

Carrick chuckled. He had a feeling that when necessary, Kate Dee could be as tough as whipcord, but when she smiled, when she relaxed, she was someone very different.

"Webb." She'd been studying him in much the same way. But now the humour had gone. "Danny Rose. Does he happen to wear high-heel boots?"

"He wouldn't call them that." Carrick pursed his lips. "I've got an invitation to visit there."

"Then you could use a driver."

Carrick would rather have had Clapper Bell and two more like him. But he saw the glint of interest in Kate Dee's eyes and knew he wouldn't win. He nodded.

Jimsy Fletcher's wife gave them directions as they left, but made it plain she wasn't happy about the kind of welcome they might get.

"There's never been a Rose born yet worth trusting," was her final warning. "And they're at their worst when they're pleasant."

Kate Dee waited until they were in the car and had started moving.

"So tell me more about them," she said.

Carrick sketched the little he did know, and she hummed for a moment under her breath.

"Nice people." She steered past a big fish truck which was heading for the harbour, then gave him a sideways glance. "Do we keep it diplomatic?"

He nodded. Unless the unexpected happened, it would have to be that way.

Their destination was about a mile west of the village, part of it along what began as a narrow tarmac road, then became a pot-holed track through a mixture of scrub and heather. The track brought them down to the shore again, where a fold of land and rock formed a narrow inlet Carrick hadn't known existed. They bumped over a last stretch, towards a group of small, tin-roofed shacks, wooden sheds and what, at first glance, looked like a graveyard collection of rusted hulls. Some were beached, partly dismantled; a few bobbed listlessly close to a crumbling wooden pier, and much of the water in the inlet was covered by an oily scum.

"Your Rose garden," murmured Kate Dee. She gave a friendly smile as they passed a tall, hard-faced woman pulling two grubby children into the first of the shacks. The woman scowled at Carrick's uniform, and the older child gave a gesture which needed no translation. Kate winced. "Rosebuds too."

A small line of vehicles were parked in front of one of the larger shacks, near the water's edge. They stopped beside them and got out. Joining Carrick, Kate nudged him.

"There's money here," she said quietly.

He nodded. It showed in the vehicles, which were mostly modern and included a red Volvo station wagon. Each shack had its own television aerial, a new pedal cycle was lying in the dirt outside one door, and there were plenty of other signs.

More signs than people. He could see a few men working on the beached hulls, one of them using an acetylene cutter. But any women and children seemed to have vanished indoors.

"Webb." Kate nudged him again and he turned.

Grandpa Rose was coming towards them from the large shack, ambling along, in no hurry. A few steps behind him came a younger man, who looked less happy.

"Chief Officer Carrick—here's a surprise!" Grandpa Rose showed his blackened teeth in what was meant to be a grin, then his small, sharp eyes switched to Kate Dee. "Aye, and I heard about you, the woman sergeant." He made a noise which was part chuckle, part wheeze. "Damn it, girl, you're not ugly enough to be real."

"Thank you," said Kate Dee in a flintlike voice.

Grandpa Rose chuckled and came nearer. "What can we do for you, Mister Carrick? If there's a trouble, it's something I don't know about."

"Where's your son, Danny?" asked Carrick. "I want a word with him."

"Danny?" The old man cocked his head to one side, like a puzzled crow. "Why?"

Carrick shrugged. "You know about the Reiver yard fire?"

"And their foreman being killed." Grandpa Rose nodded. "Well? Danny was out fishing last night."

"And left about midnight."

"Before the fire." Grandpa Rose relaxed a little. "Didn't get back in till about three—plenty of witnesses to that."

"Maybe he saw something around the harbour, before he left," said Carrick.

"Maybe." Grandpa Rose nodded toward the hulks beached along the inlet. "He's working, over there. I'll take you." He glanced at Kate. "Both of you?"

She shook her head and surprised Carrick. "I'll wait. Can I take a look around?"

"Anywhere you want." He signalled the young man still lurking behind them. "Stay with the police lady, Archie. See she doesn't get lost."

Carrick at his elbow, the small figure led the way, taking a short cut route across the edge of the inlet's shingle. It was littered with a scummy detritus of old tins and plastic, broken wood and other unidentifiable fragments.

"We're no picture-postcard operation, Skipper." Moving at a steady trot, Grandpa Rose led the way past the rusting ribs of an old drifter and towards the rest of the ramshackle flotilla. "Most o' these boats are for scrapping—there's always a good price for copper and bronze an' any brasswork that hasn't been whipped away. But we rebuild one or two, even drop a new engine in, if it's worth it."

"Then use them?"

"Use them or sell them." The old man nodded ahead, where the acetylene cutter was at work. "But that's a wee repair job we've got for that tanker man Andersen—you know, the Dane over on Bochail."

The "wee repair job" was a rusty iron pontoon barge, engineless, with a tiny deckhouse. Some old plates were being cut away; a small mobile crane was grunting as it heaved one clear.

"What does he want with that?" queried Carrick.

"With his kind o' money, who cares?" Grandpa Rose gave a shrill whistle which cut through the noise, then waved. A figure on the pontoon's deck waved back. "There's Danny. I told him to chase things on a bit—Andersen's keen to get the job finished."

The mobile crane stopped grunting, the suspended steel plate still dangling, as they climbed up onto the pontoon's deck. Danny Rose met them. He gave his father a quick, questioning glance, then faced Carrick with open hostility.

"What the hell is he doing here?"

"Looking for you, boy." Grandpa Rose grinned. "Thinks you can help him about last night."

"That's right." Carrick said it casually. But Danny Rose, dressed

in a light blue sweater and dark trousers, wasn't wearing his cow-
hide boots. Instead, he had on a pair of scuffed, flat-heeled moccasins—and the lack of elevator heels left the dark-haired, scar-faced
troublemaker oddly lacking in more than height. "The Reiver fire—
did you take a boat out of the harbour about midnight?"

Danny Rose glanced at his father again, then nodded. "Three of
us did, to check some lobster lines. We'd no luck—but what about
it?"

"We're working with the police on the fire." It was near enough
the truth. "Did you see anyone else around the harbour, or over
near the slipway?"

"No." Rose spat deliberately on the steel deck between them. "If
we had, I'd tell you—I'd nothin' against Joe Petrie. But if you Fishery comedians have anything else rattling in your skulls, forget it.
Half of Dunbrach must have been out watching that fire when we
returned—an' most of them saw us."

Carrick shrugged. "If you can't help, that's all." He made as if to
turn away, then stopped and pursed his lips in mock concern. "I
hope your feet feel better soon."

"Huh?" Danny Rose blinked, glanced down, then gave a suspicious scowl. "My feet—"

"No fancy boots." Carrick gave an innocent, goading grin.
"What's the matter? Foot rot? I was told you always wore them."

"Maybe you were told wrong." The scarred face showed a flicker
of something which might have been fear, then hardened; Rose's
voice was sullen. "I got rid of them. The stitching was going."

"Foot rot, like I said." Carrick glanced at Grandpa Rose, who
looked amused. "I'd better get back to Sergeant Dee."

Dropping down from the pontoon deck, he took a few steps
across the shingle. Gears whined, a pulley block squealed, and Carrick caught a glimpse of the section of steel plate swinging towards
him as the mobile crane's jib turned. Swinging and falling; he threw
himself to one side, rolled on the shingle, and the heavy chunk of
steel bit into the sand and gravel inches from where he'd been
standing.

A cackle of laughter sounded as he got to his feet. Grandpa Rose,
thumbs tucked into the waistband of his trousers, seemed vastly
amused, and the other men around were grinning.

"Just a wee bit o' fun, Skipper. No harm in that, eh?"

Danny Rose was watching them from the pontoon's deck, his face
impassive. Whatever the signal Danny had given, Carrick knew he

was lucky to be alive—even if the steel plate had been meant to miss.

"Fun." He nodded. "Tell Danny that's one I owe him."

They started walking, heading back along the shore towards the shacks. Grandpa Rose, still amused, hummed under his breath. Then the humming stopped and he gave a surprised grunt.

Kate Dee was standing beside the black police Ford, but she wasn't alone. She had an armlock on a tall, thin teenager, bending him almost double, his face pressed against the car's metalwork. Another spotty-faced youth stood gaping and, in the background, the man Grandpa Rose had assigned as Kate's escort shuffled his feet in indecision.

"What's this about?" demanded Grandpa Rose sharply, hurrying over. He scowled at the man in the background. "Well, Archie?"

The man shrugged.

"I'll tell you." Kate Dee released her captive as Carrick arrived. "This little villain thought it would be clever to let the air out of our tyres."

"But I didn't—" began the released teenager tearfully, red-faced, his eyes on Grandpa Rose.

"Because I got to him first," said Kate, cutting him short.

"Aye." Grandpa Rose came closer. His right hand swung and took the teenager hard across the face. "That's for being a young fool." His hand swung again, in a second, even harder blow. "An' that's for getting caught."

Snivelling, the teenager slunk to join his friend, and the old man sniffed in derision.

"No respect for anyone, at that age." He glanced at Carrick. "Finished?"

"For now," said Carrick.

"Good." Signalling Archie to follow, Grandpa Rose marched away.

Carrick and Kate Dee got into the Ford. She started it, set it moving in a tight U-turn, then gave him a sideways glance as they began jolting back along the track.

"What happened with you?" she asked.

"About the same. But Danny isn't wearing his boots." Carrick settled back. "Your little friend wasn't too happy—he probably thought you were going to break that arm."

"I felt like it." Her mouth tightened for a moment; then she gave a wry chuckle. "Ernie Hume would say I was living up to my reputation."

"Meaning?"

"He has a nickname for me, when things aren't going right. He calls me Attila the Hen." Kate Dee grimaced to herself as the car jolted over another pot-hole. "I saw something that will interest you. There are some motorcycles behind that main shack. Archie didn't like it, but I looked them over—and one was a Suzuki, with the initials DR painted on its tank." She raised an eyebrow. "DR—Danny Rose?"

"Danny Rose." Carrick gave a slow, satisfied nod. If the rest of what he believed was right, it accounted for the motorcycle heard leaving the Reiver yard as the fire was discovered.

"But why?" Kate Dee's police training made her a professional sceptic. "What kind of real motive have we got?" She frowned, keeping her eyes on the track and a tight grip on the quivering steering wheel. "I know about the trawler raids, but—"

"Someone ashore is working with them, telling them when it's safe to come in, being well paid for it." Carrick shrugged. "That's theory—but some of the Rose family could fit the bill."

"Would they kill for it?"

"Maybe."

It had to be linked, yet Carrick had his own doubts to balance against the kind of money to be earned in any one poaching raid.

He thought about it while the car jolted on. Not many people realized just how much money was involved in the fishing industry. Around the British coast alone, fish worth over £170 million sterling were landed in a year. Legally caught, legally landed—and Fishery Protection guesswork estimates added several million more to that total from pirate landings.

The money motive was there.

But was it the right one?

He wished he knew for sure.

They parted at the harbour. Kate Dee had some formal witness statements to gather before Detective Inspector Hume returned.

Carrick went back aboard *Tern*. There had been no word from *Puffin*, which he presumed meant there were no fresh problems at Little Drummer. But, he discovered, *Tern* had had an unexpected visitor while he'd been gone.

"Your loss, Skipper," was Clapper Bell's cheerful verdict. "She's a real handful of woman, that one."

"Who?" Carrick gave him a puzzled stare.

"Andersen's daughter," explained Bell with grinning patience. "The blond Marget—she came looking for you, says her old man wants to see you out at their island."

"Did she say why?" asked Carrick.

Bell shook his head. "No, but she'll give you a lift over. I was to tell you, and she'll check with us later. She said she'd come over to the bay to sort out some business for Daddy aboard the oil tankers." The burly Glasgow-Irishman chuckled good-naturedly to himself. "I wish she'd sort me out—but I should be so lucky."

"Could you cope?" asked Carrick dryly. He was still puzzled. "Was she over on her own?"

"One of Andersen's men from the island was with her—and Daddy hadn't let her take the powerboat. They were on a four-by-two cabin launch."

"I'll think about it," Carrick told him.

"You'll think about it?" Bell considered him with surprise. "Skipper, this command thing isn't doing you much good."

Two long signals had come in from Department and had already been decoded by Andy Grey. Carrick took them through to the wardroom, fetched a cup of coffee from the galley, then settled down to read.

The first was mainly concerned with the oil slick, something he'd almost forgotten about. The slick itself was continuing to drift north again, well out into the Minch, and was breaking up at an accelerated rate. Laboratory examination of the samples taken south by Tim Maxwell had identified them as Middle East crude. The source had been narrowed down to a Dutch tanker. It had unloaded in Amsterdam and then had passed north of the Scottish mainland en route for the Gulf of Mexico.

International legal machinery would take care of the rest. He pushed the signal aside and turned to the other.

It mattered, even if in a negative way. First, the Department's air-surveillance flights and routine reports from the fishery cruisers in patrol areas adjacent to Box Tango showed no significant trawler sightings before or after the last Loch Ringan fishing raid, and none since. Whoever had compiled the signal added the testy suggestion that the trawl net drifting in Loch Ringan should be "disposed of as a hazard at the earliest."

But the Department headquarters staff had been busy in other ways, quietly making their own separate inquiries without reference to any police investigations. Bob Keenan, the signal confirmed, had been a highly experienced Customs officer with a good record right up to when he retired through ill health. He'd kept in touch by letter with some of his former colleagues. None of his letters had mentioned trouble or problems in his island life—but one, the last to a particular friend, had ended with a scribbled postscript: "Life isn't dull up here. Old habits die hard!"

The friend concerned, in charge of a London docks rummage team, knew nothing more.

"Old habits die hard." Carrick sipped his coffee and frowned over the phrase again. It had to mean that Keenan's curiosity had been roused by something which had happened off Little Drummer, something which—he stopped it there. Because it could be any damned thing.

The last part of the Department signal was short and curt. He'd asked about Magnus Andersen. The answer was simple and uncomplicated. Andersen had no known fishing industry interests, past or present. In addition to the two tankers anchored in Priest Bay, he had three others laid up off the south coast of England. But the Dane's oil and shipping interests were healthy enough financially to make him the envy of several competitors.

He'd asked, he'd been answered. Shrugging, Carrick reached for a pencil and paper and drafted an update report covering the abortive two-boat deception plan of the previous night and what had happened at Dunbrach while that had been going on.

It didn't make attractive reading. He went through to the bridge, added some routine status data from *Tern*'s log, then gave the signal to Grey to send off.

"About Andersen's invitation"—he glanced instinctively through the bridge windows, in the direction of the sea and the Hound Islands—"I'll take a run down the bay to those tankers and have a word with his daughter if she's still there. Where's Clapper?"

"On deck, aft," Andy Grey said. "He's getting the inflatable launched, Skipper—and I just lost a bet with him."

The inflatable was in the water, nuzzling *Tern*'s stern, Bell already aboard and waiting.

"Who said I'd need you?" asked Carrick, stepping across into the bobbing rubber boat.

"Hell, you can't go on your own." Clapper Bell's craggy face showed total disapproval. "Wrong image, Skipper."

"So now you're a public-relations expert—that's all I need." Carrick gave in with a token show of disgust. "Let's move."

Bell started the outboard engine.

Once they'd cleared the harbour it was a damp, bumping ten-minute run down Priest Bay to where the two oil tankers were lying. Coming in on the lee side of the towering black hulls, the inflatable slowed, then Carrick tapped Bell's shoulder and pointed. The *Ranata* showed no sign of life, but a small dinghy and a medium-sized cabin launch were tied alongside the *Ranassen,* close to her stern and beside a lowered accommodation ladder.

Bell swung the inflatable's tiller and they came in beside the two small craft. They were empty, but as the inflatable eased round towards the accommodation ladder, a face scowled down at them from the tanker's deck.

"What do you want?" The shout was unfriendly.

"Can I come aboard?" called Carrick. "I want to talk with Marget Andersen."

"Wait." The face disappeared, and a couple of minutes passed before the man returned. He beckoned. "All right, come on up."

Carrick nodded, gripped the accommodation ladder and began climbing its rungs. At the top, he glanced back down at Clapper Bell waiting in the inflatable, then took his first step onto the tanker's deck.

"Over there." The ship's watchman, a lanky, horse-faced individual wearing a seaman's jersey and black serge trousers, thumbed towards the *Ranassen*'s white bridge and living-accommodation superstructure. He scowled a warning. "No going for'ard of that rope."

The barrier rope ran across from port to starboard, shutting off the aft area from the several-hundred-foot length of the tanker's main deck with its network of pipes and tank hatches. Carrick nodded. It was a normal enough precaution. Few landsmen realized it, but an empty tanker could be more dangerous than one fully loaded. Gas pockets could lurk in tank compartments; the smallest spark could be enough to ignite a blast. That was one reason the watchman wore rubber shoes. And Carrick had known tanker men who wouldn't even own a nylon shirt because it might cause static.

Marget Andersen was waiting for him in a doorway under the bridge. She stepped out and greeted him with a smile.

"Morgen . . . hello, Skipper." She gave a reassuring nod towards

the man hovering in the background. "Sorry about the welcome, but my father has given strict orders, no visitors."

"I wouldn't fault him for it." Carrick returned her smile, and it wasn't difficult.

The tall, blond Danish girl was dressed in leather trousers and a matching blouson jacket, the jacket unfastened and topping a white shirt. It was an outfit which emphasized her slim figure in a totally feminine way yet remained reasonably practical. "I got your message."

"About this afternoon," Marget Andersen said hopefully. "Can you come to Bochail? My father feels it might be important."

"Then I'd better see him."

"*Tak.* That's good." She was pleased. "Afterwards, maybe I can show you a little of our island. Unless you're too busy. That fire—"

"The police are handling it; we're only involved on the fringe," Carrick told her with a reasonable degree of truth. He paused, noticing a movement behind one of the windows high up on the tanker's superstructure. The *Ranassen*'s watchmen were apparently keeping an eye on what happened to their owner's daughter. "What about you? What brought you over to the bay?"

Her blue eyes twinkled, and she ran a hand over her short, straw-coloured hair in mock despair.

"Maybe I'm supposed to be on vacation, Skipper," she said cheerfully. "But anyone who comes near my father gets put to work—no exceptions. Yesterday he thought he might need one tanker. Now he may need both, and soon."

"Even if he brings in crews straightaway it'll take time to get them ready," mused Carrick.

"*Ja.* But he's lucky. He has engineers working on both tankers right now, doing routine maintenance. I was sent over to tell them the news and how much more they'd have to do."

"That would make their day," said Carrick.

"They tried hard to stay polite," she admitted.

Both tankers. Carrick walked over to the *Ranassen*'s rail and looked across at her sister ship. She still seemed deserted. But most tankers often did, even fully crewed. Marget Andersen had followed him over, turning up the collar of her jacket against the wind, and he remembered the other reason he'd come out to see her.

Suddenly a loud screeching of metal, then a clang came from somewhere deep in the tanker's hull.

"What have they done now?" Marget Andersen winced anxiously

at the sounds, then coloured a little and laughed. "You'd think they were using sledgehammers down there."

"I've one like that on *Tern.*" He hoped Pilsudski would forgive the libel, but the noise had sounded expensive. Deliberately he glanced at his watch. "I'll have to get back. But can I talk to one of your watchmen first?"

"Now?" She showed her surprise. "Why?"

"Because they're sitting out here every night, and I'm still chasing these damned pirate trawlers."

"And you think they might help?" Marget Andersen pursed her lips. "You can ask." She looked around, but the watchman who had been on deck earlier had gone. "Wait. I'll find one of them."

She went back to the door and vanished into the companionway beyond. Carrick stayed by the rail, looking down at the steady pattern of waves coming in to swirl in frustration against the tanker's rust-streaked sides. There was deep water beneath the hull, water clear enough for him to see clumps of quivering bottom weed and darting schools of tiny fish.

Tiny fish, and some not so tiny—a dark shape showed among the weed, almost beneath the tanker, moving slowly. A skate or a ray or —Carrick tensed and stared.

A thin plume of air bubbles was feathering up from the spot. It moved again, then was gone from sight under the *Ranassen*'s hull. He waited. It didn't reappear.

But a shape like that, teamed with those bubbles, could only have been a scuba diver.

And what the hell was a scuba diver doing down there?

"Skipper."

Marget Andersen had returned. With her came a balding, dark-haired man wearing overalls that bulged with the start of a middle-aged paunch. As they reached Carrick, the man gave him a cursory glance which held minimal interest.

"I've told Frank what you want," said Marget Andersen. She shook her head. "He doesn't think he can help."

"Nothing to help with," said the man with a total lack of enthusiasm. "We're just caretakers, Skipper. We don't keep any kind of anchor watch at night. No way. We've enough to do without that."

"You haven't heard anything, seen anything?"

"Local boats now an' then," the man answered curtly. "That's all."

"How about last night?"

"Nothing." A slight grin crossed the man's face. "We were into a poker game with the engineers we've got aboard. There could have been a war going on outside for all we cared."

"Thanks." Carrick stopped it there. He glanced at his wristwatch, then at Marget Andersen. "Collect me at two P.M.?"

"Ja." She smiled. "And don't worry, we'll bring you back again."

"I'm relying on that," murmured Carrick.

He left them, returned to the accommodation ladder and climbed down to the waiting inflatable.

"Home?" asked Clapper Bell as he stepped aboard.

He nodded. Bell opened the outboard engine's throttle lever and the little boat rasped away from the tanker's side.

Marget Andersen was at the *Ranassen*'s rail and gave a wave. He waved back, and the tall, leather-clad girl turned, then vanished from sight.

Carrick chewed his lip, thinking, ignoring the way the inflatable was bucking as she picked up speed.

Something strange and wrong was happening aboard the *Ranassen*. He hadn't mentioned the scuba diver to Marget Andersen—and for a very good reason. The man called Frank might pose as one of the ship's caretakers, but he was no tanker seaman. If he had been, he wouldn't have worn a broad white metal ring on one finger—or have had an ordinary battery torch clipped to the belt at his waist. Tanker men didn't wear any kind of jewellery aboard ship, because of that ever-present dread of a spark ignition. Ordinary torches were banned, shunned, feared for the same reason.

So what was going on?

He looked round at Clapper Bell. The big, fair-haired bo'sun gave a slightly puzzled but friendly wink.

Carrick grinned, more cheerfully than he felt.

Still, at least things could hardly get worse.

Or could they?

6

Slipping back in through a thin drizzle of rain, *Puffin* returned to harbour at noon and tied up beside *Tern*. Detective Inspector Hume was the first person ashore, and he immediately set off at a plodding, weary pace towards the village.

"He's no blue-water sailor," was Johnny Walker's sardonic verdict when he came aboard *Tern* a few minutes later. "I think he'd have tried walking back if I'd encouraged him." He sighed. "It started almost as soon as we left harbour. All I did was offer him a fry-up for breakfast. After that, we just stuck him in a corner with a bucket."

"Maybe he'll charge you with assault," said Carrick. Seasick policemen were low priority. "How about on Little Drummer?"

"Nothing you didn't know from yesterday." Walker was positive. "But now he's back he's asking for a meeting—both of us, in half an hour, at Jimsy Fletcher's place."

They were there on time. The special constable's best room had been taken over for the meeting, sandwiches and coffee supplied by Mrs. Fletcher, but her husband was out on his mail round after being firmly advised he wasn't needed.

"We've several things to sort out." Detective Inspector Ernest Hume, pale-faced but still determined, took an occasional sip from a weak, medicinal mixture of brandy and water. Kate Dee sat near him in a chair; Carrick and Walker shared the Fletchers' chintz-covered couch. Hume eyed them in a way that made it plain he was still trying to work out how much he had to forgive and forget. "Kate has told me about this Danny Rose business. What do you say about him, Carrick?"

"That we can't prove anything—yet." The room had lace curtains at the windows, a geranium in a brass pot and an old rosewood piano. But the focal point for the seating was a TV set with a video recorder beneath it. Carrick thought briefly of Jimsy Fletcher, out delivering his letters. The special constable's local knowledge might have been useful, but Fletcher had been banished before he and

Walker had arrived. "If we've got Danny Rose rattled a little, that won't do any harm."

Hume grunted agreement and looked away with a wince as Johnny Walker bit deeply into a large ham sandwich.

"What about those boots?" asked Kate.

"He's not exactly Cinderella," said Hume with a laboured attempt at sarcasm. "We could blow the little we've got by waving that broken heel under his nose and asking if it fits. Anyway, the damn boots are probably dumped out in the bay by now—if he has any sense."

She shrugged and didn't argue, but wasn't finished.

"There's Keenan's gold watch—"

"Different, very different—if it turns up," agreed Hume. He nursed his tumbler in both hands for a moment. "Except, of course, we can't prove Keenan was wearing it. It could have been stolen later, from the lighthouse." He paused. "There's something I should have told you. I've had the autopsy reports on both Keenans phoned through from Inverness. Death by drowning—no doubt in either case."

"When?" asked Carrick.

"They estimate the same night as the last trawler raid on Loch Ringan," said Hume.

Johnny Walker had been quiet, content to eat, but stirred at the news, frowned, and got in just ahead of Carrick.

"I could drown in my bath if someone held me under. Any kind of secondary noises from the pathologists?"

"Very mild ones." Hume glanced at Kate Dee. "You've got the note, haven't you?"

"Yes." She lifted one of the sheets of paper lying beside her and gave it a glance. "Bob Keenan only—signs of bruising on the head and body, some showing extravasation of blood into the subcutaneous tissues, with infiltration."

Johnny Walker blinked. "I only asked. Translate, will you?"

"Some antemortem, some postmortem—before and after death." She set down the sheet and picked up another sandwich. "When you get infiltration of blood in a bruise, it means the heart is still beating. You can bruise a dead body, but you won't get infiltration."

"But it still doesn't prove anything," rasped Hume and saw Carrick's raised eyebrow. "Look, something smacked into their boat, right? The man could have been thrown clear, he could have been knocked about when it happened, and the ones after death could have happened anytime later." He snorted. "That's how the pathology mob would play it—and at that, you'd be lucky."

"And Joe Petrie?"

"We'll maybe have that report tonight. If it doesn't interfere with someone's golf." A past bitterness surfaced for a moment, then he shrugged. "We've a police forensic team arriving this afternoon. When they're finished at the repair yard, could they get a lift out to the lighthouse?"

Carrick glanced at Johnny Walker and nodded.

"You too, Inspector?" asked Walker.

"I'm finished with damned boats for the rest of my life," said Hume acidly. He switched to Carrick again, his broad face hopeful. "I've nothing else but odds and ends, the kind that will keep. Your turn, Skipper. Whatever you've got, I'll listen. Even if it's that radar thing you muttered about this morning."

"There's my radar thing," agreed Carrick. "There's maybe something else as well."

Briefly, keeping to basics, he sketched through the radar contacts Andy Grey had noted and logged. Then, while the policeman was still making unhappy noises, he added the doubts he had about the two tankers.

"The Hound Islands and those ships—" Hume quickly moistened his lips with the brandy and water, looking worried. "Hell, man, you're talking about Magnus Andersen. Even I know about him. That Dane could buy half the fishing boats on this coast and charge them to petty cash!"

"Probably. But he quarrelled with the Keenans and they died." Carrick eyed the bulky figure opposite. "Keenan wrote a Customs friend he was on to something interesting. Unfortunately, he didn't spell it out."

Hume gave Kate Dee a quick, suspicious scowl. "Sergeant, did you know any of this?"

She shook her head.

"All right." Hume was anything but happy. "You're still going out to their island, with his daughter?"

"Yes."

"I heard about her from Jimsy Fletcher," said Kate. A faint twinkle showed in her eyes. "She could be dangerous, Skipper."

Johnny Walker smothered a chuckle. Hume wasn't amused.

"And it could all be a waste of time," he said wearily. "Carrick, you're talking about a damned millionaire foreigner. You're talking about—" He gave up. "Suppose there is something in this. What about these ships of his? Shouldn't you people be keeping some kind of an eye on them?"

"We are," said Carrick.

Gogi MacDonnell was ashore. By now, unless something had gone wrong, he should be located high among the heather on one of the hills overlooking the Priest Bay anchorage. He had binoculars and a two-way radio and he'd produced his own cover story—a .22 rifle and a canvas gamebag.

"You are." Detective Inspector Ernie Hume sighed. "And the trawler raids, your illegal fishing—what the hell is it all about?"

"I don't know," admitted Carrick.

"What about you?" Hume made it a plea to Johnny Walker.

"Me?" Walker shook his head and thumbed towards Carrick. A note of satisfaction entered his voice. *"Tern* is command boat, Inspector. I just do what I'm told."

A sudden whine came from outside the house, somewhere not far beyond the lace-curtained windows. It kept on and, swearing, Hume got to his feet, then lumbered over. He stood there, staring out, not saying a word, but with his fists clenched at his sides.

Carrick joined him and understood.

A large hut occupied most of the backyard below the window. The doors were open. Hammy Fletcher had returned after his drive to deliver Joe Petrie's body to the pathology team at Inverness. The special constable's brother, in his shirtsleeves, was using an electric saw. He was building coffins. Jimsy Fletcher was there too, leaning against the door, his postman's jacket unbuttoned.

"Do they know something we don't?" asked Hume bitterly. "Or are they just hoping?"

"Business is business," said Carrick. He gave Hume a sympathetic smile. "He can't lose. If the worse comes to the worst, he'll probably convert them into coffee tables."

Hume's wintery glare showed that the notion didn't help.

They talked a little longer, partly about Hume's "odds and ends," none of which mattered. Then the meeting broke up. Hume and Kate Dee had witness statements to gather, other things to organize before their forensic team arrived. One item, reluctantly added to Hume's list, was to put Jimsy Fletcher to work at gathering in anything he could about possible connections between Magnus Andersen and the Rose family.

"But I'll keep him on a need-to-know basis," promised Hume. "I don't trust him to keep his mouth shut." He gave Kate Dee an unearned scowl. "I don't particularly trust anyone right now. Remember that, Carrick. If you've any sense, you'll do the same."

"I'm sure he will," murmured Kate. She considered Carrick and grinned. "Have a good trip, Webb. Don't let her leave you to swim back—it's a long way."

Carrick and Walker left the house together and walked down towards the harbour. They separated when they reached the patrol boats, Walker disappearing aboard *Puffin,* Carrick standing alone for a minute or two on *Tern*'s deck, thinking about what lay ahead, knowing it was a situation he'd mostly have to play by ear.

When he did go below, he showered, then dressed in a shirt and slacks and a brown windcheater jacket. The best approach to Magnus Andersen on his island retreat had to be a low-key one, friendly and mildly curious. He eyed his reflection in a mirror as he ran an electric razor over his chin and decided the same probably applied to the other member of the Andersen family—whatever happened.

When he'd finished, he went up to the patrol boat's tiny wardroom. Sam Pilsudski was back aboard, his overalls stained with soot and ash and smelling of smoke. But *Tern*'s engineer officer seemed in a reasonable humour.

"Norah's got over the worst of the shock. She's making noises about how soon she can get the repair yard back in business." Pilsudski bared his gold-filled teeth in a cheerful grin. "I think I can give her a few ideas, Skipper. You know, some better ways of organizing things."

"You can give her something else: a message from me." Carrick carefully moved the opened can of beer lying in front of the man, then sat on the edge of the table. "Tell her I'd like to know more about that last shipment of diving gear that came in for Magnus Andersen—and any details she remembers about earlier orders."

"It might be difficult. She lost most of her office files in the fire— but I'll ask. Uh—what are you looking for, Skipper?"

"With luck, I'll know when you tell me," said Carrick, and left him.

Clapper Bell had gone ashore, which probably meant he was in the bar at the Long Galley, but Andy Grey was frowning over some charts in the patrol boat's bridge, half listening to the soft hiss of static coming from the radio receivers.

"Any word from Gogi?" asked Carrick.

"Just that he's there, Skipper." His second officer made an attempt to push the charts aside, then gave an uneasy grin as Carrick stopped him.

"Let me see." Carrick checked the charts one by one. Between them they covered every corner of Patrol Box Tango in large-scale detail. "What's the idea?"

"Thinking ahead, Skipper," said Grey seriously. "I mean, it hit me yesterday when you were under that net."

"Meaning?" Carrick raised an eyebrow.

"If it happened again." Grey frowned. "You might not make it; I'd be left in command. I'd want to know what I was doing—"

"You've just made my day," said Carrick gently, and went out on deck.

Andersen's cabin launch came muttering into the harbour exactly on two o'clock, crabbed round past a couple of outgoing fishing boats, then grazed alongside *Tern,* with Marget Andersen beckoning from the stern. Carrick jumped across from deck to deck, and the launch swung out again, gathering speed. Within moments, they were clear of the harbour and the little craft was plugging her way through the whitecapped swell.

"In a hurry?" asked Carrick mildly as he followed the tall, blond girl into shelter from the spray.

"No, but I'm like my father, I suppose. Why waste time?"

If the man at the cockpit controls heard them, he gave no sign. He lounged against the wheel, a young, lazy-eyed individual wearing denims and cut-down sea boots, his thick mop of gingery hair brushing his shoulders and tied back from his face with what looked like an old bootlace. A gold ring glinted on his left ear.

"That's Willi," said Marget Andersen. "He comes over from Copenhagen with my father." Her tone of voice made it clear Willi wasn't her favourite person. "He likes to pretend he's a Viking." She shrugged. "But then, so does my father sometimes."

"Fire and sword, rape and pillage?" asked Carrick.

"Positively not." She grinned at him. "My father is a Rotary Club member. They wouldn't allow it."

They talked while the launch pitched on. Bracing her slim, leather-clad figure against the shelter cabin's bulkhead, ignoring the heaving motion and the curtains of spray drenching outside, Marget Andersen was obviously enjoying herself. But something else seemed to lie beneath her mood, her smile, the spots of colour on her high cheekbones.

Carrick listened to her, answered, watched the way Willi kept the launch on an arrow-straight course towards the islands, and found himself wondering. Whatever had sparked the change in the Danish girl, it had happened since he'd left her at the tanker. He made at least a try to find out.

"Any more news about your ships?" he asked. "Wasn't your father expecting a phone call from New York?"

"That?" She gestured vaguely. "Yes, he'll need one of the tankers, maybe both." She shrugged. "He'll wait for contracts, signatures."

"Meantime he's making sure they're ready," said Carrick. He paused while the launch lurched through a rogue, lumping swell, then asked casually, "How about those maintenance engineers you've got working on them? Are they your own people?"

Just for a moment, her blue eyes showed a flicker of what might have been caution.

"*Ja*. They are employed by the company. Why?"

"They can't have much free time. I haven't seen them around Dunbrach."

"No. They have all they need—why go ashore?" She broke off in a way that could have been deliberate, talked briefly to Willi in Danish and drew a monosyllabic grunt and a nod in reply. When she turned back to Carrick, she smiled again. "When we get to the island, I'll give you my guided tour. But I've asked Willi to give you one view you'll appreciate—you haven't seen Bochail close up from the sea, have you?"

He shook his head.

The subject had been changed. She began asking him about life on the patrol boats, the questions shrewd and knowledgeable.

Carrick answered, part of his thoughts more on the growing puzzle of the summons to meet Magnus Andersen. Whatever the real reason, he felt certain that he'd be presented with another.

But how could he get behind it?

Abruptly the sound of the boat's engine changed. Then she began to swing round, on a new course. They were nearing Bochail, a long, green hummock of an island edged with white surf and low cliffs. To the north, Carrick could see the lighthouse on Little Drummer. But they were heading south, closing with the shore of Andersen's island, yet obviously with another aim in view, one farther down.

He tried to remember the names of the other Hound Islands and knew the next to the south was Lunnain.

"There's Bochail House, home as far as here is concerned." Marget Andersen touched his arm and pointed towards the shore and a big, old two-storey stone villa. It was the one he'd seen as not much more than a glimpse of rooftop from the Keenans' lighthouse tower. Located near the shore, the house was fronted by a small wooden pier and a sheltering spit of rock. She shook her head. "But, like I said, I want to show you something first."

The launch travelled on, heading for the south end of the island, and for the first time Willi seemed slightly on edge. Muttering to himself, watching his distance from the shore, he occasionally fed the engine more power or spun the wheel to keep from going in too far.

There were reefs in plenty close under the surface, some of them plainly visible below the foam-flecked water. But Carrick sensed something more, read in strange whirls of current and a steadily increasing roar of breaking waves.

Suddenly they rounded a tall headland and he could only stare while he held on to a rail.

They had passed the southern tip of Bochail—he was looking at the channel between it and its southern neighbour.

Lunnain island was a bare, weather-scarred mass of rock, and the channel between it and Andersen's island was about half a mile wide—but that half-mile was a creaming, eddying foam of white surf and black rocks. Spray rose high in the air, and the sound of the waves blended into a single, low-pitched but constant, angry roar. It was a channel no boat could have tackled with any hope of survival.

"Willi." Marget Andersen said it quietly.

The man grunted thankfully, spun the launch's wheel hard over, and her bow swung round, heading back to safety. Tight-lipped, Carrick kept his gaze on the gradually receding nightmare of black rocks and white water. Now he knew what the charts meant by the stark marking "foul ground" between Bochail and Lunnain.

"The local name for those rocks is the Black Dogs," Marget Andersen said. "A good name. My father says no skipper he knows would go any nearer them than we did—not willingly."

"Add me to the list," said Carrick, and meant it. He drew a deep breath. "Any more surprises ahead?"

"*Naj* . . . none. But I think what my father has to say will interest you."

In a few minutes, the launch had murmured in alongside the pier at Bochail House, beside Andersen's sleek black powerboat and a couple of smaller craft. They left Willi to tie up, went along the pier, then crunched their way over a path of white pebbles towards the house.

Roof and gutters, stonework and paint all showed signs of considerable and expensive renovations. Twin radio aerials rose above the chimneys. Carrick didn't try to calculate how much money must have been spent to make it all possible, though on the way over he'd learned a little about life on Bochail from Marget Andersen. Her father employed a married couple from the mainland as full-time caretakers; they doubled as handyman and housekeeper when he visited—and on this trip, as usual, he had a few of his personal staff along.

Andersen might make loud noises about wanting to escape from his business operations. But when he did escape, it seemed he brought the controlling reins with him.

They'd been seen walking from the pier. As they reached an old wrought-iron porch, the house door swung open. A man, bearded and casually dressed, murmured a greeting to Marget Andersen. Then, giving Carrick a glance of mild curiosity, he closed the door once they'd entered and faded back to wherever he'd come from.

"This way, Webb." She led the way down a hallway, the walls hung with Victorian paintings of hills and seascapes, stopped at a door, opened it and waved him in ahead of her.

"*Kom ind* . . . come in, Skipper Carrick. Thank you for coming over," said Magnus Andersen, beaming at them from the centre of a large, comfortably furnished room. He shook hands briskly, then gave his daughter a dry sideways smile. "So—you took him on a detour, like you threatened?" He chuckled as she nodded. "Well, now you can do penance. A drink, Skipper?"

"Thanks." Carrick saw the well-stocked bar cabinet against one wall. "I'll have whisky."

"On its own?" Andersen sighed at the thought. "I love your Scotland. But you have some barbarous habits."

"We also make the stuff," said Carrick. He took a quick glance around as Marget strolled over to the bar cabinet. From walls to woodwork, even the rugs on the floor, the main colour in the room was white. But the furnishings were Scandinavian, including a big teak desk near the broad window and the deep, wood-framed chairs grouped round a low, slate-topped coffee table. The fireplace was blocked up. Bochail House had had central heating installed and it had probably been a priority. He saw Andersen expected some kind of comment. "If this is your office, it's certainly bigger than mine."

"Sometimes I indulge myself a little." Andersen took him over towards the chairs, waited until he'd settled in one, then sat opposite, the slate-topped table between them. His keen blue eyes considered Carrick carefully. "You want to know why I asked you here, of course."

Carrick nodded.

"It's because of something which I could have told you yesterday but"—the man shrugged—"hedder, one dislikes to speak ill of the dead."

"You mean the Keenans?"

"The Keenans."

Andersen stopped as Marget returned with their drinks. The glasses were cut crystal. Carrick's whisky, when he sipped it, was a mature single malt, but father and daughter were drinking sherry. Andersen raised his glass in a token gesture and sat back.

"Skipper, I believe what happened to the Keenans was some kind of tragic accident. I believe"—Andersen corrected himself—"I know they had some link with the pirate trawlers you're so anxious to arrest. Maybe they went out to meet one of those pirates but instead —" He stopped again.

"You said a link." Carrick saw Marget Andersen had deliberately moved a short distance away from them but was listening. "What kind?"

"I told you they spied on me from their lighthouse. But I saw something else they did, saw it more than once, late at night, very late—a signal lamp, Skipper Carrick, being used from the top of that tower. A few flashes, some kind of code—always out to the west, towards the Minch." Andersen leaned forward. "Let me ask you two questions, and we both know the answers. Why would they make these signals? Who might be watching for them?"

"I could ask you another," said Carrick. "Why a signal lamp? Why not use a radio?"

"First, they didn't have one. Second, radio signals might be picked up by the authorities. Meaning your Fishery Protection boats, Skipper. How long would it take you to get a bearing, to track them down?"

Carrick sat silent. As a possibility, everything Andersen had said was true. Using that old brass telescope from the top of the Little

Drummer light, any daytime move by *Tern* or *Puffin* from Dunbrach harbour could have been spied on, a boat's course followed for long enough to make an educated guess at where she was heading. Even by night, given any kind of moon and the distinctive silhouettes of the patrol boats, it wasn't impossible. In the same way, a shielded signal from the top of the same tower could have been spotted by a trawler lurking far out in the Minch.

There was just one thing wrong. Every instinct he possessed seemed to be telling him not to believe it.

"It could happen that way." He spoke carefully, deliberately giving the tall, grey-haired Dane what he obviously expected to hear. "It could explain a lot. Did anyone else here see these signal flashes?"

"Corroboration?" Andersen raised an eyebrow, then nodded. "Yes, you don't have to rely on my word alone. Two of my people can confirm it."

"Marget?" Carrick glanced over, but she shook her head.

"I have names and times, Skipper Carrick." Andersen produced a folded slip of paper from a pocket and slid it across the coffee table. "I saw the light from my bedroom window, which is on the upper floor. Your other two witnesses are accommodated in a small cottage, a short distance from the house. They had an even clearer view."

"That's it, then." Carrick took the slip of paper and tucked it away. The game still had to be played. "I reckoned we were dealing with someone in Dunbrach."

"Did this 'someone' have a name?" Andersen showed polite interest.

Carrick nodded. "But you take them off the hook, Mr. Andersen."

"Them?"

"The Rose family."

"I see," Andersen said. "Yes, I know them—any law enforcement officer's natural suspects. But they can also do a good job of work. You know they are doing some work for me?"

"The pontoon," said Carrick. "I saw it."

"A whim of mine. When we have it over here, it will make a good landing stage." Andersen got to his feet. "This is a busy day for me—that's why I had to ask you to come over. But can you stay a little longer?" He smiled at his daughter. "I know Marget will be happy to show you more of our island."

"I'd like that." Carrick finished his drink and got up. "Nobody'll miss me too much for another hour or so."

"Mange tak . . . that helps me." Andersen led the way towards the door. "The boat will be waiting for you. I have some letters I want Willi to take over to the mainland and they'll be ready by then." He wagged a finger of emphasis. "Make sure Marget shows you our one little piece of history—St. Ringan's church. You've heard of it?"

Carrick shook his head.

"Some of the first Celtic monks built it in the sixth century, when Christianity came to the islands," said Marget Andersen. "But then what happened, *Fader?"*

The Dane gave a mock sigh. "My Viking ancestors came along. They—ah—"

"Massacred the monks and burned the church down," his daughter finished.

"True. But there were business reasons," said Andersen. "Skipper, I'll tell you the story if there's time when you get back."

Andersen came with them from the room and along the lobby, opened the main door, then stopped on the iron-work porch. Murmuring an apology to Carrick, he led Marget a few paces away and they talked quietly for a moment. The discussion seemed to please the Dane. When it finished, he smiled, laid an affectionate hand on his daughter's shoulder, then went back into the house humming under his breath. The door closed.

"He wanted to know about his damn tankers," apologized Marget Andersen. She took Carrick's arm in an easy, natural way. *"Kom.* It's guided-tour time—and don't worry, we've got transport."

They walked towards one of the outbuildings. On the way, Carrick noticed a middle-aged woman watching them from one of the house windows. But as their eyes met, she gave him an unsmiling stare, then stepped out of sight. Farther along, a man emerged from a shed, closed the door, saw them, but merely nodded and walked away.

Andersen's people on Bochail wouldn't have won prizes for friendliness.

At the outbuilding, he helped Marget open the double doors. A battered but serviceable-looking jeep was parked inside, and the area behind it caught his eye. Part of the space was filled by a small diesel-powered air compressor, and a rack beside it held half a dozen scuba-diving air cylinders.

Marget saw his glance.

"Next time," she said.

He nodded, then swung into the jeep's passenger seat as she got behind the wheel and started the little vehicle.

"Hang on," she advised, putting it in gear. "Roads haven't been invented here."

It was an understatement.

Two miles long from north to south, less than half that in width, Bochail had the kind of terrain which doubled distance and where the only tracks were ruts worn by previous wheels. Within a minute of leaving, the jeep was jolting and slamming round and over hummocks, dips and outcrop rock, steering round boulders and skirting dark pockets of peat bog. A few sheep grazed where there was enough grass. The last insects before winter still buzzed and whined or spattered against the jeep's windshield.

They were heading north, the lighthouse tower on Little Drummer like a great pointer ahead, Marget Andersen handling the jeep with total confidence.

"Ever lose a passenger?" Carrick raised his voice above the battling growl of the engine as it tackled a rise. "Isn't there an easier route?"

"This happens to be it." She laughed at him, then changed gear as they topped the rise. "You heard the Drummer beating when you were at the lighthouse—now I thought you'd like to see it."

The jeep bounced on. An occasional mound of stones or the remains of a wall showed where, long ago, a cottage had stood and people had lived. Now, except for those at the house, Bochail belonged to the sheep, the seals along the shore and the gulls and terns.

The jeep topped another rise, stopped, and Marget Andersen drew on the hand brake, leaving the engine ticking.

"There." She pointed.

They were within a stone's throw of the narrow channel that separated Bochail from Little Drummer. Suddenly a white mist of spray rose like a curtain, and as it fell, a fresh boom vibrated through the air. The milky water flowed clear and Carrick saw the long, flat overhang of rock which was the Drummer's "drum."

He watched another big wave come in, to burst and boom. It was impressive. But something more important than sight-seeing was on his mind.

"I'd like to hear more about the Keenans. How much do you reckon they saw of things over here?"

"You mean when his wife played 'Peeping Tom?' " Marget Andersen shrugged. "Probably not much, but there's a cove we use for swimming, and that damn telescope my father talked about—" She grinned. "Where we come from, people swim nude if they want."

"And that's what interested her?"

"Maybe. Poor woman. And there's nothing more I can tell you." Abruptly she released the hand brake and put the jeep into gear. "Now that church—or what's left of it."

The jeep headed inland, bouncing and pitching as before until it reached a stretch of comparatively flat ground. In the middle, a tumbled weed-grown mound of fallen stonework included the stumplike remains of a round tower. They stopped there, and Marget Andersen got out of the little vehicle.

"*Kom.*" She beckoned Carrick to follow and picked a way in through the broken walls and scattered stones, swearing softly when thorny scrub caught at her leather trousers.

There were still faint, worn carvings visible on some of the stones. A dark, low arch might have been a fireplace; a wider arch framed a crumbling entrance to the stump of tower, the interior plugged with fallen debris. Carrick stopped and looked around, hearing the light wind muttering, feeling the sadness of the past all around him.

"Up here," invited Marget Andersen. She had climbed to the top of a partly collapsed buttress of stone. Sitting there, she offered her hand to help him.

"Right." Carrick gripped her hand, scrambled up and sat beside her.

The view was across the island, to the west and the wide greyblue expanse of the Minch. He saw a steamer in the far distance, tiny, close to the horizon, far out beyond the reefs, probably heading for Stornoway. Nearer, a small rain squall was darkening its way across the water and a white cloud of birds were diving where fish were close to the surface.

"It can be peaceful here." Marget Andersen turned towards him, her hair brushing his shoulder, touching his arm. "But—well, a few more days and I'll have to leave." Her voice was quiet, her blue eyes hard to read. "Yes, it can be peaceful—but how much of it is real?" She straightened. "We'd better get back. Go carefully—these stones are loose."

Carrick made his way down. She followed, then didn't so much stumble as slide the last couple of steps and suddenly was in his arms. For a moment, she stayed that way, tantalizingly close. Then, smiling, she stepped back.

"That was careless of me, Skipper." Her mouth puckered in a smile that held a touch of regret. "But it's still time to go."

They didn't talk during the drive back to Bochail House. When they got there, Marget Andersen brought the jeep to a skidding halt close to the pier, and a moment later her father walked towards them from one of the huts.

"Willi has the letters; he's ready to leave," he said briskly. "How was the tour?"

"Interesting," said Carrick, climbing out.

"You saw the church." Andersen took the answer for granted. "Marget, did you tell him—?"

She shook her head.

"Good." Andersen smiled his enthusiasm. "Skipper, what you saw may have looked just a ruin. But it's much more—it amounts to a legend, part of history. Your history and mine. I told you that was St. Ringan's church?"

Carrick nodded.

"He was one of Columba's monks. When I came here, the little I could piece together about him fascinated me." Andersen shaped a rueful grimace. "Including the way he died. My Viking forebears had nasty ways—they killed his monks, destroyed his church, then roasted him to death on a spit over a low fire."

"At least they didn't eat him," murmured Marget.

Andersen chuckled. "No. And they had reason, by their standards." He looked out at the water. "Your people have almost forgotten it. I had to burrow into the old Norse sagas to find it again— but it was there—a disappointment, a defeat."

"It doesn't sound that way," said Carrick.

"*Nej.*" Andersen made it an impatient grunt. "But listen, think of why there are names like Priest Bay, Loch Ringan, even a bar called the Long Galley—folk memories, Skipper. When all this happened, Viking longships were raiding at will through these islands and along this coast. Any church had its riches in silver, in plate, in gold."

"So any church was a target." Carrick nodded. "You mean when they got here the cupboard was bare, so they tried roasting the man who knew?"

Andersen nodded. "There was a Viking chief, a prince, named Olaf Forkbeard. He sailed down this coast with a fleet of long-ships—"

He brought the story to life, speaking with quiet enthusiasm—a grey-haired, blue-eyed modern European looking back down a long corridor of time.

When word of the Viking fleet swept down the Scottish coast, each community of monks knew what lay ahead because it had happened often before. This time several churches decided to save their treasures. They were sent to Ringan's church on Bochail, be-cause he was trusted.

But Olaf Forkbeard tortured the truth out of one monk on an-other island. His longships reached Bochail, Viking swords glinted, monks died—and the treasure couldn't be found. Ringan had hid-den it too well. The secret died with him; the last of his monks was killed on the mainland at what became Priest Bay, trying to escape.

Carrick shivered a little as Andersen finished. He told himself it was the gathering chill of the wind coming off the sea.

"You believe it?" he asked.

"*Ja.* I'd like to find it," said the Dane. "Olaf Forkbeard even knew the weight of the treasure—and more important, what it included."

"More important." Marget Andersen gave a tolerant sigh. "He always keeps this part till last."

"Maybe." Andersen smiled slightly, as if at his own weakness. "Ringan was an important man, Skipper. Important enough to have charge of one of the most important relics of the early Celtic Church —the gold Staff of the Isles. It disappeared. Suppose it was found today?"

"By you?" Carrick pursed his lips. "Have you tried?"

Andersen nodded. "In different ways."

"Out here?"

"Out here, and other places—when I've time." The man's mood changed, and he laughed. "As a hobby, it's harmless, eh? Who doesn't love buried treasure?" Pausing, he gestured towards the waiting cabin launch. "Willi's getting impatient, and you probably feel the same. Goodbye, Skipper. Come out again, any time."

Carrick shook hands with him, then with Marget Andersen. She gave him a cool, polite smile and said nothing.

Somehow, he'd expected that.

But he also wondered just how much of everything that had hap-pened to him had been stage-managed, planned in advance.

Even St. Ringan's treasure, if it existed, could have been thrown in for his benefit.

Magnus Andersen might be reasonably easy to like as a man. But trust was something else—and Webb Carrick had a small mountain of doubts on that score.

The return trip to Dunbrach was dull and uneventful, apart from sighting *Puffin* in the distance, streaking her way out in the opposite direction, carrying the police forensic team out to Little Drummer lighthouse. Aboard Andersen's cabin launch, the young man named Willi stayed taciturn and answered any attempt at conversation with a disinterested grunt.

When they reached the harbour, the launch berthed on the opposite quayside from where *Tern* was lying. Leaving the boat, Carrick walked round. The harbour was quiet, the sky was as grey as ever, and *Tern* had only Andy Grey aboard. The young second officer was reading a book in the wardroom, feet up on the table, a feed from the bridge radio patched through to an extension speaker on the deckhead.

"Skipper." Grey gave him a welcoming grin, swung his feet down hastily and closed the book. "Everything go all right?"

"I wish I knew," said Carrick. The wardroom clock showed he'd been gone about a couple of hours, though it seemed longer. He gave a pointed glance. "Busy?"

"You see it all, Skipper." Grey scratched his black, spiky hair and showed a mild embarrassment. "I've had a couple of check calls in from Gogi MacDonnell—he's still watching the tankers, but hasn't seen anything. There's been the routine signal stuff in from Department—weather, shipping movements, the usual. Nothing for us."

"Clapper and Sam?"

They were ashore, probably at Norah Reiver's yard. As far as the police presence was concerned, Kate Dee had gone out with the forensic team aboard *Puffin*. Inspector Hume had driven off somewhere with Jimsy Fletcher as his guide.

He told Grey to bring Gogi MacDonnell back from his hillside observation point at dusk, then went through to the bridge and checked through the Department signals. The weather forecast wasn't good. Patrol Box Tango could expect at least one gale during the next forty-eight hours, with rough sea conditions. Most of the other signals could wait—the civil servants who lurked in some of the administrative backwaters of Fishery Protection had strange ideas of priorities, right down to details such as check inventories of life raft equipment.

There was only one he set aside and read twice. It was that day's noon summary of fishing movements, compiled from reports by fishery cruisers and the air observation section. Some Spanish trawlers were loitering west of Barra Head, but *Marlin* was keeping an eye on them, which brought a slight smile to his lips. Otherwise, sector after sector was normal, and air observation's contribution was equally laconic.

But it had seemed that way before, and the trawler raids had still happened.

After a few minutes, he went ashore again. One of the bigger long-line boats was in, and box after box of silvery cod, then darker sole and plaice were being swung up to the quay as she unloaded her catch. With that size of catch, skipper and crew would have no problems with their grocery bills.

He walked past the bustle and the smells and the glinting fish, reached the slipway and went into the burned-out remains of the repair shed. He saw that a tarpaulin had been dragged over some of the remaining rafters to provide a corner of protective roof, then heard laughter. It came from what had been the office area, and when he got there he was in luck. Sam Pilsudski and Clapper Bell were both there, sitting on boxes among the debris, nursing mugs of coffee and grinning at Norah Reiver. The big, dark-haired woman, similarly seated, was still chuckling.

"You?" Carrick gave Bell a suspicious glance.

"Just the old story about the actress an' the antique dealer, Skipper," said Bell, unperturbed. "You know it."

"I know it. Both versions." And both were blue at the edges—but Clapper Bell had the disarming ability to tell any woman a dirty story yet somehow not cause offence. He dragged over another box and sat beside them. "What else is happening?"

"Nothing I'd call nice." Norah Reiver's amusement gave way to a practical brevity. "I had visitors—those police scientists, all plastic envelopes for gathering evidence and messing with fingerprint powder. They're finished." She indicated the makeshift canvas roof. "One of the fishing boats loaned me that, then Sam and Clapper helped my people get it fixed."

"Any time," said Clapper Bell, embarrassed. "It was Sam's idea."

"It's a start." Pilsudski gave an encouraging smile. "Better tell the skipper the bad news, Norah—get it over with."

"Norah?" Carrick raised an eyebrow.

"You wanted to know about the two boxes delivered for Magnus Andersen—the Seibe Gorman shipment."

"And anything earlier," he said.

She shook her head. "I can't. Just about every piece of paperwork we had was burned—even the threatening letters from my bank. But anyway, I told you. These Andersen shipments just arrived—all we had to do was hold them for collection. The most I could have told you were the dates they came. Unless—"

"Go on." Carrick was ready to seize any straw.

"There was usually a delivery note—you know, items dispatched, customer to check on receipt." Norah Reiver brought her fingertips together and touched her lips, obviously trying to screen doubt from memory. "Part of that last shipment were ordinary diving spares. But the delivery note said the rest were hydrophone spares." She looked at him, hoping it helped, puzzled. "Hydrophone gear—"

"Underwater sound detectors," said Pilsudski helpfully. "Listening gear, Norah. Plenty of uses, from hunting fish to—well, hell—"

"Submarines," contributed Clapper Bell. He swallowed after he'd said it and glanced quickly at Carrick. "Wait a minute—"

"No," said Carrick. "Not that."

Common sense and instinct came together on that. Patrol Box Tango was one of the last places on earth any submariner would have considered entering, unless he was contemplating suicide.

"Norah. You're sure?" he asked.

She nodded. "Does it matter?"

"I wish I knew," he admitted.

"I'll have to talk to Andersen soon." She said it tentatively, looking past him at the charred debris that stretched down the length of the gutted shed. "He wants us to overhaul the *Helga*—that power-boat of his. We were due to do it next week, while he is on a trip to London. But now—" She sighed. "I'll have to cancel the job. Maybe when I do, I could try to quiz him a little."

"You said he was leaving." Carrick leaned forward, needing to be certain again. "Marget told me she was going, but he didn't say anything."

"Magnus Andersen will be in London for three, probably four days," said Norah Reiver. "Then he'll be back. We've got exactly three days to complete the overhaul."

"When did he book the job?"

"Weeks ago."

She was positive, but knew nothing more. Carrick stayed a moment or two longer, asking vaguely, sympathetically, about the repair yard's uncertain future. When he left, he signalled Sam Pilsudski to stay if he wanted. But Clapper Bell came with him, following without comment as Carrick walked away from the harbour and out along the shore.

They went on, past the cottages. Then Carrick stopped, swore under his breath and stood for a moment looking out towards the sea.

"Gettin' rough?" asked Bell in a surprisingly sympathetic voice.

"At the edges." Carrick shrugged. "Don't ask me about the rest." He rubbed a hand along his chin. "Any local gossip?"

"None." Bell shook his head. "But I know where there's a poker game tonight—the back room o' the Long Galley." He paused hopefully. "Might be some chat, Skipper—for real."

"Try it. But I want you aboard when we sail."

Bell nodded. "One thing. Between you an' me?"

"Puffin?" Carrick hardly had to guess and had no compunction in nodding. "Better tell me."

"You might have more trouble there," said Bell carefully. "Seems Johnny Walker wants to play it straight with you, but he's feelin' the strain."

They left it at that by unspoken agreement and parted, the Glasgow-Irishman ambling in the direction of the harbour and Carrick making his way back through the village towards Jimsy Fletcher's house. As he'd hoped, Inspector Hume's black police Ford was parked outside. When he rang the doorbell, it was answered by Fletcher's sandy-haired brother.

"Jimsy reckoned you'd show up, Skipper." Hammy Fletcher blinked at him through his metal-framed spectacles. "Come on in."

Dunbrach's special constable was entertaining Ernie Hume in the kitchen, a bottle and glasses in front of them. Hume greeted him sourly, but Fletcher gave a grin and had his brother fetch another glass.

"We're drowning a wee bit o' sorrow," he said dryly, pouring a generous measure into Carrick's glass. "He wanted to see the Roses' place for himself, so I took him." Pausing, he shook his head sadly. "Man, it was unfortunate. There we were, our backs hardly turned, yet someone gets into the car and heaves a pailful o' goat's droppings over the seats."

Hammy tutted. "I didn't know they had a goat. Strange."

"Well, you know now," said Hume, his broad face reddening. "Hell, I may never get rid of that stink."

"It'll pass," soothed Jimsy.

"And all we got from the Rose mob was a total runaround," finished Hume in disgust. "But I wouldn't put anything past them—not now." He took a gulp from his glass. "How did you make out with Andersen? It couldn't have been worse."

"I got a lecture, on Church history." Carrick turned to the Fletcher brothers. "Mostly about St. Ringan's treasure."

"That?" Jimsy Fletcher gave something between a sigh and a laugh and glanced at his brother. "I thought the silly man had finished wi' it."

Hammy grinned.

"What treasure?" Startled upright, Hume blinked at them.

"Just a daft legend, Inspector," said Jimsy Fletcher. "Not worth someone like yourself bothering about. And if a big important businessman like Andersen has time to waste on childishness—" He shook his head. "Och, there was a spell last year when he was prowling over the place asking questions, studying maps. Then he seemed to lose interest. Treasure!" He snorted.

"Matthew six," murmured Hammy. "Verse—uh—twenty-one, I think."

Jimsy Fletcher smiled a little. " 'Where your treasure is—' Aye. Except maybe Luke twelve says it better."

Unimpressed, Ernie Hume gulped down the last of his drink.

"I'm going to get some air till *Puffin* gets back—blow away that damned goat reek." Gloomily he got to his feet. "Walkies, Carrick?"

Carrick left with him. Once outside, Hume paused beside his car. All the windows were open. He sighed, shrugged, then rested his elbows on the roof.

"I want to know what you've got, Carrick," he said. "I need to know—and I'll tell you why, though I don't want it spread around. I've got a preliminary on the Joe Petrie postmortem. They've established his skull was fractured, injury caused by a blow from a blunt instrument. They're still working on whether that was the actual cause of death, but it's good enough for me."

"So you've one murder for sure." It came as no surprise. Carrick pursed his lips. "All right, but my side isn't so much what I've got as things I wish I knew more about. Off the record?"

Hume nodded.

"You've heard some of it already." Briefly, without frills, Carrick told the tweed-suited policeman the rest of it. Somehow, though his broad face showed it was a struggle, Hume stayed quiet until the finish. Even then, he eyed Carrick dubiously.

"Skipper, that adds up to one hell of a load of 'ifs' and 'buts' and 'maybe' things." He shook his head slowly. "Take them away and what have we got left?"

"Not a lot." Carrick waited.

"Slightly less than that. But I've nothing better, so I'm ready to believe you—for now." Hume sighed. "Want me to take the London end, to try to get a line on this meeting? And I could do some prodding about those equipment shipments."

Carrick nodded. "Gently."

"When I want, that's my middle name." Hume grinned.

They were waiting at the harbour when *Puffin* returned. As soon as the patrol boat had tied up, the police forensic team came ashore. Three men with an assortment of small black cases, they were gathered up by Hume, who took them to one side. Then Kate Dee emerged from the bridge with Johnny Walker as a beaming escort. Walker helped her up on the quay, gave Carrick a wave, then vanished again.

"How was the trip?" asked Carrick, walking over to the woman sergeant.

"I loved it." Her eyes sparkled at the memory. "They even let me have a try at steering coming back." She hooked her thumbs, mock sailor fashion, in the waistband of her trousers. "I was pretty good."

"I'm glad," said Carrick. "These boats cost money."

"They told me." Her mood changed, became more serious. "Any luck with the fair Marget?"

"Maybe a little, once we've sorted it out. Your boss said he'd help." He nodded towards the forensic team. "Did they come up with anything at the lighthouse?"

"Nothing that helps." Kate Dee said, then her mouth tightened a little. "It was a strange feeling, being out there, being in the place where that couple had lived, knowing they wouldn't be back." She shook her head. "I don't know why, but it never hit me quite that way before."

Carrick said nothing. But he remembered and knew exactly what she meant.

The three forensic men left, got into a car and drove away. As it disappeared, Hume came back.

"Not a lot—the same story as at the repair yard." He answered Carrick's unspoken question almost curtly, then scowled at the patrol boats. "Still planning to take both boats out tonight?"

"Yes. But with *Puffin* as radar picket."

"And the same play-acting cover-up?"

Carrick nodded. "Johnny Walker will sail before dusk. We'll be in harbour until eleven."

"Selling the dummy," Hume said. "Maybe we can help. You need camouflage."

"Meaning?" Carrick raised an eyebrow.

"Her." Hume thumbed casually at Kate Dee. "You can have her on loan for the evening."

"For what?" She stared at Hume indignantly. "Now look—"

"Camouflage." Hume ignored her protest. "Carrick, stick her in a frock and she looks fairly reasonable. If you parade her around the village, as if you've nothing particular in mind—" He stopped, snapped finger and thumb together and chuckled. "No. I've a better idea. Jimsy Fletcher was rabbiting about a charity fund-raiser, a dance or something. It's in the mission hall tonight, being run by a skippers' wives committee. They nearly cancelled because of what's been happening, but they're going ahead. Take her there."

"Suppose she doesn't want to go?" asked Kate Dee.

"It's an order, Sergeant," said Hume. "You can charge expenses."

"And I sail at eleven," said Carrick.

"Eleven." Kate Dee's mouth tightened with disgust. "Remember someone mentioned Cinderella? At least she got till midnight."

Hume made what was meant to be a soothing noise.

"I've got to talk to Johnny Walker," said Carrick.

He retreated and left them to it.

7

The weather change was on the way. The signs were there—a patchy sky and a dull, almost greasy swell—when Johnny Walker took *Puffin* out half an hour before dusk. A few fishermen watched the patrol boat's departure and one or two ribald shouts were aimed at her as she left. Most of Dunbrach seemed to know that *Puffin* was heading north—the crews of both patrol boats had done their best to make sure the word was spread.

A hint here, a cheerful lie there; the deception appeared to have succeeded again.

A little later, Gogi MacDonnell returned from his hillside lookout point. The rifle slung over his shoulder, the gamebag bulging, he ambled along the quayside and came aboard *Tern*.

"Just a couple of rabbits, Skipper," he told Carrick apologetically, then shook his head. "But those damn tankers—I reckon there are a dozen men between the two of them, yet whatever they're doing, it's all below deck. No topside maintenance of any kind." MacDonnell frowned. "Yet that doesn't make sense. Maybe if I went back again, tonight—"

"No." Carrick resisted the temptation. "Did you see any sign of diving work?"

"None," said MacDonnell firmly. He patted the gamebag. "Och, well, at least we'll have stew tomorrow."

Time drifted on, a brief, savage downpour of rain came and went and the harbour became strangely quiet. Most of the smaller boats were tied up and deserted; even the larger craft were out in fewer numbers than usual. It was a brave man—or a foolish one—who would risk the combined threat of bad weather and the possible wrath of the skippers' wives committee.

At seven, Clapper Bell ambled through to *Tern*'s wardroom. Freshly shaved, wearing his second-best uniform with its row of medal ribbons, he was ready for battle.

"Back for eleven," warned Carrick. "I mean it—even if you're sitting with five aces and the rest are blind drunk."

"No problem, Skipper." Bell cleared his throat hopefully. "I'm—uh—a bit short of cash, and this poker game is sort of official duty, so—"

Carrick loaned him ten pounds, mentally added it to the other sums the Glasgow-Irishman owed him and knew that, as usual, the odds were against him ever seeing it again.

MacDonnell had volunteered to stay aboard; Andy Grey and Sam Pilsudski had already left. Taking his time, Carrick showered and shaved, put on his grey civilian suit with a pale cream shirt and blue tie, shoved what was left of his money in his hip pocket, slung a waterproof coat over one arm and went ashore.

A couple of early drunks were singing outside the Long Galley. But otherwise the village was quiet under its few streetlights. The rain had dried away with the light wind, and a tang of peat smoke drifted from the cottage chimneys to challenge the salt air. A couple walking past even wished him good evening.

At Jimsy Fletcher's house, he rang the doorbell, then waited. When it opened, Kate Dee looked out, framed by the brightly lit hallway.

"At least you collect your women on time." She eyed him dubiously. "I'm as ready as I'm going to be."

She was wearing a simple dark green cotton dress, belted at the waist, with short sleeves and a scooped neckline. Her dark hair glinted in the light, and her face and lips showed just a trace of make-up.

"I borrowed this from Jimsy's wife." She touched the heavy silver Luckenbooth pendant at her throat, on a slim silver chain. "I think she feels sorry for me."

"I don't." It was the first time Carrick had seen her in a dress, the first chance he'd had to realize that among other things, she had good legs. "Where's your boss?"

"Phoning his boss." She grimaced. "And not having a happy time." She reached for a coat hanging on a peg in the hallway. "You choose. Do we take the car and the goat smell, or do we walk? It's not far."

"We walk," decided Carrick without hesitation.

She took his arm, winked, and they left.

The way to the mission hall was back through the village almost as far as the harbour. Then they turned right, along a narrow side street. At the very end, close to the shore, the mission hall was a long, single-storey building with a flat roof. Several cars and some small farm trucks were parked outside; laughter and country-style music were coming from inside.

"Tickets." Kate Dee produced two slips of pasteboard from her purse and slapped them into Carrick's hand. "They're on Ernie Hume's expense account. The charity is Children's Aid."

The man collecting tickets at the door was a fishing skipper, grinning uncomfortably in a blue suit and neck-strangling collar and tie. Beyond him, the hall was crammed with people. Stalls and games were busy round the fringe; a kilted accordionist, a drummer and a sad-faced pianist were thumping out the music; and the ladies of the fishing skippers' wives committee bustled everywhere, each with a name badge safety-pinned to the front of her dress.

"One thing I didn't tell you," murmured Kate. She nodded across the hall. "I got Sam to talk her into coming. She needs cheering up."

Sam Pilsudski, in his shore-going best, was hovering beside Norah Reiver. He saw Carrick, gave a sheepish grin and turned away.

Within a couple of minutes Carrick found he had relaxed and was part of the noise and bustle. Mostly it was due to Kate. Smiling at everyone and anyone, obviously enjoying herself, she hauled him round the stands and games. They won a stuffed woollen animal of uncertain species at a wheel of fortune, lost at a tombola stand, queued for coffee and cake at another stall.

An elbow jabbed Carrick's side as he waited. He looked round and the broad, perspiring face of MacTaggart, the skipper of the *Blue Crest,* grinned at him.

"Thanks for coming," said MacTaggart. "That's a message from my wife—she's the committee president this year." Turning, he winked at Kate. "Hasn't he taken you for a dance yet, lassie?"

"No." She pursed her lips thoughtfully. "But he will—now."

Dragged out of the queue, Carrick found himself on the small, crowded dance floor as the kilted trio struck up a new, enthusiastic rhythm. Kate Dee danced well and danced close to him—though he had a feeling the closeness was in part protection against some of the heavy-footed fishermen being dragged around by their determined partners.

The music finished. They gave up and escaped. She was still clutching her knitted-animal prize and, suddenly, her grip on it tightened in surprise.

"Look." She nudged Carrick.

David Smith, the Bagman, had arrived. But he was hard to recognize, spruced in an old-fashioned black suit with a white, stiff-col-

lared shirt and a stringlike tie. He didn't have his shoulder bag, his
hair and beard were neatly combed, and when a woman with a
committee badge spoke to him, he bent his head gravely to listen,
then answered in a way that made her look pleased.

The Bagman moved off, drifting round the stands, drawing a few
glances. Steering Kate by the arm, Carrick edged a way through the
bustle in the same direction. They came face to face with their target
as he turned away from one stall, slipping a purchase into his
pocket.

"Good evening," said Carrick.

"Well"—the thin, bearded face shaped a slight, almost surprised
smile—"you two again?" He considered Kate with detached interest. "You'll have been told it before, girl. You look better out of
trousers."

"I've heard it both ways," she answered with a humour to match
his own. "What brought you here? I thought you didn't like people
too much."

"I don't. But I make an exception when charity is involved." The
Bagman winced as the music began again and a burly fisherman
shoved past, dragging an equally bulky woman towards the dance
floor. "Then, afterwards I can go home and be thankful to get
there."

Kate Dee raised an eyebrow. "With a few bargains from the
stalls?"

"Aye, there's that too." He paused, took the briefest of glances to
make sure no one else was listening, then said softly, "And you,
Skipper. Did your man get back from the hill in one piece—the man
you had watching the oil ships?"

Carrick stared at him.

"He was good, very good," said the Bagman in the same soft
murmur. "I caught a glimpse or two of him—but they wouldn't see
him from the ships." He shook his head. "It's a waste of time, Skipper. You'll learn little that way. I know because I've done the same."

"Then what would you do?" asked Carrick.

"What I've done. Ask myself why they're there at all." The Bagman shrugged his bony shoulders. "But maybe the answer is somewhere else."

He walked away before Carrick could reply. When they looked
for him, he had gone from the hall.

The evening drifted on and Carrick played his part as best he
could. Kate Dee certainly did her equal best to help and more than

once was dragged towards the dance floor by an enthusiastic fisherman.

But, at last, it was ten thirty. He caught Sam Pilsudski's eye, nodded towards the exit door, and a little later Pilsudski and Norah Reiver had gone. He waited a few minutes more, then he and Kate made an equally quiet departure.

The night was black and cold outside and the wind had strengthened from the northwest. But it was still dry, the sea air a tonic after the heat and the crowded atmosphere they'd left. There was a path along the edge of the beach and they took it, walking slowly, hearing the murmur of the waves and the steady piping from the scores of small, unseen birds feeding along the tide line.

"Thanks for helping in there," said Carrick. "I know you didn't exactly volunteer, but—"

"I survived it." She smiled in the darkness and gave him a sideways glance. "How about you?"

He grinned. "If I'd more time I'd tell you—in detail."

They had stopped, and she was very close, her eyes bright. Carrick kissed her gently and she hugged him. Then she took a quick step back from him and shook her head.

"My kind of Cinderella turns back into a female cop, Webb," she said in a strained voice. "Better get to that boat of yours before it happens."

She was still holding the knitted toy. Carrick looked at her for a moment, then nodded.

They walked on in silence, then parted at the harbour gates.

Things were already coming to life on *Tern* when he went aboard. Sam Pilsudski had made a lightning change back into overalls and was fussing in the engineroom; Andy Grey was taking a gentle ribbing from Gogi MacDonnell about a girl who had said good night to him on the quayside.

"I know her father," said MacDonnell. "Owns one boat, has a part share in another." He winked at Carrick under the soft red lighting of the bridge area. "He wouldn't like to know a daughter of his was keeping bad company."

"Maybe he does," countered Grey, flushing. "Now look, Gogi—" He abandoned it there as the radio crackled to life.

Puffin had completed her wanderings and was in position at her radar picket station. Now it was their turn.

Carrick went down to his cabin, got into uniform, hung his grey civilian suit in his locker, then wasted no time in getting back to the bridge. It was two minutes before eleven P.M. and there was still no sign of Clapper Bell.

The patrol boat's engines began muttering. Sam Pilsudski made a brief appearance to report he had no problems, then disappeared below again, humming to himself. Andy Grey and MacDonnell had already completed their own checks.

The second hand on the bulkhead clock was edging up towards their deadline when Clapper Bell's burly figure came racing along the quayside, dropped down onto *Tern*'s deck and almost fell into the bridge area.

"Made it, Skipper." Breathing heavily, he grinned at Carrick. "I had a good night—all round."

"How good?" Carrick motioned him into the coxswain's position and settled himself in the command chair.

"I can square that ten quid you loaned me." Bell flicked switches and made his own instrument checks as he spoke. He chuckled. "You'd have liked it—I took our pal Danny Rose for fifty quid. Took him wi' two pairs, jacks high, when he was sitting with three queens."

"And he's still there?" It mattered.

"Breathing smoke and flame," said Bell happily, and gave Carrick a shrewd glance. "But he's not short of cash. He was bettin' from a roll of notes that would choke a horse. Grandpa Rose was there too and didn't like it." He flicked another switch open, then closed, and sat back. "Checks complete, Skipper."

Another minute and *Tern* was murmuring her way out of the little harbour. Clear of the breakwater, riding the first wavecrests, she turned to starboard and took an initial drenching of spray. Then the throb of her engines gradually increased and, at half-speed, she made her way down the broad curve of Priest Bay.

They passed some distance out from Andersen's tanker ships, black outlines in the night, given reality by the glow of their anchor lights. Carrick considered them grimly as they fell astern, certain the patrol boat's passage had been watched and noted. The two laid-up ships were a positive part of the whole shadowlike cat-and-mouse play that was taking place in Patrol Box Tango. Yet the Bagman's words still stuck in his mind. Why they were there was one thing, but the real answers waited somewhere else.

A "somewhere else" that had to centre on Magnus Andersen's domain on the Hound Islands.

Soon Priest Bay lay behind them and the radar screen's ten-mile scan showed only empty sea ahead. Quietly Carrick gave the few orders necessary, and first the patrol boat's navigation lights were extinguished, then she swung on a westward course which gradually changed again until she had completed a long curve. It left her heading north, in the open waters of the Minch, two miles west of the Hound Islands.

Before midnight, she was in the position Carrick had chosen. Under steerage way, pitching, *Tern* was poised and ready north of Little Drummer Island. It was a calculated risk: it meant leaving the southern edge of the patrol box unguarded. But if *Puffin* did get lucky during her vigil, then Carrick could guarantee Johnny Walker a rapid response.

Andy Grey took over the watch as the midnight weather forecast came in. The previous storm warnings were being repeated for the whole Minch area, spawned by a depression which had passed north of Ireland. The northwest wind was strengthening, expected to increase to force six and later to seven, with scattered showers and rain. Gale force eight winds, gusting to force nine, would arrive within twenty-four hours.

Long before that happened, both *Tern* and *Puffin* would with luck be back in harbour. Carrick went aft, gulped a cup of Gogi MacDonnell's coffee in the darkened wardroom, then hand-held his way back along the narrow, pitching companionway to visit the engineroom. He found Sam Pilsudski had a stool jammed in a corner, where he could sit back yet keep a constant eye on his precious, purring diesels.

The intercom phone beside the engineer officer buzzed. Pilsudski lifted the handset, listened, then replaced it with a strange expression on his face.

"You're wanted, Skipper." He pointed in the direction of the bridge. "It's *Puffin*. Your pal Walker has gone rogue again."

Carrick reached the bridge in seconds. One glance at Clapper Bell's stony face told him part of it. The rest was there in the way Andy Grey was feverishly checking positions at the tiny chart table.

"Skipper." Grey greeted him with relief. "*Puffin* says she has a positive contact. They're in pursuit. Johnny—Skipper Walker says he'll cope on his own."

"Did he give positions?" asked Carrick.

Grey nodded. Carrick at his shoulder, he indicated on the chart and the scribbled message form in front of him.

"He reckons he has a trawler, Skipper. At about three miles' range. She's through the bottleneck, steering south-southwest, making about fifteen knots."

Cursing under his breath, Carrick studied the positions Grey had pencilled on the chart. *Puffin* and her contact were about twelve miles to the northeast, which meant the other patrol boat had already travelled some distance from her picket position before Walker had bothered to pass any kind of message.

A heavy sea sent the patrol boat lurching while several tons of water drenched across her length. Grabbing the table for support, Carrick fought down his anger and concentrated on the chart again. If the contact was a trawler, where was she heading? On her present course, she was sneaking in through one of the narrowest, trickiest channels towards the mainland coast. Once there—he swore again, this time at Walker's impetuous lack of foresight.

If it was a fishing raid, the trawler's target had to be Loch Ringan. The trap he'd planned, the two-boat operation, would have been simplicity itself.

But now—he made a quick, mental projection.

"Clapper, bring her round to zero-three-six. Speed twenty-four knots." It would be foolhardy to push *Tern* any faster in the sea conditions they had. "All systems on—I'm going for an intercept."

Bell repeated the orders; the wheel began spinning. *Tern's* three diesels opened up to a throaty roar, and the hull shuddered with the change.

"Skipper—" Andy Grey hesitated.

"I know," said Carrick wearily. "He's your brother-in-law, he means well—he's also a damned fool. But he could need help more than he realizes."

He left Grey biting his lip, turned to the radio and called *Puffin* on the Fishery secondary frequency. A moment passed, then Johnny Walker's voice answered cheerfully.

"Switch on the fan, Black Label," said Carrick curtly. He cut in the scrambler. "Johnny, what the hell are you up to?"

"Keep your cool, Whisky Straight." Walker sounded almost surprised. "I can handle this; nothing easier." There was a grunt and a pause, then he went on. "It's a bumpy ride but we're still closing. Not what we had in mind, but when something lands on your lap, that's different, right?"

"Johnny—" Carrick kept his voice level. "I'm joining you on an intercept."

"No need." Walker was indignant. "I'm just saving you some

work. And he's for real—I've had a glimpse of him. He's a middle-sized trawler and he hasn't spotted us yet."

"Stay on his tail but don't—repeat don't—do more," Carrick ordered. "He could be more than trouble. Understood?"

"Understood," came the resigned reply. "I'll herd him. Black Label out."

A soft crackle of static took over.

Pitching and shuddering, *Tern* fought her way on while the weather gradually worsened. Brief squalls of rain and hail lashed her superstructure while the waves coming out of the black night arrived with long, overhanging crests which foamed in the direction of the wind. Things were bad enough in the bridge area, even when they reduced speed, but several times worse for Sam Pilsudski down below. A freak tumbling wave met them squarely, buried the patrol boat's bow and sent her propellors screaming briefly as they bit nothing but air.

They came out of it, *Tern* shaking herself like a dog after a bath, Gogi MacDonnell thrown on the deck, cursing the world in Gaelic, surrounded by a broken debris of equipment hurled from a locker which had burst open.

Puffin had reported back twice, briefly, bare course and position updates. But Walker had closed the gap with his quarry to under a mile.

"So they'll know he's there. But they can't try to lose him till they're farther south, in more open water." Carrick twisted round in the command chair. "Try the six-mile scan, Andy. They should be coming our way now."

Andy Grey nodded and adjusted the radar set's switches. The ghostly green light of the screen flickered as it adjusted down and he peered over it. Till then they'd been working twelve-mile, but the weather and the size of the two craft ahead had ruled out any real chance of success at that distance.

"Got them—I think," he said warily after a moment. Then, puzzled, he added, "They're close together, Skipper. Better take a look."

Carrick timed getting out of the command chair to match the next roll of the boat. Steadying himself, he joined the young second officer. The two small blips of light were slightly northwest of *Tern*'s heading, pretty much where he'd expected, at about four and a half miles. But Andy Grey was right. They were close, almost together.

He stared again and blinked to clear his eyes. If anything, it was as if the two contacts were stationary.

"Call him," he said without looking up.

He was wrong. They weren't just close—they were closing, very slowly coming together. But the movement seemed to be mostly from the larger blip.

"Black Label. Come in." Andy Grey had begun trying. Nothing happened and he repeated the call, again and again, slowly and carefully, a gathering strain in his voice. "Black Label—"

There was only static and background mush.

"Keep watching." Carrick hauled his way back into the command chair. "Come round two points to port, Clapper." He glanced at the digital readouts. They were still managing to maintain a punishing twenty knots, but another band of shoal reefs lay ahead. He reached for the throttle levers. "Coming down to fifteen knots."

Clapper Bell gave him a sideways glance but said nothing.

Threading the band of reefs meant a blind reliance on electronics backed by skill in a boil of white water. But the readouts saw them through, sent them tumbling back out into open water, and the diesels could be opened up again to twenty knots.

"Radar?" asked Carrick over his shoulder.

"Still two contacts, very close," reported Andy Grey. "They're moving, Skipper. Between three and five knots—no more."

"Range?"

"Now one and a half miles and closing."

Carrick nodded. He could feel the gathering tension around him. Even Clapper Bell was affected, talking softly under his breath, nursing the wheel, peering ahead through the spray-soaked glass.

"Range one mile."

"Searchlight," ordered Carrick.

The big eighteen-inch beam, mounted overhead, suddenly stabbed the night as Gogi MacDonnell operated its controls. It wavered, swung, then steadied abruptly on what lay ahead and slightly to starboard.

"Hell an' back!" Clapper Bell gulped and his mouth fell open. "I don't damn well believe it—"

They'd found *Puffin*—and her "pirate" trawler. Except that *Puffin* was lurching and wallowing from one wavecrest to the next, being dragged along by a towline from the trawler's stern.

"Skipper—" began Andy Grey.

"Shut up, Andy." Carrick had grabbed the bridge glasses. He used them while the searchlight stayed steady.

There was no sign of damage aboard the trawler. But *Puffin*'s deck rails were a mess of twisted metal; her radar scanner, searchlight and radio aerials had gone, and one of her bridge windows was smashed. She had a list to port, and when she rolled on a swell, he could see a dark gash on her hull paint work.

"Trawler signalling, Skipper," said Gogi MacDonnell unemotionally. The blink of a signal lamp came again from the trawler wheelhouse. "Cheeky devil—single letter code, D and X, repeated. That's—"

"I know," said Carrick. " 'Keep clear—manoeuvring with difficulty. Stop carrying out your intentions.' " He slammed a fist hard on the instrument panel. "Hell, what intentions?"

The only hard and fast intention in his mind involved wringing Johnny Walker's neck, if it was still in one piece. But the gap was narrowing rapidly.

"Coming down to ten knots," he told Bell shortly, reaching for the throttle levers. "We'll take a run past them, weather side, then a slow turn round *Puffin*'s stern." He moistened his lips. "I want to hold within hailing distance of that damned trawler, on her lee side."

"Got it, Skipper," said Bell. He saw Andy Grey's worried face and winked at him. "Cheer up. The devil looks after his own."

The engineroom intercom phone buzzed, then buzzed again, insistent. Sam Pilsudski sensed something was going on and didn't want to be left out.

"Somebody tell him," said Carrick grimly. "Say *Puffin* looks sick as a parrot. He'll understand."

The trawler was Dutch, the *Zono* out of Scheveningen, according to her faded lettering. She had a dark, rust-streaked hull, a tripod mainmast and a squat single funnel aft. Her skipper knew his trade; it showed in the way the towing warp to the patrol boat astern wasn't being given a chance to snatch and the way his course didn't vary by a hair's-breadth as *Tern* sailed past at a stone's throw distance to starboard.

Some of his crew were working on deck, using safety lines. One paused, grinned in the searchlight's glare and shouted. But his voice was lost in the wind and the waves.

Then they'd reached *Puffin*, turning tight round her stern. Close up, her damage was more dramatic than critical, although she still showed that list, and the gash, just on the water-line, was exposed with every wave trough. But she wasn't totally helpless. The bridge emergency lighting was on and a pump spouted water at her stern.

Someone waved frantically from aft. Then a lamp morsed rapidly from the bridge.

"All okay," read Andy Grey tightly. " 'Radio U/S.' " He paused, the light still winking, then relaxed a little. " 'Patching. Any spare string?' That's it." He had *Tern*'s Aldis lamp ready. "Reply, Skipper?"

"Acknowledge. No frills." Johnny Walker might be putting a brave face on things, but Carrick didn't feel like games.

The Aldis clattered, then *Tern* was lurching in the lee of the trawler. Carrick reached for the tannoy microphone and flicked it to life.

"Zono. This is Tern." His amplified voice rasped across the pitching gap between them. *"Zono,* can we assist?"

A wheelhouse door swung open and a fat figure in a duffel coat balanced in the opening, blinking in the searchlight's glare. Then he lifted a battery hailer to his mouth.

"Ja, I hope so, *Tern.* I think we tow your frien' somewhere safe. Where?"

"Wait," replied Carrick. He lowered the microphone, thinking fast. Loch Ringan was too many miles away, but they had a choice of deep-water inlets nearer at hand. He saw Gogi MacDonnell's expression. "Well?"

"Seal Bay, Skipper," said the ex-fisherman firmly. "The best shelter around. I've been snug in there on my father's boat while all hell was goin' on outside."

"You'd better be right." Carrick raised the microphone again. *"Zono,* we'll lead you. Understood?"

"Understood, okay," came the reply through the battery hailer. "But maybe be more careful than your frien'."

Zono's skipper waved and vanished back into his wheelhouse. Pursing his lips, Carrick considered the trawler again. There was something familiar about her lines—familiar yet wrong. Then he realized why and smiled to himself. Maybe he had just solved one small mystery.

An hour later the *Zono* anchored in placid water in the shelter of Seal Bay. It was a narrow gash of an inlet, flanked by rock, fringed by a few trees, with not so much as a hut along its shoreline. *Tern* had led the way in, then circled slowly until *Puffin* was secured alongside the trawler. Then *Tern* eased in at her sister's stern and stopped engines with their fenders rubbing.

"Get Sam over to help them," Carrick told Andy Grey. "I'm going to check with your brother-in-law. I want you and Clapper on that trawler. You know what you're looking for?"

Grey nodded. Carrick had briefed him on the way in.

"Supposing you're right, Skipper?" he asked.

"Then I'll try hard to stay polite," said Carrick. "But I won't guarantee it."

He went out on deck. Several interested faces watched from the trawler as he boarded *Puffin* and picked his way past twisted deck rails to her bridge. Going in, he found Johnny Walker standing under the emergency lighting amid a chaos of broken glass and littered equipment. Walker had a crude bandage round his forehead, and his pudgy face was pale.

"Welcome aboard," said Walker unhappily, while the sound of hammering and other noises came from below.

"You signalled 'All okay.'" Carrick frowned at the bandage. "What's that for? Decoration?"

"We picked up a few cuts and bruises," said Walker tonelessly. "The poor damn boat took the worst of it." He chewed his lip. "Ever hit a submerged rock at speed?"

"Not yet." Carrick considered the evidence. "An unfriendly rock?"

Walker swore sadly and gently rubbed his bandaged head.

"There'll be an inquiry, I know that," he said resignedly. "But I want you to hear, now. That trawler saw me, put on speed to get away, and I did the same. I was going to herd him, sit on his tail— nothing more, the way you wanted it." He grimaced. "But I had *Puffin* too near the edge of the channel."

"Easy enough done." Carrick meant it.

Walker shrugged. "Anyway, we hit." He used the flat of his hand to demonstrate. "Hit and took off like a damned aircraft, clean out of the water. Then"—he slapped his hand hard on the command chair—"we landed, almost on the port gunwhale, and that water felt like concrete. Things broke, things vanished, things—hell, we were knocked half-stupid, with nothing working and the sea coming in—"

"But the *Zono* came back for you," finished Carrick. "If she hadn't?"

"Goodbye *Puffin*," admitted Walker. "That towline saved us."

"What's your situation now?"

"Leaks at the stern glands, the port engine shaft is like a cork-screw, the rudder situation isn't clever and there's some cracked pipework." Walker was bitter but still determined. "I'll have power on the starboard diesel any minute. I'll get her home." He paused. "What do we do about our Dutch friends?"

"Thank them first," said Carrick. "We'll do it now. Bring a bottle, if you've one left intact."

When they climbed aboard the *Zono*, a crewman saw them, shouted, and the fat figure of her skipper came hurrying along the deck. He had a moonlike face and a straggling moustache—and an indignant air.

"We've come to thank you, Skipper," began Johnny Walker.

"Then you Fishery Protectioners 'ave one damn funny way of doing it," protested the Dutchman. "I 'elp you and what happens? You 'ave men searching my ship!" He growled to himself. "But do it. We 'ave caught no fishes anywhere."

"Then there's no problem, Skipper," soothed Carrick. He nudged Walker. "We certainly owe you."

"We do." Walker pulled the whisky bottle from his pocket.

The Dutchman's face brightened, and he thawed.

"Okay." He tapped his chest. "I am Jan Kuyper. I am skipper an' part owner too. We come from Scheveningen, to fish farther out, where it is legal. No worries, eh?"

Carrick and Walker completed the introductions, and the Dutch-man led them into a small, comfortably fitted cabin below the wheelhouse.

"Glasses?" asked Walker, setting the bottle on the table.

"*Ja*, sure." The Dutchman produced them from a locker and beamed at Walker. " 'Ow is your little ship now?"

"Recovering." Walker poured the whisky—three large, equal measures.

"Good." Kuyper waved them into chairs on one side of the cabin table and settled in another across from them. He took a first explor-atory swallow from his glass, watching them carefully. "I was glad we could 'elp."

"But before that you'd been trying to get away," mused Carrick. He smiled amiably at the Dutchman. "Even though you hadn't been fishing. Why?"

Kuyper shrugged. "It was natural, to avoid trouble." He brightened. "But when I see what 'appens to you then—well, we are all sailors."

Carrick nodded, totally ready to believe the last part. Fishermen had their code, in which nationality was incidental. Any vessel, any crew in peril outweighed all else in importance. He sipped his drink, then glanced at Walker, who took his cue and topped up the Dutchman's glass.

"Your family?" asked Carrick, indicating a framed photograph of a smiling middle-aged woman and two teenagers.

"*Ja.*" Kuyper beamed and relaxed a little.

With Walker slightly uncertain but helping, Carrick kept the conversation going and ignored the ship noises around them. They topped Kuyper's glass again. Then, just as the Dutchman was showing a first sign of impatience, there was a knock on the cabin door. It opened and Andy Grey came in.

"Skipper." His young face empty of expression, he handed Carrick a scribbled note. "Is that what you wanted?"

Carrick glanced at the note, nodded and pushed it across to Walker while Andy Grey quietly left again, closing the cabin door. A moment passed in silence while Johnny Walker frowned at the note, then gave a sudden grunt of understanding.

"Trouble wit' your repairs?" suggested Kuyper.

"No." Carrick leaned forward, resting his elbows on the little table. "Trouble for you, Skipper. This is the Dutch trawler *Zono,* out of Scheveningen?"

Kuyper paled, but nodded.

"Then why did my second officer find name boards hidden away which say you're the *Asmar,* Norwegian-registered?" Carrick didn't let him answer. "Then would you like to explain the other things he found, after some small difficulties with a couple of your crew?"

"Other things—" Kuyper licked his lips.

"That's what it says here." Johnny Walker tapped the note in front of him, grinning a little. "One dummy harpoon gun, made of wood, hidden in your for'ard fish hold along with two blow-up rubber basking sharks and a lot of painted canvas." His grin became an appreciative chuckle, and he touched his bandaged head in a mock salute. "I like it, Skipper."

Kuyper's shoulders slumped and he avoided their eyes.

"I even flew over you on my way up here, didn't I?" said Carrick softly. "You were in shelter off one of the Treshnish Isles, right?"

But the Fishery Protection spotter aircraft had simply logged the sighting of a Norwegian shark-hunting boat. Shark-hunters were a normal part of the scene in the seas around the Minch. The two fake basking sharks floating beside the disguised trawler were the final touch.

He waited for Kuyper to answer. The deception made so much now easy to understand. As the sharker *Asmar,* the trawler could sail as she pleased in daylight with minimal risk of a Fishery Protection cruiser coming close alongside. Then, after a night-time fishing raid, her holds crammed, she could resume her disguise and sail out past the patrols.

"You would 'ave to prove a lot," said Kuyper suddenly. Then he looked happier and took a gulp from his glass. "Like 'ow could I fish wit'out nets?" He scowled at them. "I 'ave no nets aboard."

"Because you dumped them a few nights ago, in Loch Ringan," countered Carrick. "How would you like to get them back, Skipper? Isn't that why you were sneaking in tonight—because a new set will cost you a few thousand good Dutch guilders?"

Kuyper's moonlike face reddened. His mouth twitched, then clamped shut.

"You know, we could do a deal." Carrick took the whisky bottle and slowly and deliberately filled the Dutchman's glass. "You could tell me a few things; I could give you an exact location in Loch Ringan. You could get there, recover your nets and be well clear before daylight." He paused, seeing doubt in Kuyper's eyes. "You weren't using trawl wires—just rope. I can even let you see a couple of lengths we recovered. I've got them aboard *Tern.*"

Kuyper hesitated. "An' afterwards?"

"Johnny?"

Walker took his cue and sighed. "We owe him, or at least I do. Wouldn't be right to do nasty things to him."

Carrick nodded.

"So"—Kuyper swallowed—"can I trus' you?"

"That's your decision." Carrick smiled at him.

"Okay." Kuyper gave a reluctant nod. "The way you guess is right."

They had him started and he talked, needing only the occasional prodding question.

There were two Dutch trawlers involved, the other skippered by his brother, who had dreamed up the shark-hunter disguise. Both worked out of Scheveningen, but only one at a time was ever in the

Minch. Everything had gone well and highly profitably until *Zono's* last late-night incursion into Loch Ringan.

Then everything had suddenly gone wrong.

Just as the *Zono's* crew began to stream their trawl net, they realized there was another boat already in Loch Ringan—slightly smaller than the trawler, moving slowly, coming towards them.

"Firs' thing we know is when the echo sounder goes crazy," complained Kuyper. "Me, I've never seen it happen before—not that way. Then"—he shrugged—"our radar doesn't work too good. But we pick up this other boat, then we see it, an' it looks like a damn Fishery patrol boat." The Dutchman's indignation was almost comical. He slapped a hand on the table. "So—"

"So you cut your trawl and ran?" concluded Carrick. "Then you were told later you were wrong, that it couldn't have been a Fishery Protection boat?"

Kuyper nodded gloomily.

"But—" Johnny Walker changed his mind and fell silent.

"Two people were drowned off Loch Ringan that night," said Carrick. "You knew about it?"

"*Ja.*" Kuyper fingered his whisky glass. It was empty again. "But we didn't see them. Hell, I am fisherman, not someone crazy."

"Crazy." Carrick repeated the word. "You said your echo sounder went crazy. How?"

"Mush—everythin' total mush. Then clear, then mush again." The Dutchman rested his head in his hands, muttering to himself for a moment, then looked up at them. "If I was in some kin' of war, I would say it was like depth charges exploding somewhere."

"Depth charges?" It took Carrick by surprise.

"Okay, it makes no sense—an' we heard no noise." Kuyper shrugged. "But it 'appened."

"Then a last question, Skipper." Carrick's manner hardened. "You've a contact ashore, someone who radios to tell you when and how he reckons you can dodge our patrols. I want a name. Who is he?"

Reluctance showed on the Dutchman's face.

"I don' know him. My brother does." He drew a deep breath. "He didn' signal tonight. But I decide I have to risk things were okay, try to fin' that damn trawl. We couldn't wait any longer."

"Who is he?" repeated Carrick.

"Suppose I don't tell you?" Kuyper read the answer on their faces, sighed and gave in. "He watches the harbour at Dunbrach. His name is Joe Petrie, an'—" He paused, puzzled by their reaction. "I don' lie about it."

"Petrie is dead," said Carrick simply. "That's why you didn't get any message tonight."

"Dead?" Kuyper stared at him in dismay. "But las' night—"

"When did you hear from him then?" Johnny Walker broke his self-imposed silence.

" 'Bout eleven." Kuyper was still shaken and bewildered. "He said bot' your boats were out."

"He was killed soon after that." Carrick signalled Walker, and they got to their feet. He pushed what was left of the whisky bottle towards the Dutchman. "Keep it. You've earned it—and more."

They left the *Zono*'s skipper still sitting there and went out on the trawler's deck. One of *Puffin*'s diesels was running, the sound slightly erratic but steadying. Her upper works were still a tangle of metal, but the pump chattering at her stern had brought her back to almost an even keel. She was out of danger, even though it might be hours before she could sail.

Carrick glanced aft, to where *Tern* was lying. At last, a few things were beginning to come together in his mind. A crazy probability he should have considered almost at the start was becoming a possible reality. He thought for a moment, conscious of the splash of water against the trawler's hull, feeling the deck roll gently beneath his feet.

"I'll leave Andy and Clapper Bell to help with repairs—I need Sam with me." He drew a deep breath. "The weather is due to quieten for a spell. When it does, you can probably make Dunbrach on your own."

Walker nodded. "I can cope."

"Don't try unless you're sure," said Carrick and grinned. "Not when you'll have half my crew aboard. One of us back in harbour at Dunbrach will make things look respectable, keep the lid on a few problems."

"A few?" Walker sighed. "Are we supposed to believe that bit about depth charges?"

"He does." Carrick was certain. "We need another reason to explain it." When daylight came, Detective Inspector Ernie Hume was due for a rude awakening on several counts. He glanced at Walker, knowing the other things that were troubling him. "About *Puffin*. Headquarters will only get one version of what happened—we'll make sure of it."

Tern eased out of the shelter of Seal Bay a little before three A.M. and headed south, down the coast. It was a rough, pitching trip for the patrol boat, even at half speed and with the weather showing the first signs of beginning to moderate again. But within the hour, she was safely berthed in Dunbrach, where the rest of the world and his wife seemed to be asleep.

Sam Pilsudski vanished into his cabin and was snoring within minutes. Yawning, Gogi MacDonnell headed for'ard to his own bunk, and Carrick was left alone. He made himself a cheese sandwich in the galley and ate it slowly in the wardroom. He didn't feel tired. He knew that would come later. On an impulse, he got to his feet and went out on deck.

He'd solved what had become the lesser mystery in Patrol Box Tango. The pirate raids on the herring nurseries could be regarded as ended—in fact, now almost as incidental.

But the Dutch skipper had handed him a totally new view of all the rest. There was another boat lurking somewhere, along the coast or out among the islands, a boat that could easily be mistaken for a Fishery Protection patrol, a boat that had been in Loch Ringan the night the Keenans had died.

A boat that had to be responsible for those strange undersea disturbances which had made Kuyper think of depth charges. He swore under his breath. Because there was one possibility, and it brought him back to Magnus Andersen, and from the Dane to his two anchored tanker ships.

It would be at least two hours before the first signs of dawn. Two hours would be more than enough for what he had in mind.

Going aft along the darkened patrol boat, he lowered the inflatable dinghy into the water and checked the outboard motor's fuel tank. It was full. Going down to his cabin, he changed from uniform into a dark sweater and overalls, belted a sheathed diving knife round his waist and collected a heavy rubber torch. As an afterthought, he changed the cut-down sea boots he was wearing for a pair of light leather moccasins.

Carrick went back to the rubber boat, got aboard and flicked loose the mooring line. The outboard engine started with a crisp bark; he cut it back to a murmur, then steered away from the patrol boat and left the sleeping harbour.

The broken swell met the dinghy immediately she cleared the breakwater. He fought the dinghy out some distance from the shore, then opened the throttle another full notch and began travelling down Priest Bay, towards the two oil tankers.

The lights of Dunbrach faded. Soaked by spray, occasional wavecrests slopped aboard, Carrick strained for a first glimpse of the two anchored giants. Instead, he suddenly had to throttle back as the steady, chunking beat of another boat engine reached his ears. The other boat was heading out. He had a brief, uncertain glimpse of a small, pitching hull against the white of a breaking wave, no lights aboard; then it had gone.

The chunking beat faded. Carrick eased the outboard's throttle open again and cursed as another wave swamped over the inflatable. But a moment later there were two solid black outlines ahead and the pinprick glint of anchor lights.

Sound could carry far at night. He cut the outboard engine again, as far back as he dared, while the black silhouettes grew larger and nearer. The nearer of the two was the *Ranassen,* her bulk half obscuring his view of her sister. But the angle was gradually altering.

The inflatable rose on a wavecrest, shuddered down into the following trough, then rose again—and as it did, Carrick tensed. Now he could see more of the *Ranata,* and something else was there. He waited for the next wavecrest and was sure. A few faint, shaded lights showed close to her water-line, lights that were moving in a small area that seemed even darker than the rest of the tanker's hull.

It was a time to gamble. He manoeuvred the inflatable, crabbing her to port, aiming her blunt nose like an arrow to cut close to the *Ranassen*'s stern and bring him down from there towards the other tanker's bow. Deliberately he cut the outboard engine, grabbed one of the paddles lashed to her sides and let the wind and the sea do the rest of the work.

In a couple of minutes, he was in the shadow of the *Ranassen*'s rusty, towering silhouette, then was suddenly free of it with the *Ranata* ahead. Digging deep with the paddle, blessing the heavy cloud overhead, Carrick altered the dinghy's drifting course just enough to bring him in towards the second tanker's bow.

The faint moving lights were very plain now—and their source had become the definite shape of another, much smaller craft tied alongside her, just for'ard of her funnel. Occasionally a brighter light flashed briefly from the tanker's deck, and once he thought he heard a man's voice, loud, querulous, then immediately silenced.

The inflatable passed close to the *Ranata*'s anchor chain, then bumped and shuddered as a wave slammed it in against the tanker's

plates. He used the paddle desperately, poling his way along, beginning to hear the soft, steady throbbing of a pump above the sounds
of the sea and the creaking and groaning of the fenders protecting
the boat lying ahead.

She was half as big again as *Tern* and she was refuelling. A thick
hose snaked down to her from the tanker, swaying as she rolled. She
had a flared bow, the general lines of a large motor yacht, and
seemed to be painted grey overall. The torches moved on her deck
again, around the refuelling hose, and one blinked a signal up towards the tanker.

The wave that came in was larger than the rest. He saw it come, a
white crest in the night. Then it hit the inflatable, lifted it sideways
like a toy and threw him into the water at the same time as it
slammed the little boat hard against the tanker. There was a harsh
clang as the outboard engine's propellor hit steel plate, another violent swirl of sea, and the inflatable overturned, spun back and collided with him.

Half-dazed by the impact, he heard shouts. One of the torches
swung and found the inflatable, then a spotlight stabbed from the
motor yacht and caught him in its glare. Before he was certain what
was happening, a small boat had rasped towards him. Seized, he was
hauled roughly aboard and the spotlight went out. His diving knife
was found and tossed aside, then the small boat turned and went
back to the motor yacht.

More dark figures were waiting. Half-dragged, half-kicked onto
the motor yacht, he caught a glimpse of a big A-frame towing gal-
lows at her stern, then was being bundled down a stairwell. At the
bottom a door opened and he was thrown into a brightly lit cabin.

"Hold him," said an angry voice as the door slammed shut and
Carrick picked himself up from the deck.

An answering grunt came from behind him. His right wrist was
seized in a vicious armlock, then the tip of a fish-gutting knife
jabbed like a needle under his chin. Carrick tried to look around.
The cabin was big, plainly furnished, more like an office. The man in
front of him, considering him coldly, was a thin, hatchet-faced figure with heavy eyebrows, and no stranger. He had seen him briefly
outside one of the huts at Bochail Island.

"Any more of them?" asked the man sharply in a heavy north of
Ireland accent.

"None, Captain." The new voice took Carrick by surprise. He
turned his head, ignoring the warning prick of the knife, and Danny

Rose gave him a sneering, lopsided grin from just inside the doorway. "He was on his own."

"And we both know him." The hatchet-faced man took a step nearer and gave Carrick a scowling inspection. "Damned Fishery snoop—we should have drowned him."

"Like the last lot?" asked Carrick.

The man's eyes hardened. He cuffed Carrick hard across the mouth with the back of his hand.

"We've got his boat?" he asked.

Danny Rose nodded. "On board—or it will be, by now." He paused and scratched a thumb along his chin. "What do we do with him?"

"Keep him for now, somewhere safe." The motor yacht's captain was impatient. "He's not my decision."

Spun round, Carrick was bundled out of the cabin and along a companionway by Rose and the crewman with the knife. They pushed him into a small, bare storeroom and gave him a quick but thorough body search.

"Nothing." Danny Rose gave a grunt of disappointment and stood back. He considered Carrick for a moment, a trace of doubt on his scarred, oddly handsome face. "You had to be alone out there. But have you any notion where you're goin' now?"

Carrick shrugged. "With you for company, Danny, it can't be pleasant."

For a moment he thought the black-haired sea gypsy was going to hit him. But instead Rose made him turn, then tied his wrists behind his back with a length of strong thin line.

The two men went out, the door slammed, a lock clicked. Water still dripping from his sodden clothes and forming a pool on the bare steel plating at his feet, Carrick listened to the noises on the deck above. Then, suddenly, the motor yacht's engines began throbbing, her rolling motion changed to a pitching heave, and they were under way.

He hunkered down in a corner and took a long, deep breath. The motor yacht and the glimpse of that towing frame at her stern had been the last pieces he'd needed.

It all came back to Magnus Andersen, and the Dane was searching for something much more valuable than a clutch of lost Viking loot.

Andersen was an oilman, hunting for oil.

But for the moment it was hardly important. Carrick knew he had a more immediate problem, a simple matter of trying to stay alive.

8

At a steady speed, the motor yacht kept under way for about half an hour while Webb Carrick felt every minute drag past. The storeroom was cold, his wet clothing clung to his body, and he had quickly discovered that the line tying his wrist was knotted with typical fisherman skill.

But he kept trying until the engines slowed to a quiet murmur. Activity followed on the deck above; then the storeroom door was thrown open. The two crewmen who came in seized him and hustled him up on deck.

It was still pitch dark and raining, and they were stationary some distance off the pier at Bochail House. Lights showed ashore, and a small launch had come out to meet them.

Pushed towards the rails, Carrick was almost thrown down into the launch. Danny Rose and another man followed him. He recognized the taciturn Willi at the launch controls, and he had a last glimpse of the motor yacht's hatchet-faced captain watching from her bridge. Then as the launch swung back towards the pier, the motor yacht's engines began throbbing. She headed out, a long, grey silhouette quickly swallowed in the darkness.

He was landed at the pier, grabbed again by his escort, then was marched along the pebbled path to Bochail House. The door lay open. Magnus Andersen, unshaven, dressed in a shirt and trousers, his feet still in bedroom slippers, beckoned them in and they followed him through to the room Carrick had seen on his last trip to the island. The curtains were closed, and used glasses and coffee cups from the previous evening were being hastily pushed to one side by Andersen's bearded assistant, Bernard. The man was wearing a patterned dressing gown over red pyjamas and looked frightened.

"Stay put an' behave, Skipper," said the motor-yacht crewman. Casually he pressed the muzzle of a pistol against Carrick's side. "You understand me?"

Carrick nodded, and heard Danny Rose give a satisfied snigger.

"Be quiet, Danny," ordered Andersen. He took a step nearer Carrick and shook his head. *"Min ven,* I wish this had not happened. When I was told, it was not good news." He pursed his lips. "You were alone. I suppose you will tell me other people knew what you were doing?"

"I might," said Carrick woodenly.

"But should I believe you?" Andersen sighed and glanced at Bernard. "Are we still monitoring their radio frequencies?"

The man nodded. "We've heard nothing, Mr. Andersen—not for the last couple of hours."

"And when they do talk, they use that scrambler system." Andersen sat in the nearest chair and clasped his hands together, thinking. He looked up. "I'm a businessman, Chief Officer. I'm trying to think of you in profit-and-loss terms. As a balance sheet, you don't make good reading."

"That's the executive approach, I suppose." Carrick looked directly at him, knowing he had to unsettle the Dane. "How about your own personal balance sheet? How good are the oil survey results?"

Every man in the room seemed to stiffen. Then Andersen gave a slow, appreciative nod.

"They're reasonable, Chief Officer." His blue eyes were rock hard. *"Ja,* reasonable. How long have you known?"

"We caught a pirate trawler tonight; I questioned her skipper." Carrick met the man's frown squarely. "A few nights ago, he had hell knocked out of his echo-sounding gear in a way he couldn't understand. Then he spotted what he thought was a patrol boat— but it wasn't."

"Her name is the *Halla."* Andersen gave the information with a shrug. "German-built. She started life as a coast-guard cutter. So, you heard this story. And you decided—?"

"I remembered," corrected Carrick, then lied a little. "Not then, but later. Any oil company making a coastal waters survey could use the same technique—all you need is a small ship equipped to fire compressed-air charges against bottom rock and towing a hydrophone system to record the results. Am I right?"

"Totally." Andersen gave a grudging nod. "You could call it fishing for sounds, Chief Officer. Then we analyse the seismic patterns and can project a geophysical picture." He indicated his bearded assistant. "That part is Bernard's speciality."

Bernard smiled, pleased at the mention.

"Why the secrecy?" challenged Carrick. "You wouldn't have been breaking any laws."

"There are good reasons. They needn't concern you," said Andersen curtly. "At least your pirate trawler raids were useful, a help to us." He paused. "But before tonight?"

"Anything we had didn't make sense." Carrick scowled at Danny Rose. "We were aiming in the wrong direction."

It was a half-truth and Danny Rose grinned. But, suddenly, Carrick understood why Rose was needed. A motor yacht as big as the *Halla*, only moving by night and towing complex gear, couldn't have lasted long without a local man able to pilot her through the sector's catalogue of navigating hazards.

"How much does he pay you, Danny?" he inquired. "And how about the rest of the family—do they get their cut?"

"My arrangement is strictly with Danny," said Andersen before the man could answer. He considered Rose with veiled distaste. "His services have a certain value, even if there has been an occasional error."

"Would you call the Keenans an error?" asked Carrick.

"They saw too much—then they were foolish." Andersen shook his head. "But *nej*, Chief Officer, until there was no option I did not wish anyone hurt."

"Even Joe Petrie?"

Andersen shrugged and looked grimly in Rose's direction.

"You win some, lose some," said Rose with a nervous grin. "You know that, Mr. Andersen."

"Losing doesn't interest me," said Andersen. He turned his attention back to Carrick. "Go on, Chief Officer. I find some of your curiosity interesting—and useful."

"Like a game, *Fader?*" suggested a quiet voice from the doorway behind them.

The gun jabbed a fresh warning as Carrick glanced round. Marget Andersen came in from where she'd been standing. She wore a sweater and denims. Her face was composed, and she walked across to join her father.

"I thought you decided to stay away," chided Andersen, looking up at her.

"I changed my mind." She made it almost a challenge.

"All right." Andersen pursed his lips and gave a slight, partly disapproving nod. "You may not like it."

"When did that make any difference?"

Andersen shrugged but didn't answer.

"Why not let her take me on another guided tour," suggested Carrick sarcastically. "I almost believed some of the last one—and your treasure-hunt story."

Marget Andersen flushed, but her father's reaction was different.

"I didn't particularly lie to you, Chief Officer." He almost smiled. "What I said about the Norse sagas was true—all of it. All I did was leave out one small detail—Olaf Forkbeard's description of the place you know as Priest Bay. He called it 'that sheltered place where black fire bubbles from the earth.'" Andersen brought his fingertips up to touch his chin. "*Ja,* 'black fire that bubbles'—to an oilman, that could be a reasonable description of a natural seepage of oil."

Carrick stared at him.

"Even Marget took some convincing at first," murmured Andersen. "But that's how it began. I owe a debt to Olaf Forkbeard, eh?"

"Good old Vikings," said Danny Rose impatiently. "Sorry to mention it, but is anyone remembering you've got to get me back to the mainland before daylight?"

Andersen frowned. "What time is it?"

"Just six A.M., Mr. Andersen—no problem yet," said Bernard smoothly. He gave Rose a scornful glance. "Don't worry, we'll take care of it."

"When I finish this matter." Andersen got up from his chair, prowled the room, then came back. His whole manner had hardened. "I've wasted enough time, Carrick. You couldn't have known the *Halla* would be refuelling. So why were you at the tanker ships?"

"I'd nothing better to do," said Carrick.

Andersen's eyes narrowed. He nodded, and the silent crewman with the gun used his free hand to piston a punch into the small of Carrick's back.

"Why?" repeated Andersen.

"All right." Carrick moistened his lips. Whatever happened, he needed time and Andersen needed reassurance. "I didn't have a reason—not a real one."

Andersen nodded again. Another agonizing punch slammed into Carrick's back.

"Why?"

"Because they were there—that's all," Carrick told him. "They were there, so they had to matter."

"That's better." Andersen relaxed. "And yes, they matter. At least, the *Ranassen* does—the *Ranata* is with her because two ships look better than one." He came closer. "Would you like to know about the *Ranassen?* I'll tell you. She carries a laboratory and certain small modifications that make her almost a drilling platform. I have divers working under her, and they've been bringing out rock core samples from the bottom of Priest Bay."

"So you've got everything wrapped up?" asked Carrick.

"No." The Dane sucked his teeth and frowned. "Not as much as I'd want—the samples could be better. But there is a deadline and I'm prepared to gamble." He paused, the frown lingering. "Now, what do we do about you?"

Danny Rose gave a hopeful snort. "There's a lot o' deep water between here and the mainland, Mr. Andersen."

"Fader—" Marget took a half step forward, then stopped, biting her lip.

"For the moment, we'll keep him," soothed Andersen. He considered his fingertips with ice-cold calm. "Marget, go and find Willi. Tell him to have the launch ready to go to the mainland—but I'll see him first."

She glanced at Carrick, doubt in her eyes, then gave a reluctant nod and went out.

"Now." Andersen walked over to the window, parted the curtains for a moment, and looked out at the darkness. Then he turned. "Bernard—"

"Yes?" The man stiffened obediently.

"We may have visitors. Warn everyone. Make sure the *Halla* is totally hidden and radio the tankers." He moved around, thinking as he spoke. "The caretaker and his wife?"

"They're well paid," said his assistant. He indicated Carrick. "Him?"

"That old net store under the pier," decided Andersen. He turned to Danny Rose. "You know it?"

Rose nodded.

"Do it," ordered Andersen.

"Happy to." Rose grinned. He beckoned the crewman, the pistol muzzle jabbed, and they pushed Carrick out.

The rain was still drizzling down outside as they marched him back to the pier. A flight of worn stone steps led down at one side, and at the bottom a small, rusting steel door was set in brickwork. Rose pulled it open, then shone a torch. The door had a ventilator grille top and bottom, and the small, brick-walled cellar area inside had a concrete floor covered in damp-smelling rubbish.

"Don't expect room service," said Rose.

He was made to kneel, then his feet were tied together. A piece of grubby, oily rag was shoved into his mouth as a gag. Danny Rose stood back and inspected the results in the light of the torch.

"You'll do." He kicked and, knocked off balance, Carrick sprawled on his side among the rubbish.

The two men went out, the iron door slammed, a bolt grated home, and Carrick was left in a darkness broken only by the faint outlines of the two ventilator grilles.

But he wasn't totally alone. Carrick heard a scurrying noise farther back and realized he had rats for company. Rats didn't worry him—he'd once sailed on a rust-bucket freighter where the rats aboard were friendlier than most of the crew. Cursing through the gag in his mouth, he tried to shift into a more comfortable position and think.

He knew most of it now; most but not all. Magnus Andersen had stayed remarkably in control of his feelings, but the Dane was obviously worried, gambling and in a situation where he'd already been faced with a deadline. Whatever the reason, it had to be connected with his London trip.

The scurrying started again. Carrick listened to it, trying to assess his own situation, too well aware it could hardly have been worse. When Pilsudski and Gogi MacDonnell wakened and found he wasn't aboard *Tern* . . .

The rat had reached his feet and began exploring his trouser leg. Carrick kicked, and as the rat fled, something light but metallic among the rubbish jangled against the brickwork.

Wriggling, twisting, hopping, it took him minutes to find a rusted tin can, then as long again to get a grip of it with his tied hands. The can ended in a ragged sharp edge, sharp enough to gash his fingers. Blood stickied the metal, but he ignored it, arching his back, bringing his feet up to help hold the can, then began sawing the edge against the cords at his wrists.

He dropped the can once, had to roll around to find it again, then settled back into the same routine. At last his wrists were free, and he lay for a moment rubbing them in turn, winning back circulation. But after that, he got rid of the gag, untied his ankles and was on his feet.

A boat engine started up outside and began idling. Feeling his way across to the door, Carrick peered out through the top ventilator grille. He could see lights reflected on the water beside the pier, but nothing more.

The grille. Leaning against the cold metal of the door, he peered at it closely and felt with his fingertips. It was even rustier than the door, the frame held in place by small rivets. One at the top had fallen out; another had almost been eaten away. If he could remove the grille, he might be able to reach the outside bolt.

Carrick decided not even to try to plan after that. The grille came first, and his bare hands wouldn't be enough. He found the cords which had been used to bind him, then searched in the blackness of the net store until his fingers located what felt like a broken length from an old oar. He had his lever. Carefully he threaded the cords through the metal crosspieces of the grille, knotted them in loose loops, then fed the wooden lever through the loops.

Voices sounded on the pier. He stopped, peered out, but still couldn't see anything. Then the voices were nearer, close to the idling boat engine. He heard Danny Rose laugh. Suddenly the engine increased its beat, then Andersen's cabin launch appeared at the edge of the pool of light and began to swing out from the pier. It had to be making enough noise to cover any sounds he would cause.

Gripping the oar-shaft lever with both hands, Carrick heaved. There were two quick, loud poppings, then he sprawled backwards as the grille burst loose from the door and clattered beside him.

He scrambled up again and waited tensely. But everything stayed as before outside, with the cabin launch still drawing away. After a few moments, the lights on the pier were extinguished. Drawing a deep breath of relief, Carrick slipped his right arm through the hole where the grille had been, felt briefly and found the outside bolt. It slid back. Another moment, and he had the door open and was standing at the bottom of the stone steps with the broken oar shaft still clasped in one hand.

The rain had stopped. The incoming tide was washing around the thick main supports of the pier, and there was just enough moonlight to show Andersen's sleek black powerboat lying at her berth. But that kind of powerboat usually needed a key start and a noisy warm-up. It was the wrong answer.

He went up to the top of the steps and saw a better possibility a little way along the shore: a small white dinghy with an outboard engine. It was moored close in against a shelf of rock.

He left the shelter of the pier and crossed a first patch of open ground towards the shadow of a small hut. He reached the patch of shadow, took another step forward, then stopped and swore wearily.

Marget Andersen stood only a few feet away, looking straight at him, equally surprised. He gauged the distance between them, expecting her to call out, calculating he couldn't get there in time to silence her.

"You picked a hell of a time for a walk," he said bitterly.

She didn't move; it was too dark to see her face properly. But he heard a sound like a sigh. Then, very deliberately, she looked along to where the dinghy was moored and shook her head.

"Try somewhere else," she said quietly, then turned on her heel. She walked away quickly, heading in the opposite direction from Bochail House and the lights.

Carrick stared after her, hardly able to believe it had happened. But the warning had been real enough, and he moved on with extra care. He reached some rocks, paused again, suddenly spotted the glow of a cigarette, and grimaced as he understood. A man was sitting on one of the rocks, on lazy sentry duty, looking out towards the sea. Noiselessly Carrick eased nearer, close enough to smell the cigarette smoke. Then at the last moment a pebble crunched under his feet. The man started to turn, and Carrick slammed the broken oar shaft down on his head.

He caught the man as he fell, lowered him to the ground and took the .38 revolver he'd been carrying. From there, another dozen steps took him to the dinghy. He got aboard, ignored the outboard engine, took the oars which were lying under the thwarts, cast off and began rowing.

He was several lengths clear of the pier, the dinghy pitching in the swell, when his luck finally ran out. A voice shouted in alarm behind him, then two shots rang out in a warning signal.

Carrick stopped rowing, scrambled to the stern of the dinghy and pull-started the outboard engine. It started the second time and he yanked the throttle wide open. The little engine snarled and the dinghy bucked forward, on an angled course towards the mainland.

Behind him, he heard the throaty rumble of Andersen's powerboat starting up. Glancing back, he saw a pale white slash of bow wave as she came roaring out. Then a spotlight lanced the darkness, sweeping the sea.

They found him quickly, closed, and the black powerboat made a swinging pass across the dinghy's bows. Carrick swung the tiller and flattened down as a gun barked busily from the powerboat's cockpit. One bullet gouged wood from the dinghy's transom, and the powerboat raced in again.

This time he was prepared. He steadied the dinghy, brought up the .38 revolver he had taken from the man at the rocks and fired twice. The spotlight went out, then he was yanking desperately at the tiller, counting the seconds.

The powerboat shaved past, a bullet grazed close to his shoulder, another smacked the metal of the outboard engine. Then a wave took the dinghy sideways, lifted her and dumped her down in a trough.

Again the powerboat came in, then again, but more cautiously now the man aboard knew their quarry was armed—and their tactics had changed. Carrick realized that he was being herded back in towards Bochail, that each avoiding action he took brought the island nearer.

The sky was beginning to show a first hint of grey, losing him the only ally he had. The black boat was positioning for another run. Carrick tensed, watched the approaching bow wave, then heart-stopping splutter from the dinghy's outboard engine. It coughed a few more spasmodic beats, then died.

The powerboat slammed past and made a wide circling turn, as if the men aboard were puzzled at the dinghy's loss of power. But by then Carrick had found the reason: a bullet hole through the outboard's tiny fuel tank, low enough down to leave it drained and empty.

But the dinghy was drifting, moving. It took him a minute or two to understand fully, to realize the way he was being carried along by a current which was growing in strength. Then he understood why the black powerboat was making no attempt to come nearer, why the men aboard it seemed prepared to watch and wait.

They knew. They were satisfied. A smaller, hand-held spotlight snapped on, focused on him briefly, then went out.

He was caught in the tidal flow through the Black Dogs. Soon he could hear the gathering thunder of breaking waves, and the dinghy began to lurch and pitch in white, angry water. He saw the powerboat hang back, then turn away.

The dinghy spun as it grated a rock. Half-swamped, travelling faster, heaving, it headed straight for the fury between Bochail and its neighbour. Another fang of rock showed ahead, and the dinghy hit and capsized.

Carrick went under, came up, then was slammed against a reef,

tumbled bodily over it and swept on again. Sharp edges clawed and
caught, and all the time the merciless sea added its own punishment.
He was weak, he was failing, he had no more fight left in him.

Another obstacle was dead ahead, almost seemed to be moving.
Then two strong arms seized him.

"Man," said a soft voice he knew. "After the trouble I've gone
through, you'd better be alive."

He tried to answer, but the world became a swirling black vortex
that gave way to emptiness.

Webb Carrick could still hear the muffled sounds of the sea when he
came round. But he was warm and dry, lying on something soft,
covered by a blanket, and he had vague memories of brief moments
of earlier consciousness. His head ached, and his body protested at
the slightest move; under the blanket, he was naked.

He opened his eyes, saw only a blur at first, then things gradually
came into focus. He was in a large, brightly lit cave. The light came
from a hissing pressure lamp, and the air carried the scent of smoke
from a driftwood fire. He moved again, winced at what it did to him
and took another look around. The smoke from the fire was being
drawn up through a crack in the roof of the cave, and coils of rope,
boxes and a scatter of other items showed that someone used the
place regularly.

He heard footsteps and tried to lever himself up on one elbow.

"Easy, Skipper," soothed a voice. The footsteps came nearer, then
the thin, bearded face of the Bagman looked down at him with
concern. "Wait now."

The Bagman knelt beside him, brought a flask from his shoulder
bag, unscrewed the top and held it to Carrick's mouth. The raw
whisky made him gasp. Then the Bagman sat back on his heels.

"How do you feel?" he asked, then chuckled. "That's a damfool
question. I had to pump half o' the Minch out of you. Aches and
pains?"

Carrick nodded.

"But nothing broken that I could find." The Bagman took a swallow for himself from the flask, returned it to the bag, rummaged,
produced a grubby handkerchief and blew his nose loudly. "I
patched you up a bit, that's all."

Carrick forced himself to sit up. His head seemed to spin, then
steadied.

"You got me out?"

The Bagman nodded. "That's a while back. It's damn near midday outside."

"How—"

"You're a hell of a man for questions, Skipper." The bearded face frowned in disapproval. "First, you're on Lunnain Island. Second, certain folk on Bochail are convinced by now you're dead—at least, they've stopped watching from over there. Third"—he shrugged—"there's a few back at Dunbrach who would like to know about this cave. But nobody does. Just me—an' now you."

"But you got me out," persisted Carrick, the nightmare impossible to forget. "How?"

"I was over here. I saw you playing tag wi' that powerboat, saw you being swept in." The Bagman sucked his teeth. "That way, I'd a reasonable notion where you'd maybe end up. I know the Black Dogs. So—I found you, that's all."

"That's all?" Carrick stared at the man. "It's more like a miracle."

"I've not much experience o' miracles," said his rescuer, embarrassed. He got to his feet. "Take your time. I've no radio, and even if you were fit, there's no way I could get you out before dark. But when you're ready, what's left o' your clothes are beside the fire."

He left, disappearing along a dark tunnel in the rock.

Carrick lay back on the mattress for a minute or two, then threw the blanket aside and managed to struggle to his feet. His whole body seemed covered in scrapes and grazes. A gash on his left thigh had been bandaged, and every time he took a deep breath, his ribs felt as if they'd been hit by a sledgehammer. He hobbled over to the fire, where a black cooking pot was bubbling, and found his clothes. They were dry, even if reduced to rags, and he dressed, then took another look around the cave. It was bowl-shaped, the size of a large room, and here and there small crystalline growths showed on the dark rock. He investigated a barrel, found it held fresh water and splashed some on his face.

Still limping, he ventured towards the tunnel. It led down at a gently sloping angle and was dark for a short distance, with the noise of the sea growing. Then he emerged in a much larger cave. He could see daylight at its mouth. The sea lapped in over most of its area, and the Bagman's little *Kelpie* floated to one side, tied to a knob of rock. Carrick stopped beside the fifteen-foot open boat, saw the fresh scars on the clinker-built hull and shook his head in near-disbelief.

But he was alive.

He went on, noting the several thick lengths of rope, each tied to a stone, which ran down on all sides into the water. They gave him a good idea why the Bagman didn't want visitors, but they could wait.

The noise of the sea grew angrier as he reached true daylight at the mouth of the cave, and he saw white spray. But an outcrop of rock blocked most of the view.

"Over here, Skipper. Go carefully." The Bagman was standing a little way along a narrow ledge above the little channel into the cave. He offered a steadying hand as Carrick reached him. "That's far enough, unless you want to be in clear sight of Bochail."

Carrick looked out at the white turmoil of the Black Dogs, towards the island. By comparison with Lunnain's bare rock, Bochail was a green hillside of apparent peace.

"There were two men with a jeep over on that hill most o' the morning," said the Bagman. "Both using binoculars."

"Wanting to make sure?"

"Aye. There's some bits o' your dinghy farther down." The Bagman leaned against the rock. "Still, they won't be too disappointed. A yacht strayed this way once. The bodies were washed up a month later, over in Ireland."

Carrick nodded, tight-lipped, and felt a moment's chill.

"That's what nearly happened to me, the first time," mused the thin, bearded figure beside him. "It was years ago. The *Kelpie's* damn engine gave up, and I got pulled in. I didn't so much find this cave as it found me. Pure luck, Skipper." He chuckled and gestured out towards the tormented water. "Mind you, I know more now. There are ways through if you know your tides."

They left the ledge and went into the outer cave. Knowing the Bagman was watching him, Carrick stooped and pulled at one of the ropes running into the water. He hauled a few feet of its length out onto the rock. Dripping wet, it was a solid, encrusted mass of big, blue-black mussels.

"Jimsy Fletcher says you land the finest mussels on the coast." He let the rope and its tightly clinging colony of shellfish slide back again. "How long have you been farming them?"

"Five years now. I crop about two tons a year, sometimes more." The Bagman raised bushy, quizzical eyebrows. "Have you seen better?"

Carrick shook his head.

Rope cultivation was probably the most difficult method of mussel farming, even though it could be the most rewarding. It needed an exact balance of conditions that was hard to attain—sea water free of impurities yet offering feeding, fairly steady temperatures throughout the seasons, an equally steady level of salinity. Given them, he'd seen the tiny mussel spats originally attached to a rope grow to three inches in size inside a year and be ready for harvest in eighteen months.

"And no one has ever followed you?" he asked.

"A few have tried." The Bagman dismissed the idea with a snort. "But once I'm here they've no chance. And don't worry about that fire. The smoke can't be seen." He changed the subject. "Maybe it's more important we talk about you."

Carrick felt the same. He'd been trying to give his mind a chance to clear, to think rationally again. But *Tern*'s crew, faced with the inflatable gone and their skipper missing, were in a predicament of their own. As the hours had passed, other people must have been drawn in. Department had probably been notified; some kind of search could have been mounted.

He carried the thought on from there as he followed the Bagman back to the inner cave. If there was a search, it was probably being confined to the mainland coast. Probably Johnny Walker was in charge if he'd made it back with *Puffin*, and that held its own irony. Walker knew a little, Inspector Hume and Kate Dee knew a little— but even if they put it together, how far would it get them? The answer, he knew, was not far enough to go storming across to Bochail and Magnus Andersen.

"You'll feel better with some food in you," said the Bagman as they reached the inner cave again. He went over to the pot in the fire, lifted the lid, sniffed and was satisfied. "Only one course, Skipper—mussel stew wi' beans."

He ladled generous helpings onto two tin plates, slapped a spoon on each plate, and they sat on boxes. His host produced two twists of paper from his shoulder bag, one holding salt and the other pepper, then a chunk of hard, grimy bread which he solemnly broke in half.

Carrick was hungry enough to have eaten anything, and the mussel stew was surprisingly good. He cleared his plate rapidly, and the Bagman ladled him out a second helping.

"Now Skipper," he said, mopping his own plate clean with the last of the bread. "You're not going to try to tell me all this mayhem is over a daft story like St. Ringan's treasure?"

"No." Carrick stifled a contented belch, already feeling better even if the aches and siffnesses remained. "Suppose I say oil?"

"You mean here?" The Bagman tried to mask his surprise but failed. "Man, that's mad. Any oil talk is—"

"Is about the North Sea, where they've got the production wells, about deep-water drilling beyond the outer isles, other places. Not here—I know," agreed Carrick patiently. "But Andersen thinks differently."

The Bagman examined his long, bony fingers sadly.

"They can keep their damned oil," he said savagely, almost under his breath. "I've seen what it does, the way it can ruin a coast." He paused hopefully. "But has he found oil?"

"That's what it's all about." Carrick set down his plate. "You didn't help. You've seen a grey motor yacht on the prowl at night, haven't you?"

"Once or twice." The Bagman nodded reluctantly. "But it wasn't my concern. Or it didn't seem that way."

"Even after the Keenans drowned?" Carrick saw the man wince. "Then there was Joe Petrie—you knew he was the shore contact behind the trawler raids. That was the reason you quarrelled, right?"

The Bagman sighed and nodded.

"What a man sees and what he does about it—" He scowled at the driftwood fire. "Man, I tried to warn you. I didn't know what was happening, I didn't want to get involved."

"Then you hauled me from that hell out there," reminded Carrick quietly. "You're involved now, like it or not."

"Aye." It came grudgingly.

"That yacht, the *Halla*—it needs an anchorage, a place to hide." Carrick made a guess. "How about the west side of Bochail?"

"It's possible." The Bagman was deep in thought. "That's poor fishing ground, no local boat has reason to go round that way and— aye, there are a couple of places." He paused. "The yacht—the *Halla* —I didn't know it was Andersen's, not for sure. I thought he was only interested in the St. Ringan treasure story, and that's for fools."

"Why?" Something in the man's voice made Carrick frown.

"I'll show you something." The Bagman got to his feet and picked up the pressure lamp by its handle. "Come on."

Puzzled, impatient, Carrick obeyed. They went towards the back of the cave, then the Bagman stopped and held the light high. For the first time, Carrick saw a Celtic cross carved deep into the smooth rock.

"Mine. I did it last year—got stuck here in a storm for about ten days." The Bagman's mood varied between pride and embarrassment. "It's—well, a signpost." He handed Carrick the lamp and jerked his head towards a patch of shadow. "Over there. See for yourself. Start on the left side."

The patch of shadow was the start of another arm of the cave, a gallery of smooth rock about nine feet high and six feet wide. Carrick took a first few steps in, then stopped, hesitated in disbelief, then held the lamp higher. He was facing a roof-to-floor mural-like painting which combined bold colour and delicate detail. It had to be old, very old, yet totally preserved by the cave's dry atmosphere.

He saw a green island which had to be Bochail and a tiny, coracle-like boat approaching the shore. Then, like turning a page in a book, the next painting showed monks building a church with others tending a vegetable garden. He moved on, one panel giving way to the next in the lamp's bright light. The church was complete, with its round tower and an archway of intricately carved stone. The vegetable garden had given way to small patchwork fields, and there were sheep grazing. Monks worked, monks worshipped.

Then, as the natural gallery ended and he turned, the mood of the painting changed, became more stark, the colours fierce in their contrast.

It started with the island again, but with the dragon prows and square sails of a fleet of Viking longships heading towards it. Then the church with monks praying while the raiders swarmed ashore. Horror came next, captured by an artist who had to have been an eyewitness. Monks fled, monks died or were hunted down. Flames rose as the church burned. But there were two final panels. In the first, a tall, calm-faced monk stood on the edge of a cliff. His arms were outstretched and, falling from them, a stream of silver and gold altar plate was splashing into the sea, followed by a long gold staff. In the last, the same calm-faced monk stood alone, his church burning behind him like a halo, a dark line of raiders closing in.

Quietly Carrick went back to the fire. The Bagman was sitting there; he looked at him and gave a slow, deliberate nod.

"That's how I felt, first time I saw them." He smiled to himself. "You and I, Skipper—probably the only two humans to see them since some poor damn monk who escaped decided to leave his own record. Don't ask me what he used for light or food, or what happened to him afterwards. But Bochail in the Gaelic means 'great happiness.' "

"And Lunnain?" asked Carrick softly.

"Lunnain could translate as 'the resting place among the waves.' " The Bagman rocked with his hands clasped round his knees for a moment. "Stories get twisted. Folk have always liked to improve on them—even Vikings, eh?" He searched down into the depths of his shoulder bag and produced a crumpled pack of cigarettes. "Smoke?"

"I've stopped."

"And me," said the Bagman sadly.

They took one each and shared a light from a splinter of burning wood.

"Get some rest," advised the Bagman, drawing on his cigarette in a way that brought it flaring dangerously close to his beard. "We're here till about midnight. I've a thing or two to do to the *Kelpie*."

"Can we make the west side of Bochail?"

"The tide will be right." Removing the cigarette, the Bagman spat accurately into the fire. "But we'll do it my way, Skipper. I don't think any o' Andersen's people would give you a second chance if they got their hands on you."

Carrick nodded, but thought of Marget Andersen. She could have stopped him; instead she had warned him. Whatever her reasons, he knew her basic loyalty still lay with her father—but he wouldn't forget.

It was a nightmare which mixed the black powerboat and the sea, a brown-clad monk who suddenly was Magnus Andersen, and struggling, drowning shapes with no solid forms or names.

Then a hand shook his shoulder and Carrick wakened, feeling stiff and sore again. The Bagman handed him a mug of coffee.

"Near enough midnight. Drink that, and we're ready."

He swallowed down the scalding coffee, took a last glance round the cave, then followed the thin, bearded figure. The *Kelpie* was waiting, her engine already muttering asthmatically but her small stub mast mounted and the patched triangle of lugsail ready to be hoisted.

"My way," reminded the Bagman. "We'll motor through to the west side—the sea's always noisy enough to cover most sounds. Then we'll just use whatever wind we find."

They got aboard, the Bagman settled at the tiller, and the *Kelpie* nosed her way out towards the foaming line of white. She met it, the Bagman gave her engine a few seconds' kick of power, then for Carrick it was as if the old workboat's last moments had come. Bucking, yawing clumsily one second, almost dancing the next, she swept along through the chaos of broken water with the Bagman occasionally working the tiller but barely using the engine.

A rock rose like a barrier ahead. They almost scraped it as the *Kelpie* took a sideways lurch. The Bagman's lips were moving and, incredulously, Carrick realized he was singing to himself, the words lost on the roar of water.

Then more rocks, curtains of spray. They went through miniature whirlpools—then, as suddenly as it had begun, it was over and they were through into a calm sea with a low, gentle swell. There was a light wind from the southwest. The sky was a pattern of cloud-filtered moonlight, and the Bagman cut the engine.

"We'll have that sail up now, Skipper," he said politely.

Carrick nodded, tasting the drying spray on his lips.

"Do you do that often?" he asked shakily.

"Och, it's just a case o' knowing where you want to go, then letting the water do the real work." The Bagman winked. "Now, that sail, eh?"

The lugsail hoisted, they tacked round. Rippling, the patched canvas filled and the *Kelpie* got under way with the sea chuckling round her sturdy little hull. She kept as close to the land as the wind would allow, and Carrick frowned as he saw the high cliffs which formed the west side of the island.

"Is all of it like this?"

"Mostly." The Bagman answered him softly. "But like I told you, there are a couple of anchorages where that grey brute could be tucked away. The second would be my choice, but we'll see."

The wind faded briefly, then picked up again but was still little more than a light breeze. The storms had blown themselves out. The night sky showed the cliffs as black silhouettes. A family of wakened, indignant seals slipped quickly into the water as they rounded a point of rock; the Bagman peered past them into a notch-shaped inlet, gave a grunt of satisfaction and steered out again.

"The other one, Skipper." He scratched himself under one arm with obvious pleasure. "Aye, I didn't think I'd be wrong. Would you say they'd have an anchor watch?"

Carrick nodded. "And every other kind there is."

"I like a challenge now and again." Unperturbed, the Bagman

paid attention to his other armpit. "Well, you'll maybe have to oblige me with a wee bit o' rowing."

Another headland came up, and the Bagman took a quick glance at the moon and the slow-moving clouds. He sucked his lips for a moment, nodded to himself, then brought the *Kelpie* even closer towards the shore.

"We'll have that sail down now," he murmured. "Then the oars, man. Quickly."

On cue, a long bank of cloud drifted over the moon less than two minutes later. By then, they were silently rowing into the narrow bay which lay beyond the headland. Then they stopped, letting the boat drift. He sniffed the air, then put his hand over the side into the water and tasted the result.

"She's near," he whispered. "But where, damn them?"

Suddenly Carrick's nostrils caught the faint smell of diesel fuel. He looked around, straining his eyes against the night, then nudged the thin figure beside him. To their left and ahead, a low, dark shape lay close under the cliffs, almost merging with them.

"Younger eyes," said the Bagman ruefully. "But there's something odd about her." He peered. "It's like she's tucked up in tarpaulins."

"Camouflage nets," said Carrick. "So she's not going anywhere in a hurry."

"But maybe we should, eh?" The Bagman signalled, and they bent to the oars again.

As soon as they were clear of the bay, they hoisted the lugsail and headed north, edging out from the land. Bochail ended, they heard the soft booming of the sea against the Little Drummer rock and saw the tall, slim pencil of the lighthouse.

Still under sail, the *Kelpie* began to ease round on a new heading towards the mainland. She didn't complete it. The big seine-net fishing boat which came chunking out of the night made a business-like job of edging in, a handlamp scanned them briefly from her wheelhouse and a startled oath rang across the water.

"You're keeping bad company, Skipper Carrick," hailed a delighted voice. "I wouldn't sail wi' that old devil for a pension. You know me—MacTaggart, the *Blue Crest*. There's a few folk looking for you."

"And I'm looking for them," Carrick called back, grinning with relief.

"Then you're heading the wrong way." MacTaggart's bulky figure showed as he leaned out of the wheelhouse. "Try the lighthouse

—and don't worry, there's nobody else around. That's why I'm doolyin' around out here."

Gathering speed, the fishing boat thrashed away, and *Kelpie* turned again.

The landing stage below the lighthouse seemed empty and deserted as they nosed in and nudged against it. Carrick stepped ashore, secured the boat's mooring line, then glanced round. A torch clicked; the weak beam checked his face and went out.

" 'And the light shineth in the darkness,' " said Jimsy Fletcher, stepping out of the shadows. "That's John one, verse five, Skipper." He rubbed his hands. "Well, I kept telling her you'd turn up."

"Her?"

"Me." Kate Dee appeared from the same shadows. She gave Carrick a quick, welcoming hug. "Damn you, Webb. You had me scared sick."

"I had me scared sick too." Bewildered, Carrick looked around. "What's going on? How many more of you are here?"

"We've got one of Skipper Walker's crew from *Puffin*. He's at the top of the lighthouse, with night glasses and a two-way radio link to the *Blue Crest*. They're keeping tabs on anything moving between the Hounds and the mainland." She saw he still didn't understand. "We thought a fishing boat would attract less attention."

"We?" Carrick raised an eyebrow.

"Her, mainly." Jimsy Fletcher corrected himself quickly. "Uh— Sergeant Dee, I mean. Very forceful about it, she was." He took note of Kate Dee's warning frown and switched his attention to the Bagman, who was still sitting at the stern of his *Kelpie* and showed no particular inclination to come ashore. "Well, that's two out of three we've found. Not bad."

"Danny Rose is missing," said Kate Dee.

Carrick stood silent for a moment, hearing the Drummer sound in the background. The wind suddenly felt chill.

"Since when?" he asked.

"Some time last night." Kate Dee touched his arm in a silent question.

Carrick shook his head. "He was with Andersen. They were sending him back to the mainland."

But the signs had been there. Danny Rose had become a liability, perhaps a dangerous one, and Magnus Andersen operated on profit-and-loss factors. He moistened his lips.

"Where's *Tern?*"

"Loitering around Priest Bay, in case anything happens." She bit her lip. "We've turned the coast upside down looking for you. Then Clapper Bell wanted to charge straight out to Bochail, but—"

"Doing this was better, believe me." He drew a deep breath. "Is Johnny Walker on *Tern?*"

Kate Dee shook her head. "Young Andy has her. Walker said he wouldn't leave *Puffin.*"

Carrick smiled to himself in the darkness.

"I think I'd better stay dead for a spell," he said slowly. "But I want back aboard *Tern.* Can you fix it?"

Kate Dee winked. "Consider it done."

For the next few hours, Webb Carrick found himself treated like a package—a package handled with care, but with other people making most of the decisions and moving him around. In some ways it was a relief, in others it was an irritation. But he accepted it.

First the *Blue Crest* came in to pick them up. MacTaggart, his red-veined face still creased with pleasure, left two of the seine-net boat's crew with the lookout from *Puffin* and growled his personal guarantee that every man aboard could keep his mouth shut. Kate Dee and Jimsy Fletcher had a brief problem with the Bagman, but at last he agreed his boat could stay hidden at Little Drummer and came huffily aboard with his precious shoulder bag hugged at his side.

Half an hour later, the lights of Dunbrach a glow on the horizon to the east, they rendezvoused with *Tern.* The patrol boat came alongside with total precision, nudged fenders, and Clapper Bell's massive hand reached out to help him aboard.

The *Blue Crest* turned away with her other passengers, heading in separately. Carrick watched while her chunking engine beat faded, thinking over the quick briefing he'd given Kate Dee. He'd left nothing out that mattered—details could wait; she knew the things that had to be done and had suggested some of them on her own.

Resting his hands on the deck rail, he closed his eyes and pictured the woman sergeant's intent face, the way her dark hair had glinted under the light in the fishing boat's cabin, her quickly masked concern when she'd noticed some of the cuts and grazes he had as souvenirs of the Black Dogs. Without a word about it being said, something had happened between them in that cabin.

But that would also have to wait.

"Skipper." Worried, Clapper Bell cleared his throat. "You all right?"

He nodded and went into the homelike familiarity of *Tern*'s bridge. Andy Grey was already half out of the command chair, but he waved him back. Gogi MacDonnell smiled from the coxswain's post, and a moment later Sam Pilsudski popped up from the engineroom like an oil-stained rabbit to pound him on the shoulder in a way that made him wince.

They knew what to do. He was still dead.

Going down to his cabin, Carrick peeled off the rags he was wearing, left them lying on the deck and flopped down on his bunk.

The last thing he heard before sleep swept in was the roar of *Tern*'s diesels as she got under way.

This time, there were no nightmares.

They wakened him again at nine A.M., and the sea was mirror calm under a cloudless blue sky. *Tern* lay at anchor outside Dunbrach harbour, near enough for him to see every last detail on the fishing boats coming and going but far enough out for the patrol boat to have acquired a protective isolation. He showered, shaved, then, with a perverse feeling it mattered, dressed carefully in uniform, including a shirt and tie.

The rest of *Tern*'s crew had already eaten. Gogi MacDonnell had breakfast waiting for him in the wardroom, hovered silently until he'd finished, then quickly cleared the table and tidied around with a houseproud air.

Puffin arrived at ten A.M., dropped anchor nearby, and Johnny Walker came aboard, to grip his hand when they met in the wardroom, then say very little. Walker looked tired, but his boat now showed few outward signs of the beating she'd taken. Minutes later, a dinghy puttered out of the harbour, reached *Tern*, and Kate Dee helped Detective Inspector Ernie Hume to scramble up to the patrol boat's deck, then be shepherded to the wardroom.

"Kate said you were reasonably intact." His broad face expressionless, Hume considered Carrick through narrowed but friendly eyes, then gave her a sideways glance which held a trace of amused malice. "Pleased about it too, weren't you, Sergeant? Clutched from a watery grave—" He left it there and turned to Walker. "Told him yet?"

Walker shook his head.

"Then I will," Hume said. "That inflatable boat of yours, the one you used at the tankers, washed ashore in Loch Ringan this morning." He raised an eyebrow. "Someone trying to point us in the wrong direction?"

"Trying," agreed Carrick.

"Well, as long as you stay dead, we can go along with it—the same way as we're keeping your friend the Bagman under wraps." Hume waited until they had settled in chairs round the wardroom table, then pulled a notebook from his pocket and slapped it in front of him. "Kate gave me as full a report as she could after you got back. But I'd like to hear it from you, from the beginning, then I'll fill a few gaps."

The sun shining brightly through the wardroom windows, *Tern* swaying gently, the only outside sounds an occasional noise on deck and some gulls calling, Webb Carrick told it all again. No one interrupted. Hume made a few brief notes, and Johnny Walker sat with his arms folded and an expression of total concentration on his pudgy face. Even Kate, watching him closely, her dark eyes showing a fresh, gathering anger, said nothing when he finished.

At last, it was Ernie Hume who broke the silence.

"You weren't just lucky, you were damned lucky," was his considered verdict. "But that's behind us, right?" He flicked back a few pages in his notebook. "So let's mop up a little at the edges. Whether he's alive or dead, we can tie Danny Rose to the Keenans being drowned. Grandpa Rose got worried enough to report him missing—and that gave us reason enough to search his room. We found Bob Keenan's watch under a floorboard, and a few other things, including a wad of money."

"Try working out how Danny Rose got his hands on that wristwatch," suggested Johnny Walker with a cold, controlled anger. "They must have brought the Keenans aboard that motor yacht, then—"

Then eventually returned them to their dinghy. Carrick's stomach tightened at the thought, remembering the postmortem report on Bob Keenan's injuries. Questioned, roughed up, the Keenans must have hoped they were being set free—until the sharp bows of the *Halla* swung round to ram them.

"How much does Grandpa Rose really know?" he asked.

"Very little." Hume shook his head. "Danny is his son. He says Danny is wild but wouldn't do anything really nasty—you know how it goes. We'll have to tell him the truth sooner or later." He gestured his distaste. "And that'll include the Joe Petrie killing. You had it right, Carrick—the radar contacts that night off the Hound Islands did matter."

Carrick raised an eyebrow at the admission but said nothing.

"I leaned on the men who crewed with Danny Rose that night." Hume scowled, making it clear he hadn't made it a happy experience for the people who'd faced him. "They sailed from Dunbrach, yes. But they rendezvoused with Andersen's cabin launch off the Hound Islands. You know what happened? Danny boards the launch, they meet up with him again later, and Danny comes back aboard."

"Nice alibi." The kind that let Danny Rose sneak back to the mainland. Carrick pursed his lips. "What did he tell them about it?"

"Just to keep their mouths shut," said Hume. "None of them felt like arguing." He paused, sucked his teeth and changed the subject. "That 'black fire' Viking story—is there any kind of natural seepage around here?"

"The Bagman says no." Carrick had tried several times, always with the same answer. "I believe him."

"Odd." Hume frowned.

"A thousand years," murmured Kate Dee. "It's a long time."

"Thank you, Sergeant," said Hume sardonically. He flicked a page of his notebook. "Anyway, I prefer this—the London meeting that Andersen has scheduled. I passed it on to the Metropolitan force, asking for help. I only got their answer about an hour ago—and it seems we've set a lot of people worrying."

"Get on with it," suggested Johnny Walker. "Why?"

"Because it is government-level stuff." Hume enjoyed his moment. "The meeting is at the Department of Trade next Wednesday, a squad of top civil servants on one side of the table, a whole mob of executives from different oil companies on the other." He leaned forward. "I'm talking about an auction, the kind with sealed bids handed in. Now do you understand?"

Carrick exchanged a glance with Walker and saw the same understanding in his eyes.

"Drilling rights." It was the only possible answer. "Offshore tenancies?"

"The same way it has been done before—licensing rights. Take a damned great chunk of map, most of it water, draw squares on it, call them exploration blocks, then stand back. The top bid for one block in the last licensing round—just one block, Carrick—was over thirty million in sterling."

"I remember that." Johnny Walker frowned doubtfully. "But all the signs were good. It paid off. This time—"

"This time there are about eighty blocks to be licensed." Hume consulted his notes. "It's like a jigsaw pattern. They're mostly deep water, out beyond the Hebrides, and that's where the money boys think the action will be. There's a secondary grouping, over this direction, but with a lot less interest." Fiddling with the notebook, he added mildly, "The bottom right-hand corner of one block takes in this entire section of coast. But the experts say the geology is wrong, so who cares?"

"Except Andersen," murmured Kate.

Carrick nodded. They had it all now.

Magnus Andersen could have gone about his survey work openly and legally. But if he had stumbled across a geological quirk, if there was oil around Priest Bay, then the last thing he wanted was to draw attention to the previously scorned sector—the kind of interest that could have attracted other bidders and cost him millions.

"St. Ringan's treasure." Hume made it a snort. "Well, it's our turn now. You've seen some of his people—what are we up against?"

"A mixture." Carrick pursed his lips, considering it. "Half of them are probably technicians, just doing a job for money and not interested in anything else. The others—" He shrugged. "They're different. They've proved it. We've got three groups—the tanker people, the yacht crew and Andersen's team at Bochail House."

"The tankers can wait," said Hume firmly. "We could mop them up later, just have an eye kept on them."

"Bochail first." Carrick nodded in agreement and turned to Johnny Walker. "What's *Puffin*'s operational state?"

"We're fit." Walker was positive. "Norah Reiver pitched in her whole repair crew to help. I've no radar and we're running on two engines, but she'll do most things. And you've some extra help waiting in the wings. Headquarters have moved in *Blackfish.*"

Carrick allowed himself a soft whistle at the news. *Blackfish* was one of the newest Fishery Protection cruisers, big and fast, with a crew of thirty.

"Where is she?"

"Killing time about two hours south of here." Walker grinned. "Headquarters were moaning a little. Your old boss Captain Shannon has been screaming at them to allow *Marlin* to join in. They've told him to mind his own business, but we've also got air surveillance if we need it."

Hume stirred, unwilling to be left out. "I've a squad of armed police on the way. Well? What else do we need?"

"A plan." Carrick rested his head in his hands for a moment, then looked up. "The *Halla* is on the west side of the island, Bochail House is on the east. We have to tackle them at the same time."

"Can you?" Kate Dee shaped a frown. "I mean, suppose she tries to escape—makes a run for it?"

"Blackfish," suggested Walker, then stopped and snapped finger and thumb together. "There's a better way. We just stop her getting out."

Hume grunted. "Exactly how?"

"We need a little outside help, all the wire rope we can find and enough timber to keep it afloat." Walker beamed at Carrick. "Then we dump a boom across the mouth of that bay, keep the door closed." The idea sparked another. "We need a fishing boat—a big one—to carry it. But suppose it looked as though Fishery Protection had just caught themselves another poacher?"

"You wouldn't happen to have one handy?" asked Carrick. "Dutch, for instance? I thought the *Zono* would be well clear by now."

"She didn't get her nets back till last night, and she's lying up in Seal Bay again—or she was an hour ago," said Walker. Clasping his hands behind his neck, he eyed Carrick. "Well, *Tern* is command boat. When?"

There was a watcher on the west side of Bochail. He'd been there most of the afternoon, on the clifftop above the bay where the *Halla* was hidden; he had another hour to go before he was due to be relieved. The sea was still calm, the sky had remained blue, and his main problem had been boredom.

It had been a few minutes before four when he'd first noticed the two boats heading south, and he'd almost reached for the little two-way radio which linked him with the *Halla*. Instead, he'd used the binoculars slung round his neck; then he'd relaxed again. One of the approaching shapes was a trawler, flying a faded Dutch flag. The other, a few lengths astern, was a Fishery Protection patrol boat—and the picture was clear. The Dutchman was under arrest, being shepherded south to Mallaig or Oban.

Which was the Dutchman's hard luck.

He lowered the binoculars, only slightly puzzled at the way both vessels were sailing close in towards the shore. The word on *Halla* was that the panic of a couple of nights back was over. Their job was done; tomorrow the motor yacht would probably quit that claustrophobic bay and head back towards civilization.

The trawler and her escort came nearer and, frowning, he raised the binoculars again. That damfool fishing skipper was practically grazing the rocks down there.

Then he saw it happen. As the *Zono* came level with the north edge of the bay, there was sudden activity on her deck and canvas covers were ripped back. A heavy anchor splashed down on the end of a wire cable and, hardly slowing, the trawler rapidly paid out the rest of the cable and the heavy balks of timber attached to it at regular intervals. It took less than three minutes and finished as the other end of the cable, similarly anchored, splashed down at the south edge. The trawler gave a triumphant siren blast and turned away; the patrol boat idled along the line of the floating, impenetrable boom.

He'd seen it all, but he still hadn't warned *Halla*. Swallowing hard, the man fumbled for his radio, then groaned. Another shape, big and fast, was racing up from the south. She was still far away, but he could recognize the upper works of a Fishery cruiser.

Moistening his lips, he pressed the radio's "Send" switch.

Walker's signal from *Puffin* that the makeshift boom was laid reached Webb Carrick at exactly four P.M. The timing was right. He had *Tern* half a mile off the east side of Bochail, making an apparently leisurely passage south. Midway between *Tern* and the shore, the fishing boat *Blue Crest* was pottering along in the same direction. But MacTaggart had Inspector Hume, Kate Dee and a dozen armed police aboard—plus a few willing auxiliaries. The seine-net boat's skipper had been prepared to swear on oath he would get them ashore at the Bochail House pier without getting their feet wet.

"Go." Carrick gave the only order needed, then leaned forward in the command chair and opened all three throttles. Clapper Bell was already spinning the wheel, and as the patrol boat swung round, gathering speed, they could hear Andy Grey behind them, shouting the same one-word order to MacTaggart.

"She's on her way, Skipper!" Almost dancing up and down in his excitement, Grey pointed. The *Blue Crest* had stopped loitering and was digging a furious white wake as she also turned in towards the island. "Now?"

"No, wait." Carrick had to raise his voice above the roar of their diesels. Staring ahead through the bridge windows, he watched the shrinking distance between the two boats and the clearly visible pier. *Tern* was already close enough behind the fishing boat to be cutting across her wake; they would arrive almost together. "Right, Andy—now!"

"Now," repeated Grey, and flicked *Tern*'s klaxon switch.

The piercing yelp, several times more powerful than any police siren, was Gogi MacDonnell's cue at his station aft. Two large signal rockets fizzed to life, shrieked away and burst noisily over Bochail House. While their echoes were still fading, two more arrived and shattered the air. If any of Andersen's men ashore was in doubt about what was happening, Carrick wanted it totally spelled out.

The *Blue Crest* swung in towards the pier, too enthusiastically, and *Tern* had to veer sharply to avoid her stern, then circle round to follow her in. As the patrol boat's siren faded, the metallic sound of Ernie Hume's voice took its place, shouting a warning through the fishing boat's loud-hailer. The fishing boat collided hard with the pier, shuddered, stopped, and a wave of blue uniforms went pouring ashore.

A shot rang out, then another. The police ran forward, one helped along by two of his companions, others firing back as they reached the end of the pier and kept going.

"Hell, Skipper"—Clapper Bell kept one hand on the patrol boat's wheel as she came idling in, but gestured frantically with the other—"there's Andersen!"

On the other side of the pier, at water level, just visible through the gaps in the heavy timbers, a tall figure was scrambling aboard the slim black powerboat still moored there.

No one on *Blue Crest* had noticed; her remaining passengers were hurrying ashore and heading towards Bochail House, and the powerboat, freed from her mooring line, was already beginning to drift clear as Andersen reached the cockpit and dropped in.

"Hard round—full port rudder." Carrick took over the throttles as Bell frantically spun the wheel. They could hear the powerboat starting up as they heeled in a tight, shuddering turn which brought *Tern* almost skidding round in the water. "Andy—?"

"He's moving," reported Grey agitatedly. "But you'll get him, Skipper."

They came round the edge of the pier exactly as the powerboat began roaring away. For a moment it seemed the two craft would collide; they saw Andersen staring round, horror in his eyes, then the Dane hauled hard at his wheel.

The black hull shaved clear, the sea boiling white at the stern as she gathered speed and her bow began to rise. Clapper Bell already had *Tern* snaking round to follow, her whole hull vibrating as the diesels responded to throttles which were jammed hard against their brass stops.

There was a ripple in the water ahead, a long, lazy, finger of barely disturbed wavelets. Carrick saw it at the same time as Andersen glanced round again—saw it, knew it and reacted on sheer reflex.

"Starboard rudder, all the way—" Carrick brought the mid and starboard throttle levers slamming back as he yelled the order. "Shoal rock—"

Tern kicked and bucked, the diesels screamed in protest, and Andy Grey was thrown from one side of the bridge to the other by the violence of the manoeuvre. But Carrick was watching the powerboat.

It hit an instant later. At close on thirty knots, planing high in the water, the black hull suddenly seemed to leap into the air. Two thirds of her keel had gone, as if sliced away by a giant knife. Still airborne, her bow dropped.

Then she hit the sea again, half-buried herself in white water and exploded in a bright fireball which burned briefly, then became a rising pillar of black smoke. The smoke began to thin, and there was only wreckage.

Tern had stopped some distance away, with Sam Pilsudski boiling up from his engineroom ready to howl about damaged bearings. But he fell silent when he saw what had happened and helped launch one of the patrol boat's life rafts.

When they found Magnus Andersen, he was floating face downwards, half-submerged, and his injuries showed he must have died in the explosion. They brought his body aboard *Tern;* Gogi MacDonnell covered it with the same piece of old canvas he had used not so many days before when they'd found Mary Keenan; then they turned back towards the island.

Things were already finished there. A sullen, dispirited group of prisoners were already waiting in handcuffs at the pier. One lay on a stretcher, but most had given in without a fight.

Carrick went ashore, and a police sergeant, a rifle slung over one shoulder, met him with a cheerful salute.

"All over, sir. Here, at any rate." He thumbed towards Bochail House. "Inspector Hume is over there, and we're getting ready to gather up that yacht crew. He said to tell you we've got the Andersen girl—Sergeant Dee is with her."

"Good," said Carrick quietly. "Casualties?"

"Three of them, two of us—nothing that won't mend." The sergeant looked past him and grinned. "But this one is making enough fuss to be dying, though it's only a flesh wound."

Carrick turned. Clutching his left arm, blood oozing through his fingers, a pale-faced Jimsy Fletcher was being helped along the pier by his brother Hammy. A look of disgust on his face, two rifles slung over one shoulder, his bag dangling from the other, the Bagman followed a few paces behind.

"Bad luck," said Carrick sympathetically as they arrived.

"Bad luck?" Dunbrach's special constable gave a pained, indignant grimace. "Man, I'm probably bleeding to death. I need a doctor —and how will I be able to deliver tomorrow's letters?"

"Easy, Jimsy," soothed his brother. "You'll live—"

"And you won't bury me. That's one consolation," snapped Fletcher.

"Look on the good side," said Hammy. "You can claim compensation, maybe even sue—"

"Compensation." Jimsy Fletcher's face changed and brightened. "Hammy, you're not a complete fool. With you, it's like it says in the Book. 'Let the brother of low degree rejoice—' "

" 'In that he is exalted,' " finished Hammy Fletcher. "James one, Jimsy?"

"Verse nine," agreed Fletcher as they moved on towards the *Blue Crest.*

It was in Edinburgh two weeks later, late afternoon and raining, when Webb Carrick left the tall Scottish Office building which housed Fishery Protection headquarters.

It was the end of a series of interviews which had lasted most of the day. Some of them hadn't been easy, particularly the one with Commander Dobie, the flotilla commodore. But the last reports had been initialled, the last questions asked.

There were areas which hadn't involved him. The motor yacht's crew had surrendered with little more than token resistance; the men on the oil tankers had simply come ashore and given themselves up. Several were in prison remand cells, awaiting trial. Others, a badly frightened group of technicians and divers, had been set free.

There were still problems. Danny Rose was dead and there were confessions to prove it, but his body had been dumped off the Hound Islands and hadn't been recovered. The *Ranata* and *Ranassen* still lay off Priest Bay, silent, ugly reminders. A whole wolf pack of lawyers were left with a few years of profitable work mopping up some of the rest—and at the government concession auction, the Priest Bay block had been quietly withdrawn, "pending revaluation."

Though it might stay that way. A petition organized by a Mr. David Smith and the Skippers' Wives Association of Dunbrach was gathering steamroller strength, claiming that Priest Bay and the Hound Islands should be treated as an area of national religious and historical importance.

He thought of the Bagman and the strange mixture of allies drawn together, shook his head, then went out into the downpour. A small red MG coupé was parked at the kerb and he got in at the passenger side.

"Finished?" asked Kate Dee hopefully.

"Finished," he agreed. "You?"

"The same."

She had taken Marget Andersen to Edinburgh Airport that afternoon and had seen her board the aircraft that would take her back to Denmark and what was left of the Andersen empire. It had taken time, but a combination of legal decisions and government pressures had decided her release. The heir to Magnus Andersen's interests mattered to the outside world more than the minimal evidence against her.

"I've a week's leave," said Carrick.

"I know." She started the engine and looked at him demurely for a moment. "So have I, Skipper."

"Sergeant," said Carrick feelingly, "I'm proud of you."

Kate Dee chuckled and set the car moving.

Bill Knox is a popular and prolific mystery writer, the author of numerous novels and television scripts. He alternates stories about Webb Carrick of the Scottish Fisheries Protection Service with tales of Detective Colin Thane of the Scottish Crime Squad. A native Scot, Mr. Knox lives in Glasgow with his wife and three children.